<u>Cockpit</u>

<u>*Confessions of an Airline Pilot*</u>

<u>A DocuNovel</u>

<u>By Stephen Gary Keshner</u>

Copyright 2001
ISBN 0-9677540-9-8

booksonnet.com
P.O. Box 36
St. Augustine, FL
32085-0036

Dedication:

To the men who fly the planes.

**To my family, who suffer my absences,
and my homecomings.**

Any resemblance to persons living or dead
is purely coincidental.

Cockpit

Confessions of an Airline Pilot

A DocuNovel

By Stephen Gary Keshner

"Every couple of weeks they drag you away from your loved ones, and send you home to your wife and kids."

…Pilot humor…

Emergency

I was working my ass off, trying to hold the rocking DC-10 steady as we approached Los Angeles International Airport. We'd lost an outboard engine, unsuccessfully tried to relight it, and completed our emergency check lists.

Notifying the LAX controllers of our emergency, we've been cleared for an immediate approach. Now on final, about fifteen miles out, we are tracking the localizer inbound. We haven't reached "Roman" yet, the final approach fix at glide-slope intercept.

Everybody's sweating. It's pitch black outside, and we've endured two hours of abnormal and emergency situation struggling to land safely. Now down to only two engines, and no hydraulics in the number one system, we reach the outer marker. I begin a let down, following the glide-slope to runway two-five-right on the south side of the airport.

"Engine fire!" screams the Second Officer, as red warning lights and fire bells pour more noise and adrenalin into our already intense cockpit. The airplane yaws wildly to the right as the engineer and non-flying pilot pull back the power on the burning engine, and discharge the Halon. I increase the amount of left rudder pressure, fighting to keep the aircraft in control....my left leg is already quivering from the extra rudder pressure I've been keeping in.

Flying on one engine, I brain-fart, forgetting to get the flaps up, to firewall the power on the one remaining engine, and to dive for airspeed...speed is life right now. With our landing flaps still out, the drag is unforgiving. Shit, I've forgotten everything...our air speed deteriorates rapidly and we stall, the airplane is falling, plummeting, we are all screaming advise over each other's panicky voices. We crash!

Maniacal screams pierce the silence. L.L. Bataan, Director of Training, "Do you know how many people you just killed?" Bataan, his neck-cords popping in rage, shrieks again "...well, do you realize how many people you just killed?"

4

My silence serves to infuriate him further, so he advises that "your fucking stupidity just killed a couple of hundred people on board this fucking airplane!"

I remind him that, in fact, I probably took out another few hundred people on the ground. "Truth be told, L.L., I think my *fucking* stupidity started another riot in Los Angeles. I figure, after the looting and insurrection, I bet millions die due to my *fucking* stupidity!"

L.L.'s not amused, but he has calmed down. He gives me another double engine failure and fire, and I get it right this time, landing smoothly to end the four-hour simulator session. "Welcome aboard, son, congratulations!"

In The Beginning…1983: Where do they find such men?

"Hi. My name is Steve Keshner, and I'm an attractive female bookkeeper."

The woman on the phone laughs, "One Moment."

"Hello, this is Will Deals, can I help you?" A man's gravelly voice.

"Hi. I'm Steve Keshner, I'm an attractive female bookkeeper." More laughter, from Will this time.

That's how in 1983 I came to meet Mr. William Macon Deals, Will Deals, an even sleazier fellow than me. His illegal, sexist ad in the Jacksonville Times Union and Journal intrigued me:

Aviation Company seeks attractive female bookkeeper.

I had just moved to Jacksonville, Florida with the last of my ex-wives. I was a forty-year-old kid, a loser, selling used cars by day, an Adjunct Professor of Accounting at Jones Business College at night. That is, I was doing nothing, going nowhere. Time to settle down, settle in, get the old life in order.

Though I'm neither female nor attractive, Will Deals invites me to come in and talk about the job. Deals' Aviation, a flight school, charter outfit, and maintenance facility, was a ragtag affair located in the corrosion corner of Craig Airport.

According to Mr. Deals his bookkeeper had left him, he had no outside accounting firm, and no financial statements for the past seven months. To prevent his life from being too easy, he was also converting his bookkeeping system from manual to electronic data processing.

"You need an accountant, not an attractive female bookkeeper," I advise.

"I can't afford an accountant."

"How much are you going to pay your attractive female bookkeeper?"

"Two hundred dollars a week."

We look at each other for a while, sizing each other up. Deals blinks first, and offers me two hundred a week and flying lessons, to become his attractive female bookkeeper.

"I accept. "Will" I ask, "what led you to advertise for an attractive female bookkeeper?"

"I meet a lot of pretty girls that way," this real dry with no hint of humor.

"Oh."

That's how I became "Keshy," an attractive female bookkeeper, and how I wound up in the aviation business.

The first person Mr. Deals introduced me to was his Chief Flight Instructor, Ms. Madeleine Bruckie. Madeleine had one glass eye and a body odor problem. I later learn that this condition is an occupational by-product of the many trips made between an air-conditioned office and those hot little airplanes. Back and forth all day, sweating, cooling, re-sweating, re-cooling … B.O. Central.

Madeleine would become my first Flight Instructor. She was a remarkable woman, a single-parent who had fallen in love with flying in Ohio, working days as a waitress, and learning to fly at night. As a one-eyed wonder, Madeleine had somehow managed to obtain the waivers necessary to become not only a pilot, but a Flight Instructor as well. She was one tough, competent cookie, Ms. Bruckie.

After meeting Madeleine, I was introduced to the other flight instructors. They were all foreign born kids, in the States to learn to fly, and to eventually try to get flying jobs with any major American carrier. The flying opportunities are far more plentiful in the United States than in Europe. Unlike the rest of the world, we allow foreign pilots easy entrée to fly for American carriers. Most other country's rules are very restrictive as regards entry into their pilot pool.

When Madeleine took me out for my first flight lesson and taxied me onto the active runway, she told me to firewall the throttle, "go as fast as you can down the middle of that concrete strip." What a rush. On that first flight, I fell in love with flying, and never wanted to be an attractive female bookkeeper or anything else, ever again.

Madeleine gave me ground school training, before and after each lesson. Leaning over the charts, the center button of her flight shirt would occasionally pop open, encouraged by the weight of one of her remarkable and unsupported chests. Madeleine's nipple would poke through her blouse, and wink at me. Transfixed, I could never remember which of Madeleine's eyes was real or glass, and which would catch me staring. I was never caught admiring Madeleine's "third eye," but thoroughly distracted, I never learned much from her ground school sessions. I'm sure that if she thinks of me today, it's as a not-very-bright ground school student, with limited powers of concentration.

I was able to squeeze in flight lessons between work assignments, and I was fortunate enough to be taught not only by Madeleine, but by Maxellende DeCorte, "Maxie," a brilliant, young French aviatrix; Oystein Aaro, capable in the air, a dick-led Norwegian disaster on the ground; Stigo Brandvik, a wild and crazy Norwegian guy; and Perry Dervas, a Greek with attitude.

The day came that I finally soloed, and my heart was in my mouth. Alone, I was flying alone…what a feeling, initial niggling fear immediately washed away by a flood of freedom. After I landed (I never wanted to come back down), all these wonderful young pilots took part in the post-solo ceremony. Using a pair of office shears, they cut off the back of my shirt, the traditional "clipping of the wings" in aviation. They all signed and dated my torn shirt-back, and presented it to me, along with a Polaroid of the occasion.

After catching up his accounting mess with Maxie's help, at Will's request I created a "Rembrandt," which enabled Deals to con the purchase of a flight school on Jekyll Island, Ga., as well as the avgas concession. I was now very popular with Mr. Deals, his wife Nancy, and all the flight staff. That popularity was not to last long...what have you done for me lately?

Mr. Deals fired me after only a few months on the job. I discovered that Will was cheating his lease-back owners. Creating phony maintenance invoices, he was charging them for parts and repairs that their aircraft never received. Don't get me wrong, I don't mind deceiving institutions, banks or insurance companies, but these owners were people we all knew and liked. I was fired a few days after confronting him with the evidence of his fraud. "There must be some mistake Keshy, I'll look into it." Two days later, I was let go with the explanation that I was now superfluous.

I was no longer an attractive female bookkeeper, receiving free flying lessons. Now I had a real problem...addicted to flying, an expensive pursuit, I'm unemployed, broke, and another of my marriages is coming apart.

During the months as Keshy the bookkeeper, I'd ingratiated myself to all the flight staff. Straightening out their payroll problems, doing their personal income tax returns for free, even getting many of them a pile of money back from prior years' mis-filings.

Most importantly for these foreign flight instructors, I was good at finding them "husbands" or "wives" to marry, dealing with their Petitions for Permanent Residency, and going with them to their meetings with the Immigration Department. These sham-marriages allowed them to stay and to work in the United States.

By this time, my four-year marriage to Ilsa had come apart. Her inability to tell the truth about anything, significant or not, overcame my positive feelings for her warm affection and intelligence. I didn't love her anymore.

On the road again, I'm on my own again. Another failed marriage, no career, no savings, no credit...now how do I afford flying?

I moved in with Captain "O" and Stig Brandvik, "Stigo." Suddenly, my flying problems were solved. Oystein and his buddies were all working two jobs. They were flight instructing during the day, and flying night freight jobs in twin engine Navajos and Aerostars. Always exhausted, they would take me along these nights to do the actual flying, while they slept in the seat nest to me. These guys were multi-engine flight instructors. So they were getting paid to sleep, and I was flying twin engine, complex airplanes, logging lots of hours, and I was doing them a favor. They were also signing my log book, the record of hours I needed toward my ratings...okay!

My days were spent begging, borrowing, and stealing flying time.... anything to build flying hours towards these ratings. Eventually, I had enough hours logged to test for my licenses: private pilot, instrument rating, commercial, multi-engine and flight instructor. After accumulating fifteen hundred hours, I was allowed to take, and able to pass my Airline Transport Pilot (ATP) check-ride. I could now legally fly for pay...I had arrived.

Two years had gone by quickly and eventfully. Geri Banion, a good, loving friend I had known for years, did me the favor of falling in love with me, as I had with her. Between Geri's full time job for the Hamilton Collection, my flight instructing days, and my pizza delivery nights, we were able to afford an apartment together. Marriage seemed like the logical next best step.

My First Flying Job

Flying for the "Majors" is every pilot's Holy Grail. For me, it's pursuit required equal measures of dedication and starvation. Until about twenty years ago, all major airline pilots were hired almost exclusively from the military. Nowadays, FLAPS (Fucking Little Airplane Pilots) make up more than half the total pilot pool of all airlines.

The traditional route up-the-ladder for the FLAP begins with flight instructing, followed by flying night freight in ragged-out equipment, and if you survive, then jobs with the commuters. All this for the express purpose of building turbine time (jet multi-engine hours). 1500 hours lead to the ATP rating, and after a few thousand hours with a commuter, and with persistence and luck, perhaps an interview with a major airline.

Stigo Brandvik and I were broke as always, yet we were excited. We landed our first flying job for, Trans-Air, a Commuter Airline out of Fort Lauderdale. We would not be paid for the first two weeks of ground school nor for flight training. We would only be put on the books after our check ride, when we would then be legally able to "fly the line." That meant no money for almost six weeks from the time we hitched our ride down to Lauderdale.

Always broke, Stigo and I slept in our clothes in the Alamo Rent-a-car lounge, off the field. Early every morning, we would take the Alamo shuttle bus to the airport, head over to the General Aviation side of the field, and shower in any maintenance locker room we found open. Then we'd sneak through the charter planes parked in the hangars, scrounging for leftover sandwiches, or some half-eaten anything not yet thrown away. Nowadays, that's called "dumpster-diving" by street-people.

Somehow, we survived the training and the six weeks of starvation, until thrillingly, we received our first paychecks, at our co-pilot rate of $6.00 per flying hour, we could earn a maximum of $600 a month…heaven.

Oystein was still Flight Instructing during the day, and flying bags of bank checks or food stamps at night. Now, without me to spell him at the controls, exhaustion was taking it's toll. Coming back to Jacksonville from Charlotte, he fell asleep at the controls. He was out over the Atlantic Ocean, nearing Andros Island, when the screams of the Air Traffic Controller in his headset finally woke him up. Luckily, Oystein made it back with enough fuel to land at Ft. Lauderdale Airport.

There are any number of fatalities a year caused by single-pilot exhaustion, someone falling asleep at the controls while the airplane, properly trimmed, just keeps flying along until it runs out of fuel.

Not long after this incident, Oystein was deported...seems that he fell for Jekyll Annie Thomas, whose short shorts inspired many an aviator to fly into Jekyll Island for her specialized fuel pumping. Oystein, who was already married to a cooperative young lady for immigration purposes, was inspired enough by Annie's pumping services to divorce the first one, and to marry Annie. Annie was trouble...suffice to say she arranged to have Oystein thrown out of the country, since she secretly wanted to live in Norway.

Oystein, our beloved Captain "O," has last been seen driving cabbage trucks in Bergen, and is reputed to be smuggling a tightly controlled fish drug into Norway from Germany, flying in on fraudulently filed flight plans, listing Stigo's name as the pilot.

Timing is Everything

I'm a brand new hire with Trans Air, a commuter feeder for Piedmont Airlines. I'm heading from my home in Jacksonville to my base, Fort Lauderdale. Following aviation protocol, I've "requested the jump seat" from the Gate Agent, who sends me to ask the permission of the Captain on this Eastern Airlines jet.

The Captain, a very distinguished looking fellow in his fifties, with graying temples, in every way resembling my (and the public's) perception of the professional pilot. The Captain graciously gives me the okay. Introducing oneself to the Captain, and requesting his jump-seat, is proper etiquette in the industry. I sit directly behind him through the flight, silently admiring his smooth flying skills.

Approaching Fort Lauderdale, the Boeing 727, gear and flaps down, is lined up to land, and the cockpit has been "sterile," silent, from 10,000 feet on down. Now, descending through three hundred feet, on short final, the Captain suddenly screams "Fuck you, Frank Lorenzo, you queer cock-sucker!"

Shocked, I look over at the First Officer, catching his eye. Taxiing in, he explains that the Captain screams that out on every flight, so that in the event they crash, those will be the last words anyone ever hears on the cockpit voice recorder.

In 1983, Mr. Francesco (Frank) Lorenzo, Chairman of the Board of Continental Airlines, had "broken the code." No pilot ever started flying for the money - we fly for fun, we have to fly...flying is our joy, our life, our addiction, and now in many cases, our damnation. Having broken the code, Lorenzo then broke the unions at Continental, and he now had his sights set on Eastern Airlines.

1983 was not a good year for Airline Pilots, it was the beginning of the end of many good careers at Continental, Pan Am, Brannif and Eastern Airlines.

The Salad

Trans Air became a Piedmont commuter, so they now required two pilots
up front for safety and insurance purposes. Captain Kerry Cinder, "El
Cind" and I were paired together flying the twin-engine Cessna 402.
The 402 is open cockpit, no partition separating the cockpit from the ten
seats filled with barfing passengers.

"Low and slow," the days were long and grueling. We lived for weeks at
a time in hotel rooms in Tallahassee. Departing at six A.M., we would
fly eight-leg days, from Tallahassee to Jacksonville to Ft. Lauderdale to
Treasure Cay to Marsh Harbor, and back the same way, finishing up
about midnight, back in our cheap hotel in Tallahassee. We flew "quick
turns," which allowed only for a quick pee and a smoke, but no food.

Room service was closed by the time we got back to our hotel, but I was
too exhausted to be hungry. Days into this coffee-only existence, hunger
finally kicked in. Returning to my room one night, I was starving. I see a
used food tray on the floor, by the room next to mine. There, calling to
me from the tray, sat an untouched salad with oil-soaked croutons. I
stealthily removed the salad and a fork, trying not to alert my benevolent
neighbor. After cleaning the fork, I devoured the salad. I'm in heaven, it
seemed the best meal I ever had.

Next morning, rushing, showering and shaving at the same time, I get a
bug in my head. I don't want the maid to find the empty salad bowl in
my room. Obsessed, the shower still running, I step out of the tub, still
wet and covered with soap. I peek out my door, salad bowl in hand, only
to find that my unwitting host's tray is gone.

It's five AM, not a soul up yet. I dash diagonally across the hallway,
wanting to plant the "evidence" in front of someone else's door, and I
hear the single worst sound ever... slam-click! My door locks itself
behind me. Balls-naked, dripping wet, I'm in the hallway of a cheap
hotel, unable to get back into my room. The salad bowl has now become
my fig-leaf.

In my Hotel experiences, there has always been a maid's cart somewhere on each level, but at five AM, having searched the entire corridor, I was out of luck. I was now standing in the little niche of the service elevator, deciding whether or not to leave the floor in order to find a maid who might get me back into my room. It's one thing to be caught naked in the hallway on your own floor, but how to explain being on some other floor?

These thoughts are whizzing through my head, as the elevator starts to move on it's own, and stops on my floor. The doors slide open, and there stand, on either side of a cart, two very stout, black chambermaids. Their wide open eyes and shocked facial expressions quickly resume an implacable "We've seen it all before" nonchalance, as they look at me, naked, wet and salad-plated.

"I've locked myself out of my room." I manage, and turn towards my room.

Without a word, they follow me down the hallway. Walking with as much dignity as I can muster, our strange procession marches along the corridor. In this emotional agony, I now can't remember my room number. In desperation I point at a door, guessing that it's about where my room should be. One of the maids opens the door with her passkey. Handing her the salad plate, I say "thanks" and step inside. Thank God, it was my room.

"No meal is worth that," I tell Captain Kerry Cinder, explaining my morning's experience.

"Kid," he grins wide, "welcome to the airline industry."

Kerry was a high-tech guy, a Pan Am furloughee and Naval Aviator, flying fighter aircraft off of carrier decks. He was very kind-hearted to me, a man with a generous nature and loads of patience.

Flying: Hours of boredom punctuated by moments of extreme terror!

It was a perfect Florida morning. Cobalt blue skies, and 70 degree weather as we're descending through 3,000 feet. I always loved landing to the east at Fort Lauderdale International. The beaches, and the ocean beyond spread out in Gaugin palettes of blues and greens.

Approach control handed us over to the Tower frequency, and Tower has cleared us to land. Landing check complete and we're cleared to Land. We were fat, happy, and enjoying the view.

Captain Rehza Kehani and I loved flying together. An Iranian and a Jew in the same cockpit, what a combination. We respected each other's flying skills, and made each other roll with laughter, both of us having the same perverse sense of humor.

Now, lined up on final, we are about three minutes from touchdown. We watch as a light, twin-engine airplane begins his take-off roll, rotates and climbs into the beautiful Florida sky.

Plane: "Tower, we have an emergency."

Tower: "What's the nature of your emergency?"

Silence…nothing.

We are the spectators of this pantomime, and as we watch, the plane rolls to the right, turns over onto its back, and comes straight down, a lawn-dart, plummeting straight into the Jai Alai parking lot south of the Ft. Lauderdale field.

Smoke, dust and flames without sound, the unreality of what we're witnessing makes no civilized sense. Neither Rehza nor I say a word to each other for the rest of the day, nor do we look at each other directly. Six more legs we flew that day, all in silence.

The beginning of the end of the beginning of many new ends

Trans Air obtained ten brand new Spanish Casa turbo-props from G.E. Leasing on very good terms. The government of Spain, as part owner of Casa, was subsidizing it's Aviation Industry. To create an entrée into the American market for these aircraft, we were being allowed to use them free of charge for the first twelve months (including a free half-million dollars of parts inventory), with the first note payment not due for one year. Meanwhile, the Bent brothers, owners of Trans Air, were collecting the revenue from the use of these new planes.

Stigo and I agreed that we could predict when Trans Air would go out of business. Although the other guys didn't believe us, we figured that the Bents would disappear exactly one year from the date that the lease was signed, when the first note payment would come due. Unfortunately, as the date approached, bills started not getting paid, and our paychecks were late.

Over the loud speaker, I heard my flight being cancelled by the Piedmont Station Manager in Tallahassee. After he had taken care of the passengers, I asked him what had become of my flight? "Go look at your plane, out on the ramp," was his response. Walking out onto the ramp, I saw a Sheriff's car parked in front of my plane, and an airport van blocking it's rear. The Airport Manager and a Sheriff are taping a document across the door of the aircraft. Getting a closer look, I discover it is a lien notice "...non-payment of fuel, non-payment of landing fees..." "Hey, guys, can I get my underwear off this plane?" I ask. Smiling, they allow me to get my personal gear off.

A few times we pilots would show up at Fort Lauderdale to start our flying, and our airplane would be missing. The banks, we discovered, would send _repo_ pilots in at 2 A.M., to fly these planes away.

Trans Air's death spiral continued until finally, the only flying left was from Ft. Lauderdale to the Islands and back. This required that Kerry Cinder, myself and a pilot buddy of his from the Navy, had to drive down from Jacksonville, to pick up our flights.

One dark night, in the truck with Kerry and his friend, they ask me how old I think the Earth is? Something tells me that this question is not lightly asked. "I don't know. I've never really thought about it much, but I guess it's about four, maybe five billion years old, what with Carbon dating and such."

"**Carbon dating is a fraud**," they explode together! "The Earth is only 4,772 years old," Kerry insists!

Seems that they both go to the same church in Orange Park, a bedroom community serving the large naval aviation community of Jacksonville. Anyway, their church (I never did ask which one it was) teaches that the Bible is to be taken literally. That if one were to add up all the begats and such, and they've certainly done just that, the age of the world would be 4,772 years old.

Sitting between these two modern men, men of computers, men who've flown the most advanced, sophisticated aircraft in the Military world, I am trying to decide whether I am being put on. I am not. Kerry "El Cind" Cinder, and his buddy, genuinely believe Carbon dating to be a fraud, they and their wives and friends are raising their children to believe that the world is less than five thousand-years-old, and I am now feeling a Pariah....not an overt Pariah, mind you, they are too polite for that, but things were never quite the same after that.

The trip to Ft. Lauderdale was about four hours long. After pulling into the first fuel stop, I voluntarily moved to the bed of the pick-up truck where I sat for the remainder of the trip.

Kerry was recalled by Pan Am from which he had been furloughed years earlier. I heard, years later, after the demise of Pan Am, that Kerry was working for Delta Airlines.

I don't know whether Kerry Cinder still believes that the Earth is only 5,000 years-old. But if you do Kerry, I ask you now, what difference does it make? The only possible difference it can make, for you and your fellow congregants, is in trying to convince yourselves that (mathematically speaking) your personal interpretation of the bible is correct…so, my advice to you is, watch out for Janet Reno!

Hired on by Continental:

It's 1987, and Dave Fielding and I are "Sim" partners, training to become Second Officer Flight Engineers on the DC-10 for Continental.

Sam Prickton, a Texan in Continental's training department, is training us on the panel. He calls us "Switch Niggers," sitting sideways (facing the Flight Engineer's panel), we are pilots trained to be Flight Engineer / Second Officers, responsible for the hydraulics, electrics, fuel, pressurization, and all other "systems" on the airplane.

It becomes apparent that Dave and I are comfortably past the worst, that Sam Prickton is confident of our competence, and that he will have no trouble passing us along to the Feds for our Flight Engineer's check-ride.

Relaxed a bit now, we hit a cowboy bar in Houston. A few beers into our evening, Sammy Prickton asks, "Do you fellers know what the only good Yankee is?"

"What's that, Sammy?" we ask in tandem.

"A New Yawk Je-ew, moves to Texas, marries him a nigger, 'dopts a couple Mexicans, then moves himself and his new family back to Jeeeww Yawhk."

My breath / heart catch in my throat, unsure after the initial shock exactly how I'm going to react. We are probationary new-hires, and can be fired by anyone, for any reason.

Before I can come out of my protective, emotional capsule, Dave says: "Sam, let me show you some pictures of my family." In slow motion, I watch the fat wallet appear on top of the spilled beer and peanut shell mess on the bar. Dave flips one by one through his wedding photos.

His black-as-coal bride and her ebony family, framed by their pure white gowns and tuxes, are all smiles, enjoying the occasion, all mixed in with Dave's northern "Yankee" family.

Sam Prickton was a dead man…we all three knew it. From his shirt collar up, neck to face, all six quarts of Sam's bigoted blood flooded upwards…"red on the head like the dick on a dog," is all I can think of. Nothing more is said. Dave has no intention of turning Sammy in. Sam, sure as shit, isn't going to say anything to anybody, and I'm the asshole who ducked the draft, too late or too chickenshit to react to the anti-Semitism.

I've found out over the years that the bigotry in the cockpit is pervasive…lots of genuine racism, sexism, anti-Semitism and homophobia. Also, lots of brotherly love, based strictly on personality and professional respect.

Blacks and other obvious minorities have it easy. They know they're being talked about behind their backs, but they don't have to hear it (decide how to deal with it) directly. In my case, my looks can make me Italian, Greek, Mediterranean, anything. Very few people (other than New Yorkers, who would immediately know better) take me for Jewish. So, I get to hear all the Jew shit, and have to decide how to react to it.

Flight attendants, "…the single most important safety feature on an airplane."… Industry Humor…

"Definition of a Flight Attendant: A life support system for a pussy."
…Pilot Humor…

In our Honolulu base, we have a senior flight attendant named Wanda Decker, also known as "Thunder Pussy" to the cognoscenti. She is a quick witted, acerbic Jew-girl from Brooklyn. Wanda doesn't take any shit from anybody. She's also a great "trolley-dolly," who does a fantastic job. Today, we would be flying the Honolulu to Manila run, and Wanda was working the first-class section, as well as being our "cockpit-queen."

We are still on the blocks, passenger boarding still in progress, and Wanda is serving Champagne to her first-class guests. Wanda had no trouble noticing that one gentleman was already drunk. He had apparently gotten blotto at the VIP lounge in the terminal, just prior to getting on the airplane. Wanda cuts him off, refusing to serve him a pre-departure drink. The gentleman was Senator John Tower, of Texas.

Indignant at having been refused alcohol, Senator Tower asks, "Do you know who I am?" Without missing a beat, Wanda makes a P.A. announcement to her first-class passengers: "Ladies and Gentlemen, may I have your attention, please. The gentleman in seat 2B doesn't seem to know who he is…does anyone here know who he is, we'd like to help him out?" The snookered Senator doesn't find this to be amusing. "My," he says, "you're a real witch, ain'tcha?"

"That's right, I'm a real witch, and POOF, you're a pile of shit!"

Wanda stood her ground, and John Tower of Texas received no alcoholic beverages during the eight-hour flight to Manila.

When the expected letter arrived, on the "take no prisoners" embossed Senatorial stationary, Wanda Decker was summoned before a Company review board. The letter was read to her, and the story was rehashed to determine exactly what had happened. She was asked for her comments, and she agreed that, "yeah, that's exactly how it happened, but I don't know why he's so upset...I turned that piece of shit back into a person before we landed." She kept her job.

Six months after the John Tower incident, I am to meet up with Wanda Decker again.

"Who's working the upper deck?" This from Captain Bob Lipton (The Godfather). He wants to know which flight attendant would be our cockpit queen on this trip from Honolulu to Guam.

"Wanda Decker," volunteers our First Officer, Billy Chowder.

"Great deal," says Bob, now satisfied he's going to get all the coffee he wants, and that we'll be able to smoke in the cockpit without getting turned in.

"Hey Godfather," I ask. "How did Wanda get the handle *Thunder Pussy*?"

"Keshy, you don't know?" Bubba and Chowder both laugh. "I'll get her to show you, once we're underway."

Halfway to Guam, Bob calls Wanda up to the flight deck. "Linda, show them your act."

"No, Bobbie, I don't want to."

"Come on Linda," gruff now, "I said show them your act!"

"Okay, fuck it, give me your flashlight and turn off the lights." Chowder hands Wanda his flashlight, while Bob turns off all the lights in the cockpit. We barely see Wanda lift up her skirt, pull down her pantyhose, and squatting slightly, I watch, amazed, as the now lit flashlight is inserted up her vagina. Her pussy is glowing in the dark, the outline of some internal tubing showing through, like an x-ray photo. "Satisfied now," she asks, now smiling?

"Damn Linda, they should call you *Lightnin Pussy*, not *Thunder Pussy*, by God," says Bob.

For one of the few times in my, life I'm speechless. "What's the matter, Stevie, pussy got your tongue," asks the Godfather?

During the long night, Wanda has darkened the cabin, putting the passengers to bed as soon as the food service is completed. Six hours later, with an hour to go before descent, *Thunder Pussy* turns the lights on in First Class, as she and her Flight Attendants prepare the First Class breakfast service. One deeply sleeping gent opens an eye, and screams "Shut out that fucking light!"

Wanda, quick as a flash, advises him, "Sir, this is the 'breakfast light,' the 'fucking light' was two hours ago."

Power of Positive Thinking

A pesky cabin temperature control problem plagued us, causing all kinds of interruptions in our attempts to read our Penthouse, Playboy, or Forum's Letters. Flight Attendants calling up, all the time bitching about the damn cabin temperature. Every five minutes an irate call, "It's too hot back here! It's too cold back here." This unhappy situation would go on for the duration of these six-hour flights, seriously hampering our discussions of pussy. A maxim in aviation is you talk airplanes on the ground, and pussy in the air!

After suffering through several of these trips, I came up with a solution. I went to a local hardware store and bought a conventional thermostat, like those used in most homes, and glued four small suction cups onto it's back. I went out to the aircraft early next trip, before the crew arrived, and mounted my device prominently in the serving area of the Flight Attendant's galley.

When the Cabin Crew showed up, I brought them into the galley, showed them the thermostat, and explained "the trial modification," implemented by our maintenance department in an attempt to solve the aircraft's temperature problems. I did fail to mention that the thermostat was not connected to anything.

"Temperature control is now the responsibility of the Flight Attendants," I told them. We pilots then went through our normal departure procedures. We set the actual cockpit temperature controller to some "midway" position, and forgot about it. After take-off, we started to time how long it would take until we received the first temperature complaint. Fifteen minutes go by, then thirty minutes, nothing. An hour into the flight and not a single gripe!

I cracked the cockpit door to see what was going on. Every couple of minutes one of the girls would reach up and turn the thermostat control higher or lower; then about three or four minutes later, another of the girls, on her way in or out of the galley, would make another adjustment.

In the course of that one day, the thermostat in the galley was used more often than a real one during it's normal lifetime.

In the crew van on the way to the hotel, I casually asked the Lead Flight Attendant if she noticed any improvement in the quality of the aircraft temperature? She told me "that problem is unequivocally solved." The temperature on that flight was perfect "for the first time since they started working this aircraft, totally and completely satisfactory," they all agreed.

My bogus unit remained on that one aircraft, undiscovered, for another four weeks. The shit hit the fan, however, when one of the very senior F/As asked her boss "when could they look for this great fix to be installed on the rest of the fleet?"

For the next few weeks, whenever I called back for a cup of coffee, I invariably found one or two cigarette butts taped to the bottom of my paper cup. My next few coffees had a few choice words written inside the bottom of the cup with eye liner. I started carrying a thermos with me on trips, not wanting to be "Visine'd." Visine in the coffee is the favored manor of retribution by Flight Attendants towards asshole pilots or passengers considered to be pains in the asses...Visine supposedly causes severe stomach cramps and diarrhea.

When I think about that whole thermostat gag routine, I realize just how powerful perception can be, that whole mind over matter trip.

Cinderella

When I was first became a Second Officer-Flight Engineer, the third man in the cockpit, it was on the DC-10 based in Honolulu. We flew the international turns from Hawaii to Guam, Saipan and Narita (the new Tokyo International Airport), and back. The ground time was usually about an hour or so, just enough time to get an ice cream and a walk around the terminal.

This one month I was flying with Lee Edmonds, a quiet, unassuming Captain. The Co-pilot was Roy Steele, a face that only a mother could love, and a more successful swordsman then Warren Beatty is reputed to be....go figure. We land in Tokyo, and are parked at the gate.

Japan has a very popular TV show that airs live. A female journalist, Japan's Connie Chung, takes a camera crew to different places of business, restaurants, fishing boats and such. She interviews ordinary people about their jobs. The Japanese love it.

Our Tokyo Station Manager advises us that this Celeb is here now, and she wants to interview us in the cockpit of our DC-10. Captain Edmonds is taken aback. Although he gives his permission, he's shy, stilted, not knowing what to do or say.

The cockpit is now stuffed with the Station Manager, a camera man, "Connie Chung," the lights, and our crew - quite a crowd. I am Cinderella, sitting at my engineer's table in the corner, out of the limelight.

I pull on the sleeve of the interviewer, as she chatters away in Japanese, "Excuse me....excuse me, do you know what I do, what this table is for?"

Suddenly, the camera and lights are focused on me, the Station Manager rapidly translates my English into Japanese for the interviewer. "She wants to know what you do?" Now I am the focus of the interview.

"Have you noticed that pilots always look neat, with freshly pressed shirts and jackets? Japanese translation. "Well, this is our steam and press table, and it is my job to steam and press the pilot's shirts and jackets during each flight," More translation. "That way, everyone looks neat once we are on the ground."

The Station Manager is rapidly translating my statements for the TV Star, she is quickly repeating it all into the camera and microphone for her live audience.

We are a success. They are all very impressed, all very happy with the interview, and they make their bowing goodbyes.

So far as I know, all of Japan, or at least all of Tokyo, is now convinced that the Flight Engineer's table is a steam press, and that the Flight Engineer is in charge of laundry, to make the rest of the crew look presentable.

* *

As an aside about Japan: prejudice and pride were definitely part of my make-up as a young DC-10 Flight Engineer. J.A.L. (Japan Airlines) was our ground handler in Narita and Nagoya. That is, they took care of our fueling, passenger, gates and maintenance needs in Japan. I used to bristle with annoyance whenever a Japanese maintenance guy would come flying into the cockpit and reach for a switch on my panel. "Don't touch anything!" I would insist, knowing that nobody knew anything about these aircraft but me, especially not some Japanese guy in overalls, with limited English communications skills. After all, I had weeks of training as a Flight Engineer…who could know these aircraft as I did?

It didn't take long to discover how thoroughly well trained, and how professional Japanese Maintenance men are (as are all the other Japanese in every department within aviation), and how much more they knew about these planes then I did. Further, their integrity would never permit them to pencil-whip a problem they couldn't solve or fix… a habit all to common on the U.S. Domestic side of the industry.

Manila

During my first Manila experience, I was taken under the protective wing of B.G. "Wild Bill" Chowder. Bill was a senior Co-Pilot in those days, and he bid the Philippines all the time. Bill was our resident Manila pussy expert, the specialist (just ask him), who spent all of his time in the smoke-filled whore houses on Del Pilar street...*Misty's, Bloomers, The Firehouse*...Apparently, Bill was dating one of these hookers, and paying her family money to fix up their house.

The first night of our one week layover, I go with Chowder to his bar. He takes me into *Bloomers*, and introduces me to his girlfriend, one of the hookers there. Behind her back, Bill is flirting with some of the other girls, trying to be discreet. One night of this shit is enough for me... "shooting pussy in a barrel for Christ's sake," I tell Chowder.

I spend the rest of the week on my own, taking in the sights, smells and sounds of Manila within walking distance of our residence, the Hotel Manila, a magnificent wooden palace used by McArthur as his headquarters during the WWII.

My practice in a new city or country is to prowl the streets, trying to get lost and to somehow find my own way back. This is the best way I know to reach the soul of a new culture. In Manila, I am taken with the Chinese section's flavors and disparities.

One eerie place I visit is the Chinese cemetery, where mansions serve as mausoleums, complete with electricity, T.V. sets, furniture, and running water. All this luxury provided for the dead relatives inside. Leaving the guarded cemetery, one sees hundreds of destitute Filipino families living on the bare ground along Manila Bay's sea wall. They have nothing, no home, no money, no jobs, no future.

Most people in the "PI" are starving, while a small minority of the people have everything. Thanks to Ferdinand Marcos, Imelda and their Cronies, the Philippines is largely bankrupt. Corruption and greed were rampant in the Philippines back then, and it remains so today. Bill

Chowder would challenge anybody to "name one country ever colonized by the Spanish that isn't fucked up today?" Nobody could think of a one.

By the time we were ready to leave, I hadn't seen my crewmates for days. In the cockpit on the way home, Chowder tells me of all the fun I missed, and that he almost got caught by his girlfriend as he tried to make a play for one of the other young ladies.

"Hey, Bill," I say in disgust, "let me explain something to you. These women are prostitutes, this is not junior high school, you don't have to worry about cheating behind their backs, they get paid for sex."

Wild Bill is miffed, refusing to accept my view of his reality, convinced that when he is away from Manila, his girlfriend is faithful to him. A year later, Bill brought his Filipina honey to Honolulu, now as his fiancée. He was weeks away from marrying her when he discovered she was also about to marry a local Hawaiian lawyer at the same time.

When I first began visiting the Philippines, I would jog from my hotel early every morning, smugly watching those poor street people who allowed their representatives to steal everything from them, looting their entire National Treasury. I felt disdain towards them for allowing such a thing to happen.

Over time during my jogs, I watched as entire families woke up on the street. Mothers and fathers would get buckets of water from god-knows-where, they would bathe their children and then themselves. They would scrub their clothing in the same leftover water. Naked, they would hang their only set of clothes out on bushes to dry in the hot Manila sun. After dressing and grooming their kids, they would do the same for themselves.

I came to realize that here were people who didn't have anything, no food, not even a place to sleep, and yet every day they would wake up and take care of their children, and themselves. How strong they must be. With no hope for a job, day in and day out they continue. I don't think I would have the strength, the resilience to go on under those circumstances. I would probably commit suicide instead.

One day while walking through Rizal Park, near my hotel, I have a revelation. I own an expensive suite, bought and paid for by Continental Airlines. I am out of my room almost all day long during these six-day layovers. I could bring some deserving families up to my room and give them the luxury of hot soapy baths, clean towels, and some sleep on a real bed.

Returning to the hotel, and wanting to immediately implement my new idea, I see a family beginning their day. I stop and chat them up…

"Comustica? M'buti po." I discover their English is better than my limited *Tagalog.* I invite them to come back with me to the hotel, making my intentions understood. Happily, they follow along behind me.

Outside the gates we are stopped by Security. An argument ensues, and I ask that Management be summoned…(all this happening just outside the metal detectors and x-ray machines which guard the hotel lobby).

Although the room is mine, bought and paid for, I am not allowed to bring my guests inside the hotel. Hookers I can bring inside at anytime, as everybody does; but a certain pecking order seems to exist between those lucky enough to have jobs, and my guests who have nothing. My adopted family graciously vaporized into the general population of the impoverished crowd loitering outside, so as to save me further embarrassment.

Now, when I am stopped on the street by kids begging, I bring them to the many food-stands along the roads, treating them to as much as they can stuff down.

Except for the southern island of Mindanao, forever trying to gain independence as a separate Muslim state, the Philippines is almost exclusively Catholic. Man, where's Jesus when you need him? As my good buddy D.B. Swayde would probably say, "All it takes is people to fuck up a good thing."

I've come to admire the Filipino people for their strength, their faith, and their perseverance, and to detest the Marcos family and their friends for systematically looting an entire Nation.

The Cobra

Captain Jimmy "Rambo" Fratella is an inch or two shy of five feet tall, and he's a classic example of the "small man complex." He is a body-builder with a very short fuse. I have been in bars with him when he has gotten in people's faces at the drop of a hat, looking to show them the big man hidden inside, ergo the "Rambo" tag. Jimmy is our Captain today, backed up by First Officer Dan Johansen, and I'm the Second Officer-Flight Engineer.

Typhoon season in the northwest pacific is no fun. We are flying a standard pairing, a turn to Guam, Saipan, Tokyo, and back to Guam. The trip takes three plus hours each way, and guaranteed, a storm will be parked over "Omelet," an imaginary navigational fix on our route between Saipan and Tokyo.

Sure enough, this afternoon's weather is as expected, with the remnants of a typhoon shaking our DC-10 up pretty good. The rough ride has been going on for half-an-hour with no end in sight. The interphone "dings," and I pick up. An "Air-Mike" (Continental Air Micronesia) Flight Attendant asks, "how much longer is this turbulence going to go on, the snake is getting nervous."

"What snake is getting nervous?" I ask.

"The cobra in first class."

"What cobra in first class?"

Rambo and Dan take a sudden interest in my conversation.

Condescendingly, slowly, so that even an idiot like me can understand, the girl explains that an older Japanese woman, who boarded in Saipan, purchased two First Class seats - one for herself and one for a wicker basket, containing her cobra. "The weather seems to be making the snake nervous, and it is thrashing about inside the basket...so, when is it going to stop being so bumpy?"

Now I understand. "I'll be right back to you."

In my heart I'm sure I'm being set-up for a joke, but I dutifully explain the conversation to the guys. Dan jumps out of his seat to take a look. Two minutes go by, and he returns saying that there's a wicker basket strapped into a first-class seat back there, and for me to try to secure the lid.

Now I know that they're fucking with me. Hazardous material "Hazmat" rules call for cargo of various kinds to be secured in very specific ways in the belly of the plane. Most of us pilots remember the Hazmat classifications by a game equated to how one normally goes to the bathroom... that is "explosive-gasses-liquids-solids..." Explosives are category I, gasses category II, and so forth... I can't think of any category which permits cobras. Dangerous cargo is not allowed on board, and poisonous snakes would not be allowed in the cabin of any airplane, period!

I'm thinking that not even our luded-out Saipanese Gate Agents could be stuporous enough to allow a woman to walk into the cabin of an airplane carrying a live cobra.

As I go back to take a look, the plane is rocking and rolling in the storm, and I'm holding on to whatever I can cling to in the turbulence. I'm also trying to figure out just what kind of a gag I am walking into.

Sure as shit, sitting in the first class section is a well-dressed Japanese matron. On the seat next to her is a three-foot tall wicker basket, strapped in, but being jostled from the inside by some living creature. The basket has a lid on it, and the flight attendants have piled some blankets on top, in a poor attempt to keep it closed.

I don't believe it, I am on an airplane carrying three hundred passengers, riding out a storm at thirty-seven thousand feet, and we've got a terrified, pissed-off cobra on board.

"Holy shit, there IS a cobra on board!" I scream back into the cockpit.

"Rambo" and Dan are working hard to keep the airplane straight and level, their eyes and hands busy jumping between their radar screens and the flight guidance panel. I'm on my own. Grabbing my heavy flight bag, I race back to the snake. Gingerly, I remove the flimsy blankets from atop the lid, and replace them with my bag. Duct-taping the bag around the seat, the basket, and the armrests, I instruct the Senior Flight Attendant to move nearby passengers to empty seats, further away from the snake.

Amazingly, nobody has taken notice of the activity surrounding this scene, the flight attendants themselves seem oblivious to the danger. It's got to be Nature's ultimate valium, the betel nut they all seem to chew in Micronesia.

Every five minutes for the next two hours, I check back on the situation. Eventually we are out of the "chop," in smooth air, and the basket-wacker seems to be at rest in his wicker home.

At the gate in Tokyo, I climb out of the cockpit in time to see the lady and her basket leaving the airplane. She is calmly carrying her "pet" up the jetway, no big thing! My flight bag has been cut free, and is now resting on the first-class seat.

During refueling and cabin cleaning, we three pilots sit in the cockpit with the door closed. We finally have a chance to talk about what just went on. If Jimmy Fratella follows the rules, he will have to write up an "irregularity report," describing the entire incident.

At least four people will be fired over this: the ticket and gate agents in Saipan, the Air-Mike flight attendant who helped strap the snake in, and the gate agent in Tokyo, who blithely escorted the lady and her cobra out of the plane and up the jet-way.

"Nobody would believe this anyway," says Rambo, electing not to write up any report at all. God only knows what happened at customs and immigration, we got out of town.

Boost Pump Blues

Summertime, Manila non-stop to Honolulu, is about a nine hour flight, an all night deal. Our first two hours had been a bitch, torrential rain, turbulence, the works. In severe-clear for the past half-hour, Captain Chuck Cooper finally succumbed to his exhaustion.

While Chuck was hanging comatose in his seatbelt harness, Roy Steele, our Co-pilot was gently maneuvering the DC-10 around storm cells, using the heading select knob on the flight guidance panel.

I'm tonight's Second Officer, Flight Engineer, sitting sideways, back at the panel, monitoring systems. My mind wanders to an impression of last night's fun, and I laugh out loud. I can see clearly now Captain Chuck, balls-naked, sloshing around on a rubber mattress, slick with hot soapy water, being worked over by two Philipina girls.

Roy Steele and I have snuck the Mama-San's karaoke machine microphone into Chuck's "private" room. I hold the mike to his mouth, as he makes a noble attempt at "You must remember this, a kiss is just a kiss, a sigh is just a sigh…," particularly hard to accomplish with your dick being sucked by one girl, and you're singing through the fine, straight pussy-hairs of a second girl, who's sitting on your face.

Hearing this unique rendition over the loud-speaker system, the Mama-San freaks out! Roy and I split post-haste, and head for Rosie's café for breakfast, then it's back to the hotel for our afternoon siesta, before our flight home. I don't know what time Captain Chuck left his two friends.

As I start to nod off myself, my head growing heavy, I notice that the engine gauges for the number two engine are doing a jig, they start rolling back, and then they quit.

"Power loss #2!" I yell out.

Chuck, a former Marine Corps fighter pilot, is awake immediately, instantly focused. Roy, pushes up the power on the two remaining engines, applies rudder, and is controlling the airplane.

Three things come to mind immediately. First, we can't maintain this altitude with only two working engines (I break out the "drift-down" charts that tell us by weight, what altitude we can maintain). Second, it's got to be fuel contamination, so we are going to lose the #1 and #3 engines. And third, we are in the middle of the fucking Pacific Ocean, it's the dead of night, hours from anywhere. Ditching, injuries, blood, sharks….fuckin' Manila, what a shithole, giving us watered down gasoline.

Jet engines don't just quit for no reason. Fuel starvation should be the only cause, yet all our fuel boost pumps are on, still feeding from the 85,000 pounds of aux-tank fuel, direct to all engines. We have "source"-"force"-and "course"... there is nothing wrong, which leaves only the possibility of contaminated fuel from Manila. Anything can be in the fuel we got in the Philippines, the place is an aviation joke, but this is no joke.

As we start our drift down, we go through the emergency engine failure checklist methodically, as we are trained to do, yet terror has gripped my heart. If we do have contaminated fuel, since all three engines have been feeding from the same tank, we are only minutes away from disaster. No way will we survive the loss of another engine.

Roy Steele, out of his own anxiety, asks me if I've "been fucking with the fuel pumps?"

"No, Roy! Are you nuts?"

Chuck confirms that all the switches are as they should be, and have not been touched since takeoff.

I'm burning mad at Roy's question. "How can you ask me something like that?"

"Sorry. In the Air Force I had a guy fuck with the switches out of boredom, I was just checking…." (this said with a twinge of embarrassment.)

We attempt an air restart of the number two engine, and it lights back up, shit-hot. Back in business, we divert, making a bee-line for Guam. The Chamorrons we have working for us in maintenance cannot find any reason for the engine failure. The fuel filters are clear, no metal shavings or other contaminants. Houston Maintenance Control clears us to continue to Honolulu, and so we leave Guam for Hawaii, with the remainder of the flight uneventful.

Next day, I return to Guam on a new pairing, with Captain Stan Poyner, a truly class guy. Stan had worked for MacDonald Douglas as a test pilot, and he listened with interest to my story about the engine failure.

Checking in at the Tumon Bay Hilton, one of my buddies from another crew comes over, wanting to know if I've heard about "the shitbird second-officer who had been fucking with the fuel system, almost causing us to lose a DC-10?" He was talking about me, though he didn't know it, and Guam based mechanics had been spreading this bullshit.

Furious, I am ready to confront the entire maintenance crew at Agana, when another friend, Captain Craig Chapman, gives me some good advise. "Forget it. If you go out there and create a scene, it will only make it worse."

Flying from Tokyo to Saipan, Stan Poyner tells me that "turning off the boost pumps would not shut down the #2 engine, anyway. It's a myth. That engine would still suction feed fuel, even sixty-feet up in the tail."

On our climb-out from Saipan to Guam, Stan turns and indicates to me with his fingers (so that no words get on the cockpit voice recorder) for me to shut off the #2 fuel boost pumps. Aghast, I shake my head "No!" He commandingly gestures this order again. I reluctantly shut-off the engine #2 fuel tank boost pumps. We fly all the way back to Guam with the #2 switches and pumps off, yet the engine keeps running, not even a hiccup... but who could I tell it to?

Stan had taken this chance with his rank, and his career, just to make me feel better, to make me know that even had the switches been turned off, I could not have been responsible.

There are some wonderful and insane people in this business of aviation. Stan Poyner is one of them.

Monsters:
The Ace of the Base

Captain Eddie Levine, an Israeli-American with dual citizenship, and with seven different opinions on any given subject, is a former New York Air pilot, now working for Continental.

He's a very hard person to get along with, another way of saying he's a total asshole in the cockpit. There are stories that followed him from his New York Air flying days. He so alienated the co-pilots at New York Air, that the Chief Pilot called him into his office one day saying, "Eddie I have a problem, perhaps you can help me with?"

"Sure, boss, what's up?"

"Well, I either have to fire two-hundred co-pilots who refuse to fly with you, or I have to let you go, what do you think I should do?" the Chief Pilot advised Captain Levine.

Eddie became a more tolerant human being for a while as a result of that conversation. Now with Continental, he's reverted to form, invariably chewing somebody out, every leg along the way. Either he's yelling at Air Traffic Control, at one of the crewmen, or at some ground handler. Eddie needs to show everyone who's boss.

Anyway, we have a wonderful First Officer, Dan Johansen who lives in Miami, and commutes to fly out of the Honolulu base. Johansen, was once Mr. Teenage Norway - he's a huge, physically fit fellow, but as are most men who don't find it necessary to prove themselves, he is a pussycat of a guy. We'd recently flown together for a month, and I came to really like Dan Johansen as a class act.

For this last trip of our month together, there's been a Captain change. Dan and I are to fly with Captain Eddie Levine. Though neither of us have ever met or flown with Levine, we know him by reputation.

Dan and I show up at the Ops (Flight Operations) office an hour before the flight, as we're supposed to, and there's no Captain. We wait some more, still no Captain Levine. Finally, we can wait no longer, so Dan grabs the paperwork, and I go running out to the airplane to do the "walk around," the exterior airplane inspection. As I get up into the cockpit, there is Captain Eddie Levine. I stick my hand out to introduce myself. Disregarding my hand, he asks "Where's that son-of-a-bitch First Officer, he's got my paperwork."

I explain that we were trying to cover for his late arrival, since he hadn't shown up at Operations….that Johansen was still at Ops, doing all the paperwork for him.

He blasts, "Well, if you guys had bothered to check with the Dept. of Agriculture, you would have known that I was within the airport environment!" This guy's a fucking maniac…Agriculture?… Jesus Christ, everybody's first and only stop is at Ops, for check-in. Keeping my mouth shut for a change, I know that Dan is in for a tongue-lashing when he turns up with the flight plans and weather.

Dan enters the cockpit, and sticks his hand out to introduce himself. I have no time to warn him, and I find it painful to watch as Captain Eddie just rips Dan a new asshole. Smart, Dan just keeps his mouth shut.

That's the way this four day trip from Honolulu starts, and it goes down-hill from there. It's a very cold working environment, and my stomach is in knots for four days.

On the ground in Newark, the plane is being refueled for our non-stop return to Honolulu. We calculate that we've received a few thousand more pounds of fuel than the Captain ordered. So, Captain Eddie points at the guy on the ramp, you know, the fella in the greasy green overalls. He waves for him to come up to the cockpit. Complying, the guy comes running up the ladder.

Foaming at the mouth, mad-dog Eddie reams this guy's ass for five minutes. "….how come you gave us too much fuel, I'm the Captain, not you, and the Captain's words and wishes are golden, they must be obeyed exactly!" and he demands an immediate explanation. "Well, what do you have to say for yourself?" he screams, infuriated by the man's calm silence.

Finally, the guy says, "Hey, I'm not your fueler, I'm the baggage handler!"

Johansen and I almost pee ourselves, trying hard not to lose it. Captain Levine has added to his shining legend. During the last leg of the trip, flying from San Francisco to Hawaii, Captain Eddie lets us know he's been a hero of the Israeli 1967 war. Proudly he exclaims that he was shot down three times, during the six-day war.

Finally, I can't help it....looking him in the eye, I ask "If you're such a hot-shit pilot, how come you got shot down three times by a bunch of Arabs?" That was it, Dan Johansen bit through his lip, and there was not another word said for the rest of the trip.

I'm a probationary pilot, it's my first year with the company, and I can get fired at the drop of a hat. I was sure I was going to be fired upon our arrival back at the base, but nothing came of it. The next time I got called out to fly a trip with Captain Eddie, he was terrific to me. Probably forgot about the whole damn thing.

Ed Malone

When I was first based in Honolulu by Continental Airlines, the very name Ed Malone inspired fear in all us new hires. Captain Malone had a reputation for being a tyrant in the cockpit of the DC-10. People were totally afraid to fly with this guy.

I had never yet flown with him, and when I heard that Captain Ed Malone had transferred over to the 747, I said a little prayer of thanks, since I would never have to fly with this reputed ogre.

Four years later I became a co-pilot on the 747, and of course there came a day when I was called out to fly with Captain Ed Malone. I accept the trip wondering how this is going to shake out. Over the years, I found myself getting along real well with people that others have considered trouble. The industry standard for assholes runs about 2%, but wide-body airplanes attract a larger percentage of twisted sisters... you know, the big watch, big airplane, small pecker variety of assholes.

Down in operations, I introduce myself to Ed Malone. As we walk out to the airplane, I tell him I'm new on the 747, "..so if you think I'm too slow, or not doing what you want, just put your foot in my ass and give me a shove."

Malone stops in his tracks and falls over laughing. We have the most wonderful two weeks together. He's a terrific guy, a lot of fun, both inside and outside of the airplane.

The trips we flew in those years were non-stop to New Zealand. After spending two days in Auckland, we'd fly turns to Brisbane or Sydney, and back to Auckland. Two more days on the ground, then fly back to Honolulu.

During a layover in Auckland, Ed drove us to a restaurant in the Mission Bay area, the swank section of town, for some Italian food. I thought Malone was an Irishman, but it turned out that he was an Italian, (Ma-Lo-Nay).

The restaurant was honest-to-god called The Mafia, and Cheech and Guido are the proprietors. Funereal, in double-breasted, sharkskin suits, they greet Ed at the door like a lost brother. As we're ushered to a booth, it's hard to miss the baby grand piano in the middle of the floor.

A Chinese woman is playing music from an Italian opera. A tuxedoed, Chinese gentleman is standing next to her, singing arias in Italian. Our *Paisans* explain that these people are refugees from China, and they don't speak a word of English. They are, however, classically trained musicians.

Here we sit in New Zealand, *manging* fine Italian food in The Mafia restaurant, and two Chinese people who don't speak a word of the local language, earn their keep singing and playing Italian opera. Welcome to Puccini's Twilight Zone.

Half-way through my *eggplant parmagiana*, I ask the waiter for extra napkins and a pen, forever conducting my business on paper napkins. Hiding what I'm doing from Ed, I write out a contract between myself, Stephen G. Keshner, as Agent for the Chinese couple. The document guarantees, for a fifteen percent commission, that I will have them on the stage of Carnegie Hall, in New York, within two years. Further, the gentleman must sing under the name *Refugio Chinko*. I sign as agent at the bottom of the contract, draw lines for *Refugio's* signature, and for that of a witness.

Between sets, I demurely carry the "writing" and the pen over to the lady pianist, showing her where to sign, as if asking for an autograph. Smiling, she signs her name in both Chinese and English characters. Next, I perform the same ritual with my new client, the singer, who also graciously signs his name, again both in Chinese and English.

Returning to the table, I produce the executed document for Ed Malone. I am now the proud agent for *Refugio Chinko*, promising to get my talented discovery onto the stage of Carnegie Hall.

We toast to the success of my new career, and ordering some more *Chianti Ruffino*, we finish our meal, con gusto!

Ed also had shares in two warbirds, a Trojan and a Harvard, hangared at Ardmore airport, near Auckland. It seems that New Zealand's laws, unlike those in the U.S.A., prevent frivolous liability lawsuits. As a result, the cost to own a plane is very reasonable, and for about $8000 kiwi dollars apiece (about $5000 US), Ed had a share in these two airplanes.

Since we had a few days off in Auckland on each trip, we would tear up the skies in his aircraft...great fun! Also, the local warbird enthusiasts have a clubhouse on the field in which the hospitality and beer flow freely.

The Revolution

Darius "D.B." Swayde grew up dirt poor in Hardscrabble, Texas, a white, trailer trash community. "As kids we amused ourselves by taping two cats tails together and tossing them over a clothesline. Them cats hung by their tails on either side of that line and tore each other up. My dad near beat me to death when he found out we were doing that, and we used our own pet cat. That cat near died."

D.B.'s sharper than a tack, but he talks l-ah-k t-h-i-s, a lazy drawl, coming across as slow farm-boy….watch your wallet.

D.B. supported himself, and his youthful flying habit, by playing drums in a rock and roll band, and doing crop-dusting, lying to the planes' owners about his flying experience… "shit man, if you survived, you knew a little more!"

Hired at a young age by Texas International (eventually to become Continental Airlines), D.B. was a Co-Pilot. "Man, felt lahk I'd cut a tall hog high on the ass!"

Darry and his Captain, another Texan, often flew turns, Houston to Guatemala City and back. Day after day, same guys, same route, and, it seemed, the same crew of Flight Attendants in the back.

One morning, down in the operations room, they're going over their preflight paperwork, checking the weather, their fuel requirements, and the NOTAMS, (Notices to Airmen) describing anything out of the ordinary. Normally they are re-fueled at the gate in Guatemala City, before taking on their Latino load of passengers bound for Houston. Today's NOTAMS indicate a change in the normal fuel operation. Instead of refueling at the gate down there, they must taxi empty over to the other side of the field, refuel, then return to the original gate and pick up their passengers. Also mentioned are fires and smoke close by the airport. Piles of tires and trash are being disposed of by the City. About half way down to Guatemala, these two miscreant pilots look at each other, smile and hatch a scheme.

There are three flight attendants working in the back of their DC-9. D.B. and his Captain call up their Senior Momma, the head flight attendant, and soberly explain that they've just been notified by Air Traffic Control there's a revolution going on in Guatemala, the rebels have the airport surrounded, and the airport is under siege.

Since they've passed the ETP (equal time point), the point of no return, they must continue on to Guatemala City. "We've got no choice but to go on and land."

They instruct her to get the passengers off as quickly as possible, once at the gate…."and then we're just going to get out of Dodge." Then they want the flight attendants to slam the door, get down on their bellies under the seats, and keep their heads down. Our two hero pilots will get them the hell out of Guatemala City, hopefully before the rebels have taken the airport and shot up the plane! "Don't worry, we've both been in combat before." She goes rushing out of the cockpit.

As expected, not two minutes later, all three flight attendants are crowded inside the cockpit. They've been briefed by the senior flight attendant. They are fearful, but they know what to do. The pilots are busy, but allow the girls to stay in the cockpit on descent, and as they get in range, they point out the smokey fire-fights and the rebel locations, surrounding the airport. The girls are fascinated, and scared shit-less.

Landing smoothly and pulling quickly up to the gate, the Captain yells back, " OK, get 'em off, get em off!"

The flight attendants stampede their passengers out the door. D.B. hollers out, "Close it up! Close it up! Now get down! Get down under them seats!"

The three flight attendants, scrunched down on their bellies beneath the seats, are crying their eyes out. The two pilots behind the closed cockpit door are crying too, while laughing hysterically as they taxi across the field to get refueled for the trip back to Houston.

Fifteen minutes later, when the truth comes out, the remainder of the flight is taken up with vigorous oral sex between the pilots and flight attendants.

"Fuck you, Darius!"

"No, fuck you! "

D.B.'s Mid-life Crisis

D.B. and I are together all month, based in Guam, flying to Saipan to Narita or Nagoya and back, every other day.

Geri and I have known D.B. and Lois, his Flight Attendant wife, for years. She's the big-hearted, adventurous type. We've attended their "orphan Thanksgiving" parties, for people with no family on Oahu, many times.

Beautiful Tumon Bay is always sunny and hot. At the Tree-Bar, poolside at the Hilton Hotel, D.B. and I are drinking Jack and Coke. D.B.'s mournfully focused on a table of six young Japanese girls, obviously on holiday here in tropical Guam, clerical types escaping the harsh winter in Narita. They are all giggling, drinking "whiskey," which to the Japanese is any alcoholic drink except beer.

D.B.'s first sexual encounter, at about age eleven, was at the instigation of an older neighbor boy who took Darry into a back bedroom of the other kid's trailer. He starts to play with and suck on D.B.'s dick. "Hey, man, if he wanted to do that, I weren't gonna' stop him."

Suddenly, they're caught by the neighbor kid's 35 year-old mother. She pulls her son's head off of D.B.'s dick, and drags her kid by the hair into another bedroom. D.B. is shitting, not knowing what she's going to do to him. She comes back in, closes the door, and gently pushing Darry back on the mattress, she goes down on D.B., finishing him off in her mouth. D.B. smiles, remembering. "That went on for awhile, don't remember why it ever stopped."

Earlier that afternoon, walking the beach, D.B.'s confided "I don't have it anymore, man." Now in his fifties, he's still a good looking man, with white, unruly hair, a twinkle in his eye, and a great physique. He's going through some kind of mental male-menopause, doubting his own good looks, and his sex appeal. Nothing I've said to D.B., or can think to say, dissuades his self-doubt.

49

"You see all these Nipper girls? I've never had one of those Nipper girls, in all these years we've been coming to Guam." I know that some of our younger pilots have scored, or claimed to, with these Japanese girls, away from home on holiday.

Later now, during the course of the evening, tables are pushed together as we are joined by other flight crewmembers. The six, now tipsy Japanese secretaries are now part of our party. Eventually, the party moves to D.B.'s room. The "Jack and Coke" on the rocks has been flowing. D.B. is glowing, one arm around a friendly Nipper girl, the other holding his cigarette and drink.

I'm happy for him, knowing he's finally gonna get some Nipper Nooky; and we last four revelers leave D.B. and his new friend to themselves.

En route to Narita next evening, D.B. looks over, grins, and says, "You ain't gonna believe it man."

"What?" He's obviously happy, but we haven't talked yet about his night with the Nipper chick.

"Jerry, Steve, you know how sometimes good luck can be bad luck, and bad luck can be good luck?" We wait for the story.

Seems that shortly after D.B. was left alone with his girl, she became nervous, and no longer wanted to be in his company. She left, no kiss-kiss, no Nipper-nooky, no nothing."

He was so upset that he finished the Jack Daniels, put on the "Do Not Disturb" sign and collapsed alone into his bed.

Guam's Hotels hire staff from all over the Philippines and Micronesia. They are famous for disregarding 'Do Not Disturb' signs. Many mornings, at six or seven A.M., I've had to shoo away the mini-bar man…."Just want to check your mini-bar, sir;" or housekeeping staff, getting an early start on the vacuuming and sheets.

At six A.M., someone is knocking on D.B.'s door. "Go away," he manages, still drunk and comatose. Louder knocking. "Go the fuck away!" D.B. shouts, giving himself a worse headache, "I don't want any!" The knocking becomes more persistent. Fully awake now, his head throbbing, Darry flies out of bed, throws open the door, ready to strangle the mini-bar man.

Pushing past him into the room is his wife, Lois, who has taken it upon herself to surprise him. Her own charter trip was cancelled, so she hopped the Air-Mike flight from Honolulu, arriving at Agana Airport at 5 a.m. "Surprise, Honey!" They hug and kiss, as D.B. thinks of what the scene would have been had he "gotten lucky."

"Holy shit!" is all anybody can say. D.B. had been cured of his lack-of-nooky despondency, and he was his old self again. Back in the cockpit with Jerry Lovell as Engineer, I say:

"Hey, D.B., tell Jerry about the "doggy with no legs."

"Man walks into a bar carrying a doggy with no legs, sets him the doggie on the bar..." Darry is now exaggerating his Texas twang. "...bartender walks over and the man orders a drink. Bartender pets the doggy and says, "Nice doggy, what happened to his legs?"

"Nothing happened to his legs, he was born that way."

"Oh," says the bartender…"What's your doggy's name?"

"Ain't got no name."

"Ain't got no name?"

"Don't make a shit, can't come if ya call him!"

Yeah, D.B.'s back to himself for sure, that's his favorite joke, and he's been telling it for years.

My mind wanders back to my first ever flight with Darry Swayde, years earlier. He and I were alone in the cockpit, he was a distinguished Captain, and I was a lowly new hire, Second Officer, Flight Engineer. The co-pilot had stepped off the flight deck for some reason or other.

D.B. turned to me and in the serious, confidential tone of a man imparting some wisdom:

"You know young fella, I must have painted...I don't know, maybe a hunnert, a hunnert and fifty houses, but no-one ever called me a house painter. And, you know, I bet I helped build about a hunnert barns and silos, but nobody's never called me no carpenter...." Now, leaning forward, he places one hand high on my thigh as he says, "....but you know, just suck one dick...." He smiles.

I was so scared and uptight, that it took a few seconds for me to get the joke, but I fell in love with D.B. right then, and I've loved him ever since. God, it's been 10-15 years, longer than most of my marriages.

Returning to Honolulu, someone cuts an outrageous, stinking fart. We all reach for our oxygen masks, nobody admitting who did it, another advantage of a three man flight crew.

"Man, what crawled up inside you and died," Jerry asks D.B..

"Hey, it wasn't me, man."

"That's the worst fart I've ever experienced," I said.

D. B. proudly confides that his wife's poisonous clouds can "take the paint off the cockpit walls. You know, one time, I was down there, eating her out, and she farted and singed the hairs in my nose."

Two month's later, D.B. and I are matched up again, and Lois tags along with D.B. on a trip to Guam. It's going to be fun, a room for a week at the Hilton Hotel, snorkeling on Tumon Bay. We're doing morning turns to Japan, and we'll be back early every evening, a vacation.

Tradition has it that we have a debriefing session upon our arrival into Guam. The eight hour Honolulu-Guam flight gets in at about 5 a.m., it's still dark by the time we check into the Hilton. So, most of the crew gather on the beach to greet the gorgeous sunrise, while drinking from stolen mini's, or from their own bottles.

A couple of hours later, the sun's been up for a while, and D.B., Lois and I are the last ones left "debriefing." The sunrise has been beautiful, and the bantering conversation has been fun. We're all in our cups now, tipsy, and Lois says, "you know, I think it's wonderful how close you guys all get, like family, knowing so much about each other, I think it's great, that male-bonding thing."

I can't resist...."You know, you're right, Lois. Just the other day, one of the guys confided in me that "...there he was performing oral sex on his wife, and she cut a fart like to burn the hairs out of his nose!" D.B. groans. Lois looks at the two of us, then throws her glass of ice and Jack Daniels at us both, "You Sons of Bitches!" Seconds later she starts to laugh. We all do. No wonder D.B. married her. She's a good shit, one of the guys.

The King of Tonga

The King of Tonga, His Royal Majesty Taufa'ahau Tupou IV, was snoring heavily, drool moistening the collar of his "Aloha shirt." A grossly overweight man, this last true Monarch of the Pacific, filled his first class seat completely. The King's wife, his Crown Prince son, and their retinue, had purchased exclusive use of the First Class cabin for our flight from Guam to Tokyo.

Captain D.B., Wild Bill Chowder, and I were the crew flying this royal assemblage to Japan, to attend Emperor Hirohito's funeral, in January of 1989.

En route, I told D.B. of a story I had read as a kid, one which stuck with me all my life. Jim Thorpe, the American Indian running star, had been sent to Europe at the turn of the century, to represent the United States in the Olympics. Having won a number of gold medals, this young kid, right off the reservation, was on the receiving line being introduced to the King of England. Jim Thorpe said, "Hi, King," The London Times famous banner headline screamed "H I,   K I N G" and Jim Thorpe became the toast of Europe.

D.B. raises an eyebrow, he knows this story's been goin' somewhere.

"Darry," I ask, "may I?"

"Hey Kesh, not many real Kings left," D.B. says, granting me his permission, with this bit of wisdom. Before I leave the cockpit, I carefully straighten my tie, put on my pilot's jacket, and adjust my hat.

"Very pretty." D.B. says.

"Thanks," I agree, leaving the cockpit.

Everyone's asleep in First Class, including His Royal, snoring Majesty. Decision time....Fuck it....I tug gently on his sleeve... nothing. In for a penny in for a career, I pull on his cuff more insistently. His poached-egg eyes roll down, focusing on me as he comes awake. Sticking out my hand, I say, "Hi, King." Graciously, the mountainous Monarch shakes my hand.

As I reenter the cockpit, D.B. looks back at me. Giving him the thumbs-up, I say, "Thanks, D.B."

"Hey."

Initiation

"Oh my God, he came in my ears!," screaming, she rips off the headset, the sticky, white fluid dripping from her ears, and down onto her collar. In a panic, Cyndie runs from the cockpit, slamming the door behind her.

D.B., Jerry Lovell and I were crying too, hysterical with, laughter.

Cyndie, the new-hire airhead, was thus initiated to aviation on the last leg of our pairing, Guam back to Honolulu. The rest of our flight attendants were in on this bit of mayhem.

We had recently received a series of memos concerning the "do's" and "don'ts" of sex discrimination, written by our in-house Sex Cop, Vice President of Sex, or whatever her politically correct title was. Pilots, being the most irreverent of God's bastards, say whatever they want to say, whenever they want to say it, political correctness be fucked.

Cyndie was a newbie, a brand-spanking new flight attendant. Working first Class, she had come up to the cockpit a number of times over the past week, bringing us our meals, and our coffee. It didn't take long to discover the empty universe that lived between her ears.

"If'n that little girl tried to blow her brains out with my pistol, the bullet would travel in endless circles forever, looking for somethin' to hit," declares D.B.

"Hell, D.B., she sticks her head out her moving car's window to get herself a refill," I add.

"I don't get that," D.B. says. What's that mean?"

"You know, refill, air in the ears, 'airhead'…" I stop myself seeing him grin at me, he's got me again.

"We got to do her!" Our Captain has made a command decision.

D.B. concocted some gizmo in his room during our last day in Guam. Taking a headset from cabin class, the old-fashioned kind, with the rubber-tube ear-pieces, he cut off the last couple of inches. Filling a balloon he bought at Gibson's with just enough milk, creating a little bladder, he inserted the end of the headset into the neck of the balloon, and secured the whole apparatus with a rubber band.

Now, we're established at altitude, on our last leg, the flight home to Honolulu. D.B. carefully tucks the entire affair down his uniform pants, and puts the phony headset on. He's sitting in the left seat, a very still spider in it's web, waiting patiently.

Cyndie, the fly, finally buzzes into the cockpit, and starts chatting with me and Jerry Lovell. D.B., all the while, remains studiously uninvolved, monitoring the instruments, seemingly oblivious to us. Eventually, Cyndie eyeballs the tube running down the outside of the Captain's black tie, and disappearing into his trousers. Fascinated by the cabin-class movie headset on D.B.'s head, Cyndie flys into the spider's web. "Captain Swayde, what are you listening to?"

D.B. blushing, shyly looks over at her, and says, "It's kind of embarrassing to talk about, but my wife Lois and I have been trying for kids for a number of years now. We've gone to all the doctors and the specialists, you know. This last specialist, he's come up with some new technique, and he's taught me how to listen to my sperm count, to see if it is 'proper.' So, on the last leg of every trip, I listen to my sperm count. If it's a good count, I go home and we try to make a baby. You wanna' listen to my sperm count?"

Cyndie, saying yes, leans her head close, as D.B. now gently places the headset over her ears. When he's done, and she's concentrating, he gives the bladder buried in his pants a little squeeze, and the milk squirts out of her ears.

"Oh my God, he came in my ears!" Cyndie screams, ripping the headset off, charging from the cockpit.

"Mission accomplished," D.B. says. "I sure do hope we're in compliance with the Company's policy for ..."

"We're in real fuckin' trouble," is my only response.

"Hey, Chubby," Lovell asks, "Why do women fake orgasms?"

"Okay, why?"

"Because they think we care!"

"Lovell," D.B. asks, "you know why the bride's smilin' as she's walkin' down the aisle? It's 'cause she knows she'll never have to suck his cock again. But, why's the groom smiling?"

"Because he doesn't know it yet!" I beat him to the punch-line.

A male flight attendant, with severe female tendencies, brings us up our coffees, and quickly minces out of the cockpit.

"Fuckin' fudge-packers!" says Jerry Lovell, "We got more fuckin' fagots then girls on this crew."

"That's the industry," I say. "They hire their own, the guys with cock-in-mouth-disease....they've killed sport-fucking, that's the problem."

I have always sold myself out for acceptance, and I'm still doing it. I actually consider our group of gay males to be some of our best workers, conscientious, and dedicated to giving fine service.

D.B. says, "If we all just woke up everyday and shot a faggot in the face, wouldn't be no more problem."

"Didja hear about the ground controller in San Francisco who asked the Southwest guy on ground frequency "what that animal was painted on his plane's tail?"

"No."

"Southwest pilot says 'I dunno' then thinks for a second and says 'I guess it's a gerbil.'"

"Yeah," Jerry adds "the City of Brotherly Love, it used to be Philadelphia, must be San Francisco now."

Janet from Another Planet

Captain Jimmy Walken, is a florid-faced, bow-legged stump of a crazy Irishman. The name Walken doesn't sound very Irish - but he's as Irish as you can get - maybe he's German! Anyway, Jimmy is always in a good mood, walking around with his head and hat both cocked to the side, eyes flashing.

Came a day when we were paired together as a crew. Continental flew two flights from Honolulu to Los Angeles and to San Francisco, both departing at 8:00 AM. Our DC-10 had pushed back from the gate, and we were heading out to the active runway, the "reef runway," in Honolulu, which is quite a long taxi.

This plane is packed, every seat and every flight attendant jump-seat is occupied. There's a knock at the cockpit door. It's the Flight Service Manager, the chief flight attendant. He asks if we could allow "Janet-from-another-planet," one of our spaciest flight attendants, to sit on a cockpit jump-seat. In her ozoned condition, Janet had gotten on the wrong plane. She was supposed to be working on the San Francisco flight. Now, mistakenly on the Los Angeles flight, there was no seat for her anywhere in the cabin. To be legal for take-off, she needed a place to sit, and with a seatbelt on.

We are cleared "into position and hold" on the active runway, about to take off. Jimmy turns and says, "Janet, so long as I have a face, you'll always have a place to sit." A typical Walken remark, as he grants her access to the cockpit. She sits on the jump-seat and buckles herself in. Jimmy has saved her job. We take off, and the rest of the flight is routine.

It turns out that "Janet-from-Another-Planet," offended by Jimmy's remark, writes a letter to the FAA and to the Company, accusing Jimmy of some kind of sexual infraction. We are called in to see the Honolulu base Chief Pilot, Brock Pyle, a typical "office-puke." He's an ex-marine, with a close-cropped buzz cut, and that anal, meticulous nature with the personality of a dial-tone.

Brock asks Jimmy if there's any truth to this story, showing him Janet's letter. Jimmy looks at him, his hat cocked, and with those flashing, smiling blue eyes, says "Brock, I've been saying that to flight attendants for twenty-five years. If I told you I didn't do it this time, would you believe me?" The office staff broke up, Pyle included.

Weeks later, Jimmy was called before an F.A.A. Board of Inquiry. The board consisted of five members, all of whom happened to be men, and the circumstances of the story were once again reviewed.

Jimmy was ultimately cleared of any regulatory infractions. After the official verdict was rendered, and we were all leaving the room, one of the F.A.A. guys booms out, "Captain, the next time you ask a flight attendant to sit on your face, just make sure you tell her to put her seat belt on, as well!"

Delicious

While in cruise, on a back-of-the-clock flight from Melbourne to Honolulu, Captain "Filthy" Farnsworth and I decide the time was right to play a joke we had all ready, just waiting for the right new-hire flight attendant to show up. Now we had one.

I've disheveled my appearance, dampening my face and hair, generally making myself look sick. Then Filthy calls this new hire up to the cockpit, pointing out my condition. "He's sick."

This lady became immediately concerned with my illness. "What was the problem? What could she do? How did it happen?"

Farnsworth tells her that I had eaten something bad, that I was very sick, and anything she could do to ease my condition would be much appreciated, since he's busy with the plane. She leaves the cockpit to gather up anything she thinks might help me out.

Meanwhile, in the cockpit, we've taken my uniform hat, lined the inside with a shower-cap to protect it, and dumped a steaming hot can of chili into it.

When the girl returned, I seemed to be in the final stages of up-chucking into the hat. Her look was one of grave concern. Filthy commented that hopefully I would now be feeling better, having vomited, and would she please take the now brimming hat out of the cockpit, "dispose of this for us will you?"

Averting her eyes, she reaches out and gingerly takes the hat from my lap. Just as she starts to withdraw, Filthy stops her, grasping her wrist. He peered curiously at the mess in the hat. Looking directly into her eyes he says, "Christ, this whole thing has made me hungry!" With that, he sticks two fingers into the chili, and starts eating.

The girl's shade of green can't be accurately described. Gagging several times, covering her mouth with both hands, she groaned and took off for the lavatory like her ass was on fire.

For the rest of the trip she was totally out of commission. Curled up on a blanket in the rear galley, she took some hot tea and a sleeping pill, getting up only to go to the lavatory every hour or so, continually proclaiming, "If I live to make it back to Honolulu, I will tender my resignation immediately upon arrival!"

"Pretty formal speech for a sick young lady." I tell her, "I'd be saying I fuckin' quit!" I can't get her to laugh.

She didn't quit, and she's still with Continental, a little older and wiser to the shenanigans of pilots.

A few years later, when I was a co-pilot on the 747, I ordered the fish for my meal. One of the flight attendants brought up my tray, with the main course plate covered in foil, which is common practice.

Removing the foil covering, I am staring at the bony skeleton of a fish. My face must have reflected my puzzlement, my mouth hanging open. I'm surrounded in laughter and the joke's on me this time, as I look back into the face of that flight attendant from long ago.

The Engine Sir

I was going into my fourth year with Continental, and had spent all that time in the engineer's seat on the DC-10 in Honolulu. Not flying the plane was driving me crazy, and my scan (the practiced, patterned review of the flight instruments) had gone to shit.

My last job had me flying six and seven legs a day for Eastern Metro, Jetstreams without autopilots, in and out of Atlanta-Hartsfield. I had been at the top of my game. My scan had been developed to a point where I saw all the instruments at once. This mid-focused Zen state allowed me to know everything about the airplane's performance, without consciously realizing it. Now it was all gone, replaced by rust and lethargy.

At that time, Singapore Airlines was hiring expatriate pilots for their 747-400's on five-year contracts, and I was more than ready for the change. My FAX and phone correspondence paid off, and I was invited out for an interview in Singapore. They provided tickets for me, and I arrived in Singapore with a few days to spare before my appointment.

To get my weight-to-height just right, I went at it whole hog, jogging for months. I rented a suit for the interview. Some friends from CAL Honolulu base had preceded me out there, and I lunched and had dinners with them, to catch up on old friendships and to pick their brains for information about Singapore Airlines and life in Singapore.

Wishing to have a good night's rest before my important interview the coming morning, I booked a massage through the hotel, for six in the evening. This was to be a legitimate massage, not the "steam and cream," so common in the orient.

At six P.M., I dutifully present myself at the hotel's health spa, and I'm introduced to this gnarled, chestnut-colored Malaysian woman who was to do the honors.

Disrobing in her private cubicle, and positioning myself face-down on her table, I was almost asleep by the time the old lady nudged me to turn over. This was going to be perfect. I was going to have just enough energy to crawl into my own bed for a great night's sleep. Lapsing back into my stupor, I was totally relaxed when her mouth engulfed my penis. My entire body levitated off the table. My mind, racing to catch-up with this unexpected sensation, directed my mouth to say, "What? What?"

"Theengensahr."

"What?"

"Theengensahr."

She pointed to my unresponding member…"You have to make certain that the engine is working."

I mentally slap my own forehead, oh "The engine, sir" is what she had been saying, while offering me this extra service.

The speed of thought is faster than the speed of light, I've always believed. Unbidden, my brain instantly asks my dick and my conscience, in that order, whether I can lay here with my eyes closed, pretending a young, pretty girl was fellating me for love, not for money. The answer came back, and "no thanks" was my response.

I've told this story to Geri, who finds it hilarious, as I do.

Once, I told it to D.B., and when I was finished telling him the story, he looked at me in his shit-eating, fish-eye way. "Now Steve, your tellin' this story to me now, not to your wife," waiting for me to confess my guilt.

I broke out laughing, not saying another word.

Continental 747 Upgrade

Although I was offered the job, Singapore Air required a thirty-five thousand dollars cash deposit, as insurance against my leaving early on the five year contract. I didn't have the money, and it never worked out at Singapore, however my luck soon changed at Continental.

Most airlines pay "wide-body" or differential pay, the larger the equipment, the greater the pay. Not so in those days at Continental. Nor did Continental pay extra for international flying as is common elsewhere. Therefore, there's no incentive to move to Hawaii to fly large equipment.

When the new equipment bid came out I was thrilled and stunned to learn that I had been awarded a right-seat job on the 747. It had gone junior, since none of the senior guys in LAX, Houston, or Denver wanted to commute, or move to Honolulu without a pay increase.

Now I was faced with the challenge of getting through upgrade training on the largest airplane in the world, without having flown a lick in four years.

It wasn't pretty. After three weeks of systems ground-school, and two weeks of simulator training, having worked my ass off, I came out the other end of the process as a marginally acceptable 747 pilot. I was now the most junior co-pilot in the Honolulu 747 base. I was on reserve, but I was in pig heaven. I was flying airplanes again, no longer a panel-nigger or switch-nigger, in the unfortunate vernacular.

Since neither my sim partner nor I had ever flown right seat in a large swept-winged jet for a "121" outfit before (F.A.R. part 121 refers to the regs covering major airlines), Continental had to give the two of us a couple of hours of touch and goes in the actual airplane, and in the presence of an FAA examiner, before we could legally fly the line carrying passengers.

Amazingly, one night we took an empty 747, filled it with a few hundred thousand pounds of fuel, and took off from Houston to Reno. There, we spent a few hours taking turns doing touch and goes, that is taking off and landing, continuing the landing roll right into another take off, and so forth…what an eerie experience it was to look back into that cavernous shell and all those hundreds of empty seats.

Machismo

The very first time I was called out for a trip, it was to be with Captain Psycho Saroyin. Jerry Paddy Lester would be our Flight Engineer.

Courtesy and common sense dictated that, as I introduced myself to the Captain in the Ops office, I made a definite point of telling him that this was to be my first actual flight on the 747, and that I hadn't flown for a number of years. In other words, watch your ass, and mine, I might be dangerous. Saroyin's face registered no emotion as he grabbed his flight bag, a tennis racket, and headed for the airplane.

Our trip was to be from Honolulu-Sidney, layover for two days. Then Sidney-Melbourne-Sidney, layover, returning once again to Hawaii. In my excitement, I never noticed that both Saroyin and Lester had gathered up pillows and blankets as we entered the plane.

The Captain elected to take the first leg, HNL-Sidney, which was fine by me. It would give me the opportunity to watch him operate, as I got more comfortable with the airplane. As the PNF, pilot not flying, my duties were communication, navigation, and to back-up the Captain.

Pyscho took off from runway 8 right, the reef runway, turned right to an assigned heading, and we climbed to our initial altitude of 5,000 feet. Throwing on the autopilot, Saroyin says "you have it," and both he and Paddy build cocoons for themselves, actual nests of many blankets and pillows, and they both drop immediately into a sound sleep.

This is going to be interesting, since winter flying north-south across the equator is a bitch. The storms that band the globe from 10 North through 5 North, and from 5 South to 10 South are brutal. The cells can be thirty miles thick, stretch for hundreds of miles, and climb above forty thousand feet.

Most passengers think that all a plane has to do to avoid weather is to climb above it, or to go around it. Not true. Indiscriminate climbing is out of the question, since the weight of the airplane determines how high you're capable of going. The initial altitude a fully loaded Boeing 747 is able to reach is about 29,000 feet. Burning about 25,000 pounds of fuel an hour lightens the plane gradually, allowing the pilot (assuming the concurrence of Air Traffic Control) to climb an additional two thousand feet every few hours. No way however, could we ever climb high enough, given our weight and time en route, to climb above the kind of storms we were going to face this evening.

As to deviation, when you take off on an eleven-hour-plus journey, fuel conservation is a real concern. Deviation must be kept to a reasonable minimum if you want to have enough fuel to reach your destination, plus some in reserve.

I was now "alone" in the cockpit, brand-spanking new, having to fly, communicate, navigate and do weather avoidance, constantly scanning the weather radar. On a moonless night, which this was, there is nothing to be seen out the windscreen, zero, nada, a black hole.

We were about an hour into the flight, only at 29,000 feet, when the first band of storm cells appeared on my scope. Playing with the radar, adjusting it's pitch and range settings, showed me that we were not going to top these storms. I was going to have to decide the best way to penetrate this line of death, which stretched across the entire horizon of my radar scope. Choosing a path towards the yellows and greens, avoiding the pinks, reds and violets, I turned on the seat belt sign, put on the sparklers, (the ignition switches to "flight start" - continuous ignition), the nacelle anti-ice, and prepared for the worst. I also called back, and told the cabin crew to take their jump seats.

The plane bucked and kicked at first, and rocked and rolled. We were finally being tossed about by angry gods, a child's toy in a whirlpool. My two companions' snores continued from under their blankets. Saint Elmo's fire was dancing off the windscreen, and it's strange blue light traveled between the flight guidance controls and my hands when I reached for a switch or control knob.

I'm flying while weighing the degree of perceived danger against my ego-driven need not to wake Captain Saroyin. I decide that I can handle it, the hell with those guys.

The mechanical bull in Gilly's Saloon in Texas was tamer than our ride became. Turbulence in aviation is measured in very specific terms. Light, moderate, heavy, severe and extreme, all have their meanings. Light is that uncomfortable chop we've all experienced, while extreme means the plane can no longer be controlled. We were in moderate and severe. Not once did my two fellow travelers open their eyes.

About four hours into the ride, we finally emerge into calmer air. I had been so busy flying, trying to control the airplane, navigate and call in position reports, that I never noticed how desperately I had to pee.

Now in smooth air, I reach over and wake up the Captain, indicating that I have to jump back to relieve myself. He might have sat up, I don't honestly remember, so great was my need to go.

As the flight attendant opened the cockpit door for me to get back onto the flight deck, I used my body to block her view of the two corpses up front, swaddled in their shrouds...nobody's awake, nobody is flying the airplane.

Now, with the luxury of an empty bladder and a full cup of coffee, I check the fuel balancing and fuel used, satisfying myself that our fuel burn is on flight plan.

An hour and a half later, having crossed the equator heading towards five-south, we're approaching storms again. The Sleeping Beauties, as I was now thinking of them, were still out cold. I alerted the purser to put all the carts away, and to have all the flight attendants once again buckle in, since the approaching storms appear even more intense than the previous mess had been.

I had my hands truly full this time. We gained and lost a thousand feet of altitude at a time as the heavy rain and hail beat the plane, a maddened

Gene Krupa on a set of steel drums. At the worst of it, flying in turbulence with Saint Elmo's fire dancing around me, I am deviating as best I can. The Captain pokes his head out and opens one eye. The eye looks at me, at the flight control panel, then withdraws back under the covers. I guess I'm doing okay.

Flying is described by some pilots as hours of boredom, punctuated by moments of extreme terror. This night became hours of terror, punctuated by moments of boredom!

I started a decent about twenty minutes out of Sydney. I was about to wake the Captain, when Saroyin suddenly sprang up, folded up his camping gear, grabbed his DOP-kit, and went back to the lav.

Five minutes later, now level at 5,000 feet, I'm on a radar vector to intercept the localizer for the ILS at Sidney. Captain Saroyin returns to his seat, adjusts himself in, and says, "I have it." He is shaved, smells of shampoo, his damp hair is combed back, he has brushed his teeth and he is in control.

A few minutes later we land in Sidney, eleven hours and twenty minutes after take-off, and the Captain has said a total of six, count 'em, six words to me. He and the Engineer have been awake about fifteen minutes.

On the crew bus to the hotel, I exhaustedly sink towards oblivion. In my last moment of consciousness, I overhear my two crewmates planning to meet to play tennis in half-an-hour's time. It turns out that these two guys are tennis freaks who buddy-bid, and pull this shit all the time.

It's no fucking surprise to me that they call him Psycho Saroyin. We lived through my virgin flight, and although we were never in imminent danger, no sane pilot would allow an experienced man to handle that load by himself, no less a novice like me. For my part, I was wrong to allow my stubborn pride to win that particular game of "chicken."

My flying rust disappeared fast, my spooling-up process was so accelerated that I never wanted anybody else to touch anything in that airplane but me. As it turned out, I had no worries in that department, since those two guys pulled the same stunt on me heading back for Honolulu a few days later.

Jurgenson

Jurgie, Captain Gary Jurgenson, is a pussy-hound pilot who adopts a
smooth, shy persona. His little boy face, and Clark Kent style haircut,
portray an innocence that allows him to get away with anything. Before
every flight terminating with a hotel layover, Gary would disappear from
the cockpit for the half-hour before departure, trolling through the school
of passengers that swirl near the gate, he would eventually show up in
the cockpit with his catch of the day.

The attractive blond woman taking the jump seat today, whose name I'm
told is Beth Wagner, is returning to Guam from Tokyo. Jurgie had done
it again, here he is, radiant and shyly making the introductions. Miss
Wagner, is an Air force Officer, no less. Gary instructs her on the proper
use of her seat belt and oxygen mask, and jumps into his Captain's seat.

Although the FAA strictly forbids any unauthorized people in the cockpit
during any phase of flight, Jurgie always has a companion on the
jumpseat for every take-off and for every landing on every leg. It's
amazing. One report, one mention of this behavior, and his career is
over, along with we fellow crewmembers who were present during the
occurrence, us; but he's even got us mesmerized, cobras facing ferrets.
Jurgie is so blasé about the matter, he has never risen a hint of resistance.
It's my leg back to Guam, so as we take off north from Narita, I'm busy
flying the Narita reversal. I'm tuning VOR's, setting radials, talking on
the radio, doing it all because Gary's busy pointing out the sights to our
guest, as usual when he's entertaining an attractive guest, he's paying no
attention whatever to the flying.

We are finally established on the airway and at altitude, so Gary asks me
to show Miss Wagner the plane, indicating with a sweep of his hand all
the "buttons and bows" up front.

The light test is always impressive, since holding the switch to the test
position illuminates all the red, green, blue and amber lights up front, so
I show her the "Christmas Tree." Beth Wagner, underwhelmed, just
yawns.

"Gary," I say, "Allow Ms. Wagner to sit in your seat for a moment..."
Gary and Beth switch seats, and we position her into the Captains seat,
close to the yoke, the steering wheel, so to speak.

"Would you like to see the world's largest vibrator?" I ask.

She beams, "Yes."

"Put your hands on the yoke," I instruct, showing her my hands now on
the steering-wheel.

As she puts her hands firmly on the yoke, I reach up and test the stall-
warning system. The entire yoke and control column in front of both
flying pilots vibrate and buzz vigorously in her hands. "You are now
holding an 800,000 pound vibrator, the world's largest."

Without hesitation, Miss Wagner shoots back, "May I have a moment to
reposition myself?"

We fall over, and we know that Jurgie has caught another live one, and
will likely mount his catch in his hotel room later in Guam.

Rita Sex

Filthy Farnsworth, Jerry Lovell, and I were heading for Sidney. As usual, we would be staying for a few days at the Sheraton Wentworth, a stately, five-star jewel which is only a block from the Circular Quay, the Rocks, and the Opera House. The rest of the pattern would be two days in Papeete, Tahiti, then back to Sidney for two days, then a return to Honolulu.

Layover time spent with Farnsworth would be fun, but could be hazardous, since Filthy was a heavy drinker/philanderer. Young girls were his specialty, the younger the better, and his "rep" was further polished by the hint of a cocaine habit. I was still a light-weight drinker, and faithful to my wife, Geri.

Lovell was always a lost cause to us on layovers, since he invariably had an advance babe set-up, no matter where we wound up. I'm convinced that Jerry Lovell would have a woman ready in Mombassa, Mumbai or Kabul, were we heading there.

Sure enough, on the flight down, Jerry is tantalizing us with descriptions of his Sidney sweetheart, who he had dated only once before. He's alerted her to his impending arrival, and now he was salivating with anticipation. Jerry loved to drive me crazy, teasingly refusing to tell me anything about his girls. I just got that Cheshire grin of his, and his patented "life is good!" routine.

After a shower and a nap, I'm down at the bar expecting Filthy to show up, but he's missing in action. He must have hooked up too. Just as well, at least I'll be staying out of trouble. To my surprise, Jerry Lovell enters the place. He's alone, seemingly crushed, the body-language wind is definitely out of his sails.

"What happened to your date?" I ask, half in disbelief, half secretly glad that he's struck-out.

Jerry orders a Long Island Ice Tea, explaining the components and proportions to the bartender, who's eager to learn how to make this Yank concoction.

"Keshy, there's no accounting for the wondrous ways of the female animal," Jerry begins...

It's going to be like that, so I switch from beer to double Stoly's, rocks, with olives. "Okay, I'm ready" I say.

Jerry smiles, it's going to be good, and he begins: "For months I've been joking around with those girls behind the registration desk, here at this hotel. Never thought much of it, just funnin' around. Three months ago, I'm opening the door to my room, and the phone is already ringing. It's Rita, calling me from down in the hotel office. "Can I meet her for a drink? Can I be discreet? Nobody in the hotel must know, all that...."

"Yeah?" Anticipating the juicy parts.

"It's jammin' at the bar she told me to meet her at that night, Aussies wall-to-wall. She's in a sexy, white-knit dress, sitting at the bar watching for me, and she's saving a seat for me. She greets me with a wet kiss, we have a drink, she excuses herself to go to the loo. When she climbs back up onto her barstool, her dress hikes up some, beautiful bare thighs. She leans close and whispers 'put your hand under my dress.' As I slide my hand up the inside of her thigh, she opens her purse on her lap to show me that she's removed her panties when she went to the bathroom."

Jerry slurps an impossible amount of his Long Island Ice Tea up the two straws. I find that I have forgotten to breathe. My dick hasn't. It's filling it's lungs with blood, waiting for the payoff.

"Chubby, as she closed her leather purse, givin' me that pure evil, Mona Lisa-sitting-on-a-dildo smirk, she opened that velvet, warm, woman-purse thing of hers for my hand. My God, did she know what she was doing to me, it was like liquid gold in there, peaches-and-cream ice cream, put in a microwave for just twenty, thirty seconds.

"She takes my wrist gently, removes my hand from under her skirt, slowly brings my fingers up to her face, slides her lips all the way down those fingers, and sucks off her own juices, never taking her eyes from mine. 'Buy a bottle of vodka and let's go,' she says."

"Goddam, Jerry!"

"Wait…. You know that the bottle shops and bars are normally separate deals here in Sidney, but this bar includes its own bottle shop, near the entrance."

Jerry's ready for another Long Island Ice Tea, and the place is empty except for us, so this time the bartender allows Jerry behind the bar, watching carefully as Lovell professionally brews the otherworldly concoction.

My erection is now a nagging embarrassment, preventing me from leaving my bar seat. I beg another double Stolys, breaking the bartender's concentration from Lovell's demonstration. Glancing down at my newly arrived drink, I realize that my first glass is still half-full. I Close my eyes, finishing my first vodka in one long slow pull, then I start working on the olives and ice. Squeezing the pimento and juice into my new glass, I suck the remnants off my fingers and am jolted back to visualizing Rita and Jerry's fingers, and I feel a pulse surging between my legs.

Jerry settles back in. "I pay for a bottle of Stoly's, brandishing it in the air above the crowd, and Rita and I grab a taxi to her place. It wasn't far, but she was holding the bottle in one fist and me in her other the entire trip. I think my dick was harder than the bottle.

"We're into her bedroom and out of our clothes so fast, I only have time to notice what a real playground it is, room for elbows and knees, a huge bed. Stevie, for hours we are devouring each other everywhere. She has these swollen strawberry nipples, a pretty, trim golden-red little pussy, with tiny, close-set lips. Her clit was gorgeous, a half-hooded, lightly-oiled oblong pearl, and at the center of her perfect cheeks lived a rose-

77

bud asshole, it pulsed open and closed like an expensive camera lens, and it had a mind of its own. She enjoyed getting on top, with my dick deep in the tight rings of her throat, my tongue probing, working between her cunt, and that perfect, puckering asshole.

More tea, I watch the tan liquid travel up the straws into Jerry's mouth. My face, I realize, is flushed, I feel dryly feverish, slowly rolling the cold, perspiring outside of my Stoly's glass along my forehead and lips.

"Stevie, what she loved best of all, was to get on her knees, her face buried in soft, cool pillows, her arched back presenting her butthole to me. She told me to put it in deep and slow, wanting me to withdraw and re-enter each time, all the way in, all the way out. I learned quick, I don't have to tell you. Watching those fingers of hers dancing on her clit and jamming in and out of her cunt, while my dick, bigger than it's ever been, is driving slowly all the way in and out of her warm ass was in-fucking-credible.

"At the height of all this, she's saying 'it's so pink, it's so pink….,' and she goes on to describe her girlfriend's pussy-lips and cunt, how she only just had her first three-way with a girlfriend and some guy. It was her first experience down there, and she loved it. Now her eyes are tight closed, her face screwed up with concentration as she's fantasizing the coral and pinks of her girlfriend's sex."

Jerry is face to face with me now, our drinks forgotten. "Then she starts to spasm, her whole body is orgasming, and she screams 'Jam it deep, jam it deep…' It was one of those magical nights for me, my cock never went down. I don't even remember if I came after that first time in her mouth, but God, it didn't matter. We stopped long enough to damp towel off, order a pizza, and break open the bottle of vodka. She was fun, to boot, she has this great, quirky sense of humor, and we both knew it was all shits and giggles."

"So what's the problem?" I ask, "What happened with her tonight?"

"Wait," he says, now ordering some tap beers for the two of us. "When the pizza arrives, we only eat a slice each, but we start in again. She's *manging* down on my dick after slapping a slice of pizza around it, I'm feeding cheese pie up her tight little hole and chewing her and the pizza out at the same time, it was fun, it was great, and we finished it with another serious session.

"This thing lasted until morning, when she had to get ready to go to work. We both shower, she dresses for work, and we have enough time to cab it to New York, New York, that breakfast place over at the Circular Quay. Over breakfast, we both laugh about how sore we are. My knees and that little knot under my tongue are startin' to sing their complaints to me. But we're both grinning, knowing how good it was, how light, how much fun. She was great, she was the best.

"She doesn't want me to walk her back to the hotel, because she's real serious about not wanting anything to affect her position there. Apparently she's in line for some kind of promotion, and I'm glad she's got those kinds of priorities.

"Before she leaves, she says, 'Look, I don't want to crowd you or anything, and no pressure, but can we see each other again, next time you get to Sidney?'"

"Jesus Christ, what a terrible request" I laugh, as I notice that my body is finally starting to relax. "So, come on Jerry, what the fuck happened tonight?"

"Keshy, I told that little girl that I'd love to see her again, and we agreed to do just that. Remember, this whole thing happened three months ago. So, I've been bidding Sidney trips, and my luck, suddenly I can't fuckin' buy a fuckin' Sidney trip. Finally, after three months, I get this trip, and I send her a card to let her know I'm coming down.

"I get to the hotel and she's not behind the desk, but I don't want to ask the other girls for her, I want to respect that discretion thing of hers. When I get to my room, I'm really expecting for the phone to be already ringing, but it's not. So I sit on my bed and wait, and wait, and man those minutes are tickin' by slow. So, I busy myself with unpackin' and shaving and showering and dragging each process out. No Rita, no call.

"I'm in a dilemma man, how do I call downstairs to ask for her, and yet not upset her applecart with her mates, and her job at the hotel? Finally, after two hours, I call down to registration and ask in some business-like voice, 'Rita, please.' Some little girl down there says, 'Oh, she's in the accounting office now, hold on, I'll transfer you…'

"'This is Rita, may I help you?' Great, I think, I got her on the phone personally, with nobody the wiser…It's me, I say, Jerry, and I'm in for a few days, room 1217, did you get my card? 'I'll call you back,' she says, very professionally…I'm set, Chubby, she knows I'm here, nobody's the wiser, and I'm just waiting for her to call me back from somewhere safe. I nap, I wait, finally the phone rings, I'm like a high school kid I'm so excited. Her tone tells me immediately that something's wrong, and I listen, focused now as she says that she's spoken to her girlfriend, and she doesn't want to get serious with me, and her friends advise her against it, and all this blather is pouring out…and I'm trying to equate what all this has to do with the lighthearted fun and sex we had just three months ago…

"Rita," I says, "it was just shits and giggles for us, you know, light-hearted fun…we both agreed on that, and we enjoyed each other's company, and you even asked me if we could do it again the next time I came to town. What's all this about?'"

"There's this pause, and she says, 'I let it get too serious… I just can't go through with it, it won't ever go anywhere, so I've got to stop it now.'"

"I told her 'Hey, Rita, I like you as a friend, sure, whatever you say, no hard feelings, take it light'…and we hung up."

"Holy shit, what's that all about," I ask Lovell.

Jerry says "Hey, buddy, no shit! I sat there for a solid ten minutes, stunned, my mind is trying to put it all together, to make some sense of it…I have no idea what that was all about."

"Geez, Jerry, I'm sorry." Now I genuinely am.

"Hey, like I said, there is just no understanding the wondrous ways of the female animal."

"You know, Jerry, I think she's in love with you, you were just too good."

"Life is good," Lovell says, smiling now and lifting his glass in a toast.

Willy, Silly & Bali

We were lounging about at the _Sri Ratu_ pool on _Jalan 3 Brothers Road_ in Bali. We'd just been introduced to the hotel's new owner, an Australian named Sid, who'd just bought the place from Chugai Boyeki, the Chinese gent, who also owns the Dew Drop Inn on _Legian_ (pronounced _Legyan_) Street. Sid is the picture of the perfect Hotelier, round and jolly, he loves good drink and good company.

Willy and I were finishing a bottle of _Arak_, which we had bought on the street for 1800 _Rupiahs_, known affectionately as _Rupes,_ less than $1. Returning to the hotel pool, we drank while walking, passing the bottle back and forth, weaving to avoid the pesty vendors, "_Diedat ablee_" "Get lost, we don't want any!"

Now properly lubricated, we are continuing our endless discussion of the Clintons, as Sid ambles over to listen. Silly is starkers, absolutely naked, enjoying the pool, while I'm expounding:

"Do you realize that poor bastard, is waking up right now, having to decide which power-tie to wear with what suit? He's going to have meetings, change shirts, make a few speeches today, and he's doing it because he wants to be President. What a fucking asshole, he could be here with us in Bali, doing…what are we doing?" I ask Willy.

Willy suggests that we're doing, "Nada, Baby."

Sid starts comparing Australian politicians with American politicians, "They're all the bloody same, bunch of thieving barstards," We fall instantly in love with Sid.

"Yeah," I continue, "they all spend millions of dollars, their own, and other people's, in order to be elected to a job that pays $100,000 a year." Passing the _Arak_ now to Sid, who takes quite a slug out of the bottle, "They're obviously doing it out of civic virtue mate, pure altruism."

Sid spits _Arak._

"You know we Airline Pilots have to be tested for alcohol, drugs, and competency. We take first-class medicals every six months, proficiency checks, line checks...the public expects competent, sober, healthy pilots, and they deserve that. We only expect one thing from Senators and Presidents...integrity!"

"We should pay those bastards $1,000,000 tax-free dollars a year, for life, and we should demand only one thing from them, lie detector tests! Before and after every vote, we hook them up to the machine and ask only one question, "Are you voting your conscience on this issue, or are you being paid off, or expect to be paid off, for your vote?" Then maybe we'll get some relief from the bastards...it'll be cheaper in the long run. What do we have 100 senators, 500 congressmen? About 650 people, if you throw in the President and Governors...at a million a year each, that's only $650 million. Hell, the first vote would probably save billions in giveaways."

"Spot on, mate, but they'd steal some more, anyway!"

"Yeah, you're probably right, look at the Marcos family... it's human nature... they couldn't take a few million, or a hundred million, no, they took everything."

"Have you been in Bali long, Sid?"

"No, mate, been here on holiday with the Mrs. over the years... we're from Perth, a stone's throw, but we had us a hotel in Borneo."

"Borneo, I've never been. Do you still own that hotel as well?"

"Hell, no, we had to get rid of it, they ate my manager."

A long pause of incredulity, a sidewise look at Willy.

"No, Stevie. It's bloody true! They did eat him, and he was a skinny-fucker, too!"

Willy and I were fascinated by Whitestar's girlfriend's armpits. The women around the pool, mostly Aussie's and Europeans, went topless matter-of-factly. At first, we would study this new terrain, pretending to be casual about our sweeping glances. After a while, the 'white-tips,' as Sid called them, became too familiar to be titillating.

Whitestar's woman, however, had trimmed her underarm hair. Unshaved, yet unthatched, they were barbered, and perfect. Something about the texture, color, shape and buzz-cut of her pits, sent a direct message to "sex-central," releasing all the heart-tripping chemistry of my uncontrollable lustbuds. I would have fought and killed to be able to run my nose and mouth through her armpits.

During our *Arak* walk-abouts, Willy confessed to the same obsession. From then on, we would bracket her chaise lounge, as casually as possible. Not interested in her breasts, which I can't even recall, only for our chance to worship her armpits. To us, their siren song was a command to view, without focus. When "our Miss Pits" was at poolside, we were mesmerized, unable to look elsewhere.

She, for her part, would sprawl, completely relaxed, her face protected by a towel, arms thrown back, casually, behind her head. Whether she was aware of the power of her pits or not, is subject for debate. Willy thinks not, but I believe she knew their effect on men. We never knew her name. I don't remember her ever speaking.

Whitestar himself was an interesting creature. How we came to meet and befriend him, I can't recall. We've visited his gorgeous Balinese spread of homes, behind the huge security fences, and walls. Whitestar is in his fifties now, with no apparent source of income, however it is whispered that he started the flow of "ice" and "ecstasy" into Hawaii.

He had traveled off-beat paths as a young man, and he was now telling us the tale of one of his early treks. Seems he and four or five like-souled young men, were on walk-about in Tibet. Avoiding the well-traveled paths, they were in joint, yet uncommunicated pursuit of the unusual, the exotic. One of their number, Guy (say Ghee), a French-Canadian, was their misfit. Whitestar and most of his buddies were quiet and unassuming in their quest, invisible visitors from another galaxy, taking everything in unobtrusively. The *Canuk* was pushy, his camera always present, upsetting the serenity. They could not shake him, yet no one would coach him on their unspoken etiquette.

After weeks of intentionally climbing further into Tibet's vast remoteness, they hear talk of an old Buddhist Monk who spends his days in a trance, his eyes rolled back into his head. It was said that this Monk was more than 100 years-old.

Whitestar and his band, after an arduous two-day climb, find an unassuming monastery, guided there by some villagers. Easing within the room, they now see an ancient man in saffron monk's robes, seated lotus style. His head is back, his eyes are rolled up inside his skull. He is a living still life. The old man is being attended by an even older woman, who brushing cobwebs aside, soundlessly beckons them close.

Reverently, they shuffle near the tranced-out ancient one. Guy, the insensitive fellow with the incessant camera, walks right up on the monk, clicking away from every angle. This desecration horrifies Whitestar and his mates, who freeze in place. As the rude young man continues clicking away, the old monk's eyes roll down into focus. It is a silent summons to the old woman, who places her ear close by his whispering lips. She withdraws, and whispers into Guy's ear, as the Monk's eyes, once again roll upwards, showing only their whites.

"Finally," Whitestar thinks "that asshole is finally gonna' get his comeuppance."

Later, passing back through the remote village, and down the mountain, Whitestar asked Guy, "What did the old lady say?"

"She said that the old man wanted to know if I could send him some copies of the pictures I took."

I tell the group of my experience at the temples in Narita, Japan. Over a course of two years, every few weeks I would have an opportunity to visit the Buddhist temple, which is actually a sprawling, yet serene collection of wooden temples, hand-carved over the centuries. Near the massive, stone-lintled entryway, stood a grated incense burner, open on all sides. I mimic the gathering, and washing of the smoke over my face and head that I see being done by the Japanese worshipers, to bring them luck.

Each visit, I take in another building or two. They are fascinating to me, what with their indecipherable script and symbolism. One huge wooden building is covered about, on all four sides, with carved heads and faces. It is said (a sign says in English and Japanese) that if you look at these thousands of faces carefully enough, you will recognize one of your parents or grandparents, that it will be them. I spend an entire day, able to study only half the building, with no luck, so far.

Another of the buildings looms three stories high, lattice-sided. Narrow passages have been carved, allowing entrance through all four sides. Inside it is empty of people, yet there, taking up the entire center of this building, is a massive three-story high top, a *dredl*-like cylinder, pointy-end down. Pigeon-holes, stuffed with parchment, envelop it's entire surface, and it is supported through it's central axis by a forty-foot pole, anchored top and bottom. This mysterious affair, which must weigh tons, has horizontal poles, chest high, protruding every few yards around its perimeter.

Along one wall is a countertop with a slot for coins and paper money built in. A sign behind the cash slot explains that the "if you turn the wheel three revolutions around its axis, that you'd derive the same benefit as having studied all the written works of Buddhism." Seems that the parchment documents stuffed into the pidgeon holes contain all the sacred writings of Buddism…. "Donations are customary."

Pushing some yen through the slot, I approach the behemoth. Over the years, a circular path has been scrubbed through the tiles by the feet of countless believers. Taking a grip on the pole nearest me, I notice that it too has been reshaped by thousands of earlier hands, also anxious for wisdom. Planting my feet firmly, putting my back into it, I start to shove, part of my mind registering (for the three count) where I've begun. The monster begins to move, far more easily than I expected, and I complete my three revolutions, adding half-again as insurance. Leaving the building, passing from its darkened, cool interior, to the warmer light of day, I feel an indefinable, yet convincing, something... I sense that I am now secret heir to some mystical wisdom.

As is my custom, on my last visit to the temple grounds, I head for a building I've not yet visited. Getting closer, I pick up sounds, Japanese voices, strange and high-pitched. "What fascination will be revealed to me today?" I wonder, almost at the building itself. Removing my shoes, entering with deference, I am facing a magnificent shrine of golds, reds and burnished wood. A light trace of incense delicately registers, as I turn now towards the sounds. Seated in a row, are three monks, their heads shaven. On a shelf in front of them is a color television, at which they stare transfixed, watching Disney cartoons, dubbed with Japanese voices. Elmer Fudd, his shotgun at the ready, is chasing Bugs Bunny. On the counter, nearby, is the slot for donations.

"I never went back," I conclude.

Guam

"It's called the 'brown tree snake.' It started off in Indonesia actually. Most likely island-hopping on freighters." The herpetologist has been expounding on the problems caused on Guam by these climbing snakes. The young scholar has been brought in by the U.S. Navy on Guam, as a favor to the Chamorro people of Guam. "The snakes cause power outages, brown-outs. They climb the electrical poles and slither from wire-to-wire, that shorts out the system. The bird population is disappearing as well."

Captain Bubba, ordering us another round of beer, says "Snake-suicide, is that it?"

"Well, kinda'" admits the snake-man.

"I've been coming to these islands for thirty-years off and on, and I've never even seen a snake, brown or otherwise."

"Well, that's not unusual," explains the expert, these snakes are nocturnal, only active at night."

"So's Bubba," I tell him, sipping the last of my Kirin.

Chuckling, Bubba tells us he knows that the snakes are nocturnal. "Last snake-man they brought in didn't know shit, though. Know what he done? Brought in Mongoose…mongeese…is it mongooses or mongeese?" asks Bubba, suddenly concerned with his grammar.

"Mongoose is the singular as well as the plural, like fish."

"I say 'fishes,'" says Bubba,…"Anyway, this last expert, your predecessor, brought in mongooses to fight the snakes. What he didn't know was that mongooses, they're 'di-urinal' like us, the snakes being nocturnal, they never meet."

"No," Bubba says, "your electrical problem is the "Chamorons," don't know shit about power plants. They're just blamin' the snakes for their own stupidity.

"What about the declining bird population?" the professor asks.

"guess what a mongoose's favorite meal is?" chortles Bubba.

"You sure don't think much of the indigenous population, Bubba." I muse, wondering why Bubba believes that the Chamorros are "Chamorons." I always thought these slurs were said in jest.

"Any morons that celebrate 'Magellan Day' as their biggest holiday of the year after what Magellan did to them, they're just plain stupid!"

"What?"

"Keshy, when Magellan sailed into these Marianna's Islands, with his entourage of those good old boy Jesuit priests, there was millions of Chamorros on these islands. After those holy-rollers got through with 'em, only a few thousand were left alive, and I'm not talkin' 'bout any fancy, European disease germs, neither! Nope, ain't for no reason that these islands are the most shark infested waters on Earth. It was accept Jesus or off the cliffs they went."

"Jesus!"

"Just so," he says.

Desert Storm

Radio check is coming due, as we approach the F.I.R., the air boundary between Cairo and Jeddah control.

"*Sa'allah'm Alahem*, Jeddah Control. MAC 3-1-3-1, checking in FL 350, estimating *Abdul Azziz* at 2130Z, *Insh'allah.*"

"Roger MAC 3-1-3-1, radar identified, flight level 350, contact military control on 128.2."

"Roger, MAC 3-1-3-1."

We've been flying MAC support for Desert Shield and Desert Storm, ferrying doctors, supplies and Marines into Kuwait City and bringing troops and equipment home.

The war has been over a few months, and tonight we will bring home the "lost battalion," so dubbed in the editorial pages of the New York Times, and the Washington Post. This Marine Corps reserve outfit is a troop of infantry, 'grunts,' who are primarily civilians with a monthly military obligation. Cooks, teachers, bottle washers, playing soldier. This battalion, from Baton Rouge, Louisiana, is the only ground reserve unit to see combat, suffer casualties and dead. Their mission was to dash north from Western Saudi Arabia to a crossroads in Northwestern Kuwait, and to hold that roadway.

Somehow, in the mysterious way of these things, they've been forgotten out in the desert. After months of maintaining their position, nursing their wounded, and grieving for their dead, they've dropped through the cracks. Nobody knows that they are still out there. Calls to H.Q., calls to wives begging assistance from local politicos get no results. Finally, a company clerk writes letters to the editors of some big city news papers. "The Lost Battalion" has been found, and with the speed of a white house scandal, they are packed up and ordered home.

D.B. asks, Who said it's easier to make a million dollars than it is to steal it?"

"Willie Sutton?"

"No, Keshy," that was Mr. P.T. Barnum, and he was right."

"Okay, D.B., so how come we're always broke?"

Jerry Lovell adds, "You know, W.C. Fields hated Philadelphia. Back then, Vaudeville traveled city to city putting on shows. For one reason or another, W.C. Fields hated going to Philadelphia, something about the city…" "Top of decent fuel is 41.5…" I don't even bother to write that number down. "…Anyway, know what's on W.C. Fields tombstone? His epitaph?… 'I'd rather be in Philadelphia'… it was his last prank, and he played it on himself."

I'm trying to decide what that has to do with anything, as we start our descent towards the Kuwait airport.

On the ground now, we've a few hours to kill, waiting for refueling, unloading, reloading and paperwork. We will be operating the first leg, Kuwait City to Cherry Point, N.C. Some other crew will fly our 'lost battalion' the rest of the way to Baton Rouge.

"Hey MAC 3-1-3-1, what are you carrying tonight?" asks Shannon Oceanic Center, as we coast out west, out over Lands End.

"We're carrying the 'Lost Battalion,'" I respond.

"Standby 3-1-3-1."

Minutes go by, as we wait for our oceanic clearance. Finally, "MAC 3-1-3-1, cleared present position direct Cherry Point, North Carolina."

"Holy Shit, we're famous, this is a first for me. Maybe Air Force One gets clearances like that," D.B. says.

On a MAC flight, the rules don't apply, so it's open cockpit, and the Marines come and go freely, sharing their stories, sharing their lives. A bizarre unreality washes over me as my mind drops back twenty-five years. Then, I was a twenty-four-year old marine grunt, being brought home from another war, at a time when flying planes had never occurred to me, now I'm the pilot flying these Marines home from their war.

"...so these tractors with these huge tires on 'em, they've got these snow plows welded to their front-end, they just drive along on either side of the trenches, filling them in with sand." The lieutenant grins as he explains, his photo-album of corpses and burnt-out vehicles, still open on our 'pedestal,' the instrument panel between the two flying pilots. He's been sitting in the jump seat explaining his maneuver.

The Iraqi's had dug miles of east-west trenches, and had hundreds of thousands of their young soldiers in them. These kids and their rifles were facing south towards Saudi Arabia, ready to repel our invasion.

Unwilling to be there, drafted, kidnapped off the streets, these young kid soldiers had Sadam's Republican guards sitting behind them. They were told to stay and die for Sadam, or if they bolted, be shot in the back of the head by Hussein's loyal butchers.

For twenty days and nights, these poor, young bastards endured the B-52 Carpet bombings all along their lines. Terrified, deaf and shell-shocked, they were finally buried alive, as our sand-pushing tractors filled in their Maginot Line in the desert.

"How long were the trenches?" I ask.

"I'd say about a hunnert, hunnert-fifty clicks," answers the Looey.

That's about 60-90 miles.

D.B. and I look at each other, then back to our cockpit visitor. We know that hundreds of thousands of Iraqi mothers and fathers, people who never wanted war and had no say in it, would never see their sons again.

Would never know where their sons died, how and where they were buried.

God & Beliefs

I have a secret, I am spiritually bankrupt. The reason I tell you this upfront, is that I've always worried that it showed.

Commercialing, sitting in any airline passenger seat, I try to establish a pecking order of importance with my neighbors. Peeking at their paper-worked laps or their laptops, deciding this one's a lawyer, that one's a Corporate V.P.... I start playing my head-games.

I'm better than he is, smarter, more worldly than that one, but close calls require that I pull out my passports, with their stamps and visas from all over the world, pretending to need some info from these passports (busy work), I break the tie... See, I'm the biggest dog, look where I've been, fool!

Considering my need to do this, I have little hope for my future growth towards emotional or spiritual maturity...I'm not better yet! When I try to think why I'm thus driven, I avoid looking too closely. It's very uncomfortable.

I asked Kiley to listen to my CD of Rach-3 from start to finish...I told her, if she listened to my Rach-3, I would listen to whatever she wanted me to listen to. I wanted (really) to get her impression of the piece, since I love it so.

To give her credit, the first movement is more than 15 minutes long, and the whole more than half an hour. She declared, after the second movement, and unable to sit through any more, "it doesn't go anywhere!" (too slow moving, is how I interpreted her critique.)

I understood. At her age, she didn't have the patience to allow the three movements to develop, and to therefore appreciate the whole.

I remember my father calling me over in Synagogue to point out the English versions of passages he must have found particularly meaningful. All the "praise God, Glory to God" stuff...I couldn't believe it. He seemed like an idolater. Didn't he realize, I thought, that any real God wouldn't need to hear all that bullshit?

I don't think much about God, but when I do, I'm always brought back to a dark night, in a rain soaked jungle. I am standing still, wet through for days, numb, exhausted beyond caring, I have shorted out. The rain, coming straight down now, pours through the flash suppressor ports of my M-14, slung upside-down from my sopping shoulder.

Staring straight ahead, unseeing, I'm quits. Suddenly, standing there in front of me, within my pool of darkness, is a man. The fact that he's wearing a Marine Corps khaki poncho and fatigues doesn't yet register. He is facing me, and sees through my eyes and into my heart. We say nothing, but he knows... without a word, he takes my weapon, then removes the heavy pack from my back. He strips me to my waist. In my pack, he finds a towel and some dry shirts, rolled within my poncho. Briskly, he towels me dry. Working quickly now, he pulls a dry t-shirt over my head, buttons me into a new fatigue shirt, and pulls my poncho down, into place.

Instantly, I begin to come alive, the warmth floods life back into me. The man eases me back into my pack, and re-shoulders my rifle, now with my help. He looks me in the face for a moment, and then he's gone. That man in the jungle, thirty-five years ago, was Jesus Christ. Through the years, my New York cynic, Jew-brain has twisted and turned-upside down, all religious conviction. I've tried every way I can to explain this experience to myself, even believing it to be the delusional byproduct of my then wretched condition.

No... the one thing I'm sure of, as sure as I am of any real thing, is that that was Jesus Christ there, in those fatigues, saving me.

As I said, I don't dwell much on God, and I hope, after all I've done since then, that he doesn't spend much time thinking about me.

Months later, I'm home, watching the Gulf War Victory Parade on T.V., our proud troops are marching down Pennsylvania Avenue, in Washington, D.C. My stomach involuntarily rebels, and I choke back the vomit until I just make it to the toilet. On my knees now, spitting the final, sour acid juices from my mouth, I'm wracked with tears, trying to feel patriotic and proud of what we've done over there.

Chris Smith's First Trip

Chris Smith, a better looking Tom Selleck, was a crash pad buddy and flying colleague over at Eastern Metro. Married to a devout Baptist woman, father of two children (his family lived in Charlotte, heart of Jesus' Heartland), Chris was always being chased by the ladies, sometimes successfully.

Chris was the first of our gang to be hired by a Major Airline, every Atlanta based Commuter pilot's first choice, Piedmont Airlines. He came back to visit all of us at our College Park complex, after completing Initial Indoctrination. We were rapt as he described the President of Piedmont's greeting to Chris' new hire class on their first day: "Welcome to Piedmont, the last Airline you'll ever work for!" Man, that sounded great, what a lucky guy.

Months later, we meet up again, and he tells me about his first trip as a brand new Second Officer/Flight Engineer. "The Captain and everybody were great, all real nice to me," he says. It was a five day trip, and he's not sure, but he thinks the girl Sue, serving the coffee and meals to the cockpit, is coming on to him. "She's been kinda brushin' up" against his back, arm and shoulders as she goes forward to hand the Pilot's their coffee and meals, he's not certain, but "some of it might have been unnecessary," and he's heard all the stories about layovers and such.

On their third night out, now in Savannah, the crew gets together in the evening for drinks... they're not flying again until the next evening. Everybody's chatting and sipping, and suddenly a real mellow live band kicks up in the cocktail lounge. The whole crew jumps up together, all ready to dance. They laugh at their own eagerness, this is great, nice people, laid back. Eventually, Chris is dancing one number with the cockpit queen that he thought may have been coming on to him. She is very reserved on the dance floor, very proper, but when nobody is looking, she slips her room key into his pocket, whispering for him to wait at least an hour after she leaves and before he shows up... be discreet... Holy Shit, it's gonna happen.

Chris waits about half an hour after the girl, Sue, has left. He excuses himself, says goodnight and goes to his room. While he waits, he brushes his teeth, applies more deodorant and recombs his hair. Finally, gently, he lets himself out of his room, and quietly makes his way to Sue's room. Knocking softly, he lets himself in... she's in the shower, yelling for him to get himself a drink (there are minis and ice on a sideboard), and to join her in the shower. Chris knocks back a fast vodka, rocks.... "it hasn't even had a chance to cool down, but I needed it for my nerves," he laughs. Then he strips naked and pulls back the shower curtain. "Welcome to Piedmont Airlines!" the whole crew yells, sitting, hiding on the floor of the tub in their bathing suits, Sue standing there in hers. They are laughing and pointing with glee... Chris is the only one balls naked, he's been had. It turned out all right he shyly smiles, finishing his story.

Last time I saw Chris, he and his very Baptist wife, Kathy, visited me and Geri at our apartment in Honolulu. While the girls were shopping, Chris and I walked along Kapiolani Park, up the trail to Diamond Head. Chris was real upset as he told me "the latest," and I could tell he had been holding back, wanting to get me alone for this. Seems he had taken up with a Flight Attendant who had her home in Atlanta. On layovers in Atlanta, schedules permitting, they would shack-up at her house, a few bedrooms of which she rented out to two openly gay, male flight attendants. She was a "liberated, sex-loving lady," he says.

One morning he wakes early in her bedroom suite. He's got an early morning show, she's got the day off. So as not to wake her, he's quietly using her master bathroom, going through his routine... he shaves, showers and dresses in uniform, "all real quiet like, so as not to disturb her rest."

As he re-enters the bedroom, he is instantly repulsed. She is doing the two gay male flight attendants in her bed, the bed Chris crept out of only an hour earlier. She's taking them both at the same time, one in the mouth and the other in her pussy." The guy whose dick is in her mouth, is deeply tongue-kissing his buddy, the other guy, "over the top." Chris wants to puke.

This is the age of AIDS, it's 1987, and his lady friend never felt it necessary to tell Chris that she was also fucking the two gay guys. Chris is crying, sobbing now in my arms, as he finishes his story. He really loves his wife. They have been married eight years, have two young sons, and she's a devout Christian woman who attends church regularly, in Charlotte, their home town. "I know," he says through his tears, "I did it to myself, but God, I don't want to do this to her!"

I hold him around, comforting him. He doesn't know if he's got AIDS, worse, he doesn't know if he has passed it along to his wife. There are no quicky tests as yet, and prevailing wisdom is that at least five-years must pass before you'll ever know. He is wracked with guilt, faced with indecision. Should he tell his wife, or not?

God, I feel for him, another pecker-induced mistake, common to the airline industry.

Marcos

While still based in Honolulu, former Philippine President Ferdinand Marcos, his shoe-loving wife, Imelda, and their son, Bong Bong were living in splendid exile on Oahu. When Marcos died, the Philippine Government refused Imelda's requests to allow her, and the family, to return to bury Ferdinand in his home island city of *Ilios Norte.*

Responding to accusations of larceny on a grand scale (the Marcos' were reputed to have looted the Philippines of about $35 billion), Imelda would gather the reporters together on the porch of the mansion in which she was forced to live, and tearfully protest their innocence, their poverty, and the injustice of it all. "They were getting along," she would declare, "due to the handouts from, and kindness of friends."

Imelda, never underestimating the stupidity of the masses, kept Ferdinand's body on ice at a fancy cemetery near Kailua Bay. Once a year, on Ferdinand's birthday, his body, cryogenically convenient in it's crypt, would be brought to her Hawaiian mansion-prison. She would invite hundreds of *Marcoista's* to Ferdinand's birthday party, and I have it on good authority, that at some point in the evening, Imelda would call the gathering to order. Ever the entertainer, she would sing "Happy Birthday to You" to Ferdinand's frozen corpse.

Five years after Ferdinand's death, the Philippine Government relented to the pressure of the masses. It was announced that Ex-President Marcos would be allowed burial in *Ilios Norte.*

I was taking Willy and Silly, good friends for many years, on "buddy passes" to Bali. Buddy Pass trips are on a space available basis, and this trip required a flight from HNL-Guam, then from Guam to Denpassar, Bali. Calling Continental reservations, I confirmed that tomorrow's DC-10 flight from HNL-Guam was "wide open." Good, tomorrow's first leg had plenty of empty seats.

Next day we check our bags at the Continental ticket counter, produce our passports for verification, and proceed to the gate. It is cordoned off. Hundreds of passengers are being herded back, kept at a distance from the gate. We move to a waiting area one gate over, trying to figure out what the fuck is going on.

Television cameras are trained at the ramp area, focusing beneath our flight's DC-10. Honolulu's local Jane Pauley approaches me, microphone in hand. Her cameraman, shoulder-cam rolling, brackets us. "Jane" asks me: "What do you think of Ferdinand Marcos' body being returned to the Philippines for burial?"

Oh shit, as fate would have it, Marcos' body, now being belly-loaded (in an ordinary baggage container), is heading to Manila via Guam, on our airplane. Worse, hundreds of *Marcoista's*, including his son Bong Bong, are accompanying their dead hero for burial in the Philippines.

I respond, "I can't believe that after twenty-years of fucking over the Philippine people, now five-years after his death, Ferdinand Marcos is going to fuck me and my friends out of our trip to Guam!"

"Cut!"

We make it onto the airplane after all, but it was close, with only a few seats remaining. Celebrating our success, Willy and Silly break out the Evian water bottles they've filled with Stolys. We drink for the first half-hour of this eight-hour leg, ordering only Bloody Mary Mix, and ice from the flight attendants.

My mind begins to wander. We are sitting on an airplane carrying Marco's body, his son and hundreds of their corrupt cronies who have sucked billions of illicit dollars out of the country, all of them on board this airplane. A niggling thought creeps and grows in my head...How many Filipino's out there would love to see this airplane blown out of the sky?

"Willy," I say, "More vodka!" I suffer through the remainder of the flight, trying not to dwell on the worst case scenario.

Our fellow passengers are partying hearty, standing up all over the plane, smoking, schmoozing and completely disregarding seat belt signs or instructions to put out their cigarettes. These are rich, happy campers, at a party.

Silly is seated next to the only dour gentleman on the airplane, and she begs me to change seats with her, and I do. After perhaps an hour of silence, the seventy-ish gentleman turns, and introduces himself to me, "Father Gomez, at your service," (do I hear boot heels faintly clicking?). He hands me a business card, as well. It seems the good Father is also a General of the Philippine Air Force, and he has a Canadian address.

"Are you part of the group accompanying ex-President Marcos for burial?"

"Yes, I was his priest."

Never shy I ask, "Did you used to take former President Ferdinand Marcos' confession?"

Pause..."Yes, I did."

"Did it take a long time?"

The remaining five hours of the flight were spent in silence.

The five hour flight from Guam to Bali was uneventful, and Willy, Silly and I were anxious to meet up with our old comrades at the *Blue Moon Cafe*, off of *Jalan three brothers* road. The Specialty of the House at the Moon is the "Blue Thunder" Mushroom Soup. Twenty minutes after slurping down this delicious delicacy, the familiar stomach cramping begins. It's not too uncomfortable and doesn't last long. The Blue Thunder mushroom trip lasts half a day, and the psychedelic colors and patterns are proof positive, as to the inspiration behind Balinese patterns and fabrics.

Balinese, by tradition, are only supposed to have up to four children. They name the first born *Wayan*, next *Mahdi*, then *Nyoman* and finally *Katut*. Should they, by chance, have additional kids (no sin), they start over again. Number five is *Wayan*, number six, *Mahdi,* and so forth. Differentiating girls from boys is easy. The prefix *Ni* is sometimes designated, as in *Ni-Wayan* Kiley, but is not required.

"*Wayan* Steve ," asks *Mahdi* Willy, "have you seen *Ni Katut* Silly?"

"No Willy, last I saw she was in the pool."

Silly surfaces, insisting we join her in the pool. "Wait till you see the colors and textures underwater," she insists, and disappears to the bottom, again.

Mahdi Willy follows her in. I am satisfied to sit at poolside at *The Sri Ratu* Hotel, watching as multi-colored horns grow out of the other patrons heads, and snakes of all colors and patterns wind through their legs. "Blue Thunder" is a powerful hallucinogen, but there is no fear associated with it. While tripping, you are aware of your own situation, always in control and able to completely enjoy the experience.

Willy and Silly surface, smiling, *Lucy in the Sky with Diamonds*, Willy announces. It seemed to me that they were gone for hours.

Next day we travel by "Motor transport Sir" to *Candidasa*, to visit our buddies at *Ida's (eedah's) Homestay*. On a football-field size greensward, at the aqua-green water's edge, sits *Ida's warung*. Three hand-carved, two-story, thatched-roofed dwellings, they are beautifully made of stone and bamboo.

On the road side, high above us, it's top lost in mist and cloud, looms a huge mountain. Ancient, terraced rice-paddies cascade down its sides.

Ida Bagus Wijanah greets us warmly, and shows us to the two *'huti'* we will occupy. Willy and Silly in one, and I in the other. Each of the three dwellings comprising the *warung* can sleep seven.

In the morning, when the staff, an entire Balinese family living on the *warung* grounds, sense we are up and about, they greet us with hearty, smiling *salamat pagees*. They are bearing heaping platters of steaming *Nassi-Goring* (delicious mounds of fried rice, chopped scallions, and fried eggs on top), pots of delicious Balinese coffee, yogurt, fruit and nuts.

"Salamat pagee, Wayan-Steve, welcome back. Abaca bah?"

"Baik-Baik, Salamat Pagee, tereema cassi banya," I greet and thank him in return.

Over the centuries, as Islam crept inexorably eastward across Indonesia's 16,000+ islands, the remaining Hindu's fled further east, just east of Java, they settled on the island of Bali. Bali is the last bastion of Balinese, and Balinese-Hinduism, which is far different from the Indian Subcontinent variety of Hindu people or religions. The Balinese people are beautiful inside and out. They are a truly loving, generous people, who are sincere in their favors, not fawning or smarmy. Further, there is no word for art or artist in the Balinese dialect, since everything they do or touch is done with love, and automatically becomes a work of art.

Silly is a great artist. Add equal parts of Picasso and Chagal in a blender, set on "high," panache onto large canvass, that's Silly's style. Breathtaking, and one of a kind, her paintings capture your soul forever. God alone knows what she is trying to create, since Silly is crazy, but controllable. "They've adjusted her dosage," is Willy's response, when I complain about her abusive tirades towards me.

"Control your *monkey*," I insist in a thick, nasal French accent, harkening back to the blind organ-grinder routine, in an old Inspector Clousseau movie.

Back on Tumon bay in Guam now, we're spending the day at the Pacific Star poolside, waiting for our evening flight back to Honolulu.

Bubba and his crew, Herr-Lippi and Jerry Lovell are laying over at the hotel as well. They will be the operating crew taking us home. Herr-Lippi and Lovell are chatting up some women in the pool.

"Can I ask you a question?" Herr-Lippi approaches two of the girls.

"Sure."

"We've been noticing for most of the day now the t-shirts you're all wearing, the ones that say "NOA" and for the life of us we can't figure it out. What does NOA stand for? Is it Biblical?"

Some of the women, on chaise lounges nearby, whisper briefly to each other. The lady Mark's addressing, a thirty-something with dark, curly hair, deliberates, then: "Okay, I'll tell you ,but it's not a joke to us, it's not funny, and we would appreciate it if you would understand that, up front."

"All right," Mark, serious now, "we'll respect your wishes. So what does NOA mean, it's not a biblical reference, is it?" .... concerned.

"No, no...we belong to an organization, a self-help group, similar to AA, NOA, called Nymphomaniacs of America." She explains that these women are from all over the U.S., and that they meet monthly at local chapters. Once a year, however, they pick a foreign location to hold their National meeting at, and this year it's Guam.

"You have to understand, this is a disease. Most of us had childhood experiences which destroyed our feelings of self-worth. Some people take to drink, our members reactive symptoms are nymphomania.

Giving your body away, to be used by anyone, anytime, is a form of self-punishment." This lady has obviously spoken on this subject before.

"Oh," Mark says.

Our guys, and the women, relax back now, just ordinary people kicking back, getting to know each other. They chat about careers, ambitions, places back home, while sipping soft drinks. Over the next few hours, comfortable trust has built up, and they are at ease with each other.

Bubba has his guitar out, and has been "plunkin'" for Willy and I. Silly's off being Silly somewhere.

"Hey, Keshy, you visit the Buddhist complex at Narita a lot, don't you?"

"Yeah, it's beautiful, Bubba, all those ancient, hand-carved wooden temples."

"I've got a song I wrote, mentions it."

"Let's hear it, Bubba."

"I call it *My Sweet Narita Conchita*," Bubba starts to play and sing:

> My sweet Narita Conchita,
> she takes good care of me.
> She's my Japanese cowgirl,
> really knows how to please.
>
> We stroll the Temple by day,
> Chow down on Miso butter-corn.
> Compai lots of Asahi beer,
> and then it's time for some porn.
>
> My sweet Narita Conchita,
> she takes good care of me.
> She's my Japanese cowgirl,
> really knows how to please.

My Japanese cowgirl,
she hog-ties me to the bed.
Oils up my body,
saddles up my head.
Rides me like a wild Brahma,
past the count of ten.
A rodeo-rama,
she gives to few cowmen.

(Finishing with a flourish)

My sweet Narita Conchita,
she takes good care of me.
She's my Japanese cowgirl,
and...she...really...knows
how to please,
she really knows how to please!

Willy and I applaud wildly, as Bubba bows deeply from his seat..."I know, I know, it's great."

"You should get that done in Nashville." I say, knowing Bubba's already connected down there.

"No, no, Kesh. Ever been to the Mount Fuji Country Western Music Festival?"

"Never even heard of it."

"Yeah, last year on layover at Narita, we had a mechanical, kept us there three days waitin' on parts. I found out that the Nippers are crazy for Country Western, and their annual Mount Fuji Festival was underway. Well shit, I had to get up there. It was a friggin' zoo! Millions of drunk-on-their-ass Nippers, all dressed up in these designer cowboy outfits, enjoying the hell out of country western music. Hell, I know half of them didn't understand a word that was sung, but they loved it.

"They even got them a Nipper Country Western Super-Star, Charlie "*Call me Johnny*" Nikatani, he ain't bad neither!"

"Bubba, you're shittin' me." Falling now into his vernacular.

"No joke, Steve. That's what inspired '*My Sweet Narita Conchita*.' Got my agent contacting his agent, want him to do my song."

A swim later, and Herr Lippi and Lovell greet Willy and I, although they try to avoid introducing us to their new lady friends in the pool. Lippi, however, has already told me the circumstances of the NOA T-shirts, so we remain properly respectful.

"Can I ask you a question?" I ask Mark's lady friend in the pool, the one who did the talking early on.

"Sure."

"Well, as a result of your group's … ah, uh "affliction," you've all done lots of men, all types and races?"

"That's true," some of the girls gather closer now.

"In your discussion groups, have you ever compared, you know, what race or creed of men make the best lovers?" It's a valid question, academically asked.

Some of them blush, or giggle. "As a matter of fact, yes, we have discussed that, and we mostly agreed that American Indians make the best lovers, they're the longest lasting ...but there are so few of them... Jewish men are a close second."

"Well, then allow me to introduce myself," as I extend my hand. "My name is Tonto Bernstein!"

Silly is back, carrying plastic bags filled with Shirley's fried rice and takeout. Great, we all ravenously descend on the feast, tables and chairs hastily thrown together.

"Who's got the hot sauce?"

"What we need is some *wasabe*" declares Bubba, who has put up his guitar.

Silly had taken a taxi to "Shirley's II" in Harmon Plaza, off of Marine Drive, and she has already eaten. Eagerly she tells Willy and the table in general, that she's met "the most interesting woman I've ever met in my life."

"The last person you ever talk to is always 'the most interesting person' you've ever met," I say joking, but caustic. There has always been an edge to our relationship. Has something to do with her jealously wanting Willy closer to her than to anybody else. Whenever Silly's paranoia tells her that someone besides herself is getting too close to Willy, she reacts. Lately, I've been the target of her venomous sarcasm. Understanding where it's coming from is one thing, being able to reasonably deal with it, another... It does not come easy to me. Feeling ashamed of my comment, I try to make it up to her... "So, who did you meet? Was it at 'Shirley's?"

Silly, recovering quickly, says, "This wrinkled up, ninety-nine-year-old woman at Shirley's..."

Bubba interrupting, "Nolan's widow! She's Shirley's Aunt. She still alive?"

"Yes," Silly continues, "she seems to sit there all day long, and is willing to tell you everything." Silly who has recently started her umpteenth business, Video Magic, is anxious to grab her video cam and run back to interview the old widow. She starts pulling away.

"Tell me first," Willy Says. "Who's Nolan's widow...who's Nolan?"

Bubba, who flew the Micronesian Islands for twenty years, tells Willy to let Silly go. He'll fill him in. Silly goes running to grab her video cam from her room.

"Noland was Amelia Earhardt's Radio Operator, her Navigator..."

"Not a very good Navigator!" I toss in.

"...anyway, his widow tells all the old stories about Earhardt and her husband. She thinks they survived the landing, but were captured by the Japs and brought to Saipan. She says they were executed as spies, at the jailhouse there, just north of the departure end of runway 7."

"Shit, Bubba, I've been in that deserted jailhouse and it does have bullet holes in the walls."

Much later, Silly's back, it's late and we're rushing to catch the plane to Honolulu. "What did the old lady tell you about Nolan," Willy asks?

Silly, dejectedly, "That he was a drunken, no good bum!"

"That's great footage," Willy says, "I want to see that interview, Viacom will pay us a fortune for that interview."

"No Willy, there's something wrong with the batteries, or something's no good." Silly pouts. "I don't think the video-cam is working."

Willy and I glance at each other, another one of Silly's businesses.

Transition

It's 1994 and Continental Airlines has been going down the shitter, They are in Chapter XI bankruptcy, furloughing hundreds of employees, and I've been knocked off the 747's 'cause they've reduced the fleet from nine to five planes.

Flying the DC-10's has been fun, big plane, same International routes, same Honolulu base, but now, to save money, Continental moves the DC-10 base to Guam. Geri doesn't want to live on Guam. I want to move to Bali and commute to Guam (only a five hour ride), Geri doesn't want to live in Bali. "It's too far from her family (in Indiana)."

"But Honey, we are Airline people, we travel free," I respond.

Truth is, she's right anyway. I'm going to be traveling a few weeks every month. She's the one, she and Kiley, now four-years-old, who actually have to live wherever we live, they are the ones who have to be happy, and safe.

Bali's great, but the health care system sucks. If you become really sick, or get really hurt, you have to get out of Indonesia for any decent medical treatment. Guam's Guam, people either love it or hate it, I love it, Geri hates it. Living in Hawaii is no longer an option. The commute to Guam, eight hours or more during the winter, would be impossible with so many more senior people than me trying to jump seat. Further, Kiley's going to be starting school next year, and the public school system in Hawaii is the pits.

A Hawaiian Professor named Trask, a local a *Kamaiina* Heroine, has guaranteed mediocrity or worse for her people, by championing the

111

cause of teaching and accepting "Pigeon" as a language acceptable in the public school systems…. this was Ebonics years ahead of it's time. The Honolulu public school system is the bottom of the barrel, grade-wise in all comparative standardized testing. The "*Haole*" hate factor is also unacceptable to me. White kids (*Haole*s) are not just discriminated against, they are in physical danger from the local kids in the Honolulu Public School system, I think so, anyway. The fruit of Hawaiian and *Haole* mixed marriages are called *Happas*, half Hawaiian, half Haole. We call Kiley a *Happa Hebrew*, half Catholic, half Jew.

We never had any trouble with the locals, always accepted, 'cause we're wild, crazy, genuine and great…. but kids, they're kids… I just can't trust the deal for Kiley. Without Kiley it was different, Geri and I were more adventurous, it's been completely different since our daughter's birth, in Queen Kaolani Hospital.

We're getting ready to check out of the Hospital room. Geri's nursing the baby, I'm packing, and in walks a Candy-Striper with a clip-board. She starts asking questions: "Mother's name?"…… I answer. "Father's name?" ……. I answer. "Mother is?"……… "Mother is 100% Hawaiian," I answer, looking over at my green-eyed, freckled, Irish-Catholic wife, who is now staring back at me.

"Father is?" the girl asks, unflinching. "The father is Alaskan Eskimo Indian," I say."

Now Geri is staring at me hard, still unable to say anything to me with the girl there. Finally, the Candy-Striper and her clip-board leave. Geri asks, "What was that all about?"

"Honey, that's for Kiley's Birth Certificate, for the Bureau of Vital Statistics, they're gonna have her down as fifty percent Hawaiian and fifty percent Eskimo, she's gonna get free land, free college…."

Geri explodes at me "You're not starting my daughter's life out on a FUCKING LIE… You're not starting my daughter's life out on a FUCKING LIE, I don't care what you do with yourself, but……."

Five minutes later I've kinda got the message that my straight wife from Indiana is serious, Geri definitely doesn't want me to start Kiley's life out on a fucking lie. Now I have to find the Candy-Striper with the thirty-caliber pencil. She is three rooms down by now.

"Excuse me, there's been a misunderstanding."

"Oh?"

"Yes, … Mother's Caucasian, Father's Caucasian."

Bent as I am, I still regret having changed the Birth Certificate back to the truth.

We are going to have to leave Hawaii, Kiley's birthplace, after eight great years, and head back to "the Mainland."

I'm in a hotel room in Houston, training (going through IOE, Initial Operating Experience) on the MD-80, and we are moving to Florida. The phone rings and it's Stigo, he's not drunk… strange, and he's got a message to impart.

"Stevo, Tower Air is hiring."

"What's a Tower Air?" I ask.

"They're the highest paid American Carrier, average two years into the left seat, a fleet of only 747's…"

Jew Stuff – Tower Air

It's my first day with my second major airline, Tower Air. I am bonding with my classmate buddies. Lots of experience and talent in this class. I am a lightweight compared to the level of experience here. There are former Pan Am, Eastern, Brannif, and Old Continental pilots in this group of about thirty guys.

Bruce Quinn, a typical office-puke, is our Ground School Instructor. On day one, he's discussing the Hasidic Jews we fly to Tel Aviv, Tower Air's bread and butter customers.

"We carry more New York Jews to Tel Aviv then El Al," he confides.

"If we have a trim problem and we're nose heavy, no problem, we just throw a dollar bill towards the tail of the airplane."

The class erupts with laughter, my new-found friends find this Jew-joke hilarious.

I write a note to myself on my yellow legal pad, "mouth shut, mouth shut," and resolve that no one here will ever know that I'm a Jew.

On my first leg, Flight Engineer Wally Hudson, better known as *Al-Wahlid* in Saudi Arabia, leans forward to ask (as I push the throttles forward to take off JFK-San Juan), "Where did you get that *Hebe* name?"

"My German father would be really upset to hear you say that, Wally," I hide behind the lie.

Manaus

Tower Air has a fleet of only 747's, three of which are exclusively freighters. This month we're flying computers and other electronic gear to Buenos Aires. We would then layover in BA for a few days, fly empty to Santiago, Chile, load up with flowers/produce and head back for Miami.

Our loads, the outside air temp and max gross weight of the plane would decide whether a stop for fuel would be required. Tonight's flight had us making a "tech stop" for fuel at some place called Manaus, on the equator in Brazil.

Being new to the company, I was excited and nervous about flying to South America, as well as meeting and flying with Captain Larry Lopes, who I had never met. We were all going to meet up in the hotel lobby at show time. Living in Florida, I decided to rent an Avis Car, crank up the radio to "Monsters of the Midday," (104.1 out of Orlando), and drive down in my shorts, t-shirt and flip flops. It was a fun, relaxing drive down to Miami. "Bubba whup-ass" Wilson and Samantha had some raunchy diatribe going on concerning her shaved pudenda on Monsters... a great radio show.

The bellhops at the Miami Airport Hilton helped me in with my bags, and my uniform, which had been hanging in the back of the car. One porn movie, a four-hour nap later, and my phone rang for my wake-up call. Meet downstairs in the lobby in one hour.

I shave, shower and dress in my uniform. Except for my shoes...my black, pilot shoes which I have forgotten at home. I've got white tennies, red rubber flip-flops, but no uniform shoes. I'm a 'newbie' a new hire, on probation, about to meet my Check-Pilot for the first time, and no shoes. Shit!

In the lobby of the hotel I introduce myself to Captain Lopes, and to Michael Marks, the Engineer. We're all cordial, and I point down to my feet (which nobody noticed) showing them that my feet are in black socks and the red flip-flops. They break-up as I explain what happened.

Larry says: "Hey, we'll be stopping in Manaus for fuel, but we're running late out of here, so we'll probably be there overnight. You can buy yourself a pair of shoes in Manaus."

Fast Air, the company in Miami whose freight contract we are flying, are having problems. "They are always having problems." Larry explains. "They are always late. We always have to wait for the freight to arrive; and then we wait a few hours more while the plane is being loaded."

We're sitting on the plane for five hours, it is now seven A.M. and we've watched a beautiful Miami sunrise. We are just about ready to go, but we still won't push back for another 45 minutes. The plane is "maxed-out," its take off weight will be about 805,000 pounds, which is no problem for Miami's 13,000' runway, especially in the cool of the morning.

Manaus, however, will be another story. Their only runway is 8000 feet long, and is only 2 degrees from the equator, in the heat of the Amazon jungle. Because of our delay, we will be arriving there in the heat of the day, about noon, and the temp will be about in the nineties. After we refuel, no way will we be able to get our airplane off an 8000' strip, not until the temp falls below 30'C. That won't happen until early next morning, so Larry tells Fast Air to make hotel arrangements for us all - two pilots, one engineer, a load-master and one of our mechanics, Sylvester, known as Sly, a slick, lanky, black fellow.

En route to Manaus, Larry, who has lived in Santiago, Chile, and whose ex-wife and kids still live there, fills me in on Manaus.

There's been nothing but jungle for hours. Then we find the little concrete strip in the middle of the Amazon, right on the water.

"Hey Chubby," what city was the richest city in the entire Americas, until about 1930?"

"You mean North and South America?"

"Yeah. Both, the whole nine yards, Americas."

"I don't know, let me think..."

"Don't bother, it was Manaus! Also, had more millionaires than anywhere else in the world."

"This place? This jungle, what did they have here, gold?"

"Better, rubber. Before vulcanization, Manaus had the rubber plantations that provided all the world's rubber. Wait till you see this place, you're lucky we're staying over."

After an excellent meal of *cerviche*, a south American fish that is prepared by allowing it to cure itself in lime juice, I go out to explore Manaus. I allow myself to get lost again, in order to enjoy the city my way. I turn a corner, and I'm face to face with *La Scala*, Milan's beautiful Opera House. My God, it is *La Scala*, an exact replica, in the middle of this city being reclaimed by the Brasilian jungle. Investigating further, I find that the inside is an exact duplicate as well.

During Manaus' heyday, Enrico Caruso had been invited to perform for this community of ultra-wealthy lovers of the opera. He promised to come on one condition, that they would build for him a decent opera house. Wanting to impress Caruso, who was then the world's foremost tenor, the City Fathers did the ultimate, they replicated La Scala in downtown Manaus. Caruso died just before the project was completed. The opera house, mansions and cathedrals, lonely in their magnificent isolation, are surrounded by millions of square miles of unimpressed Amazon jungle.

Spocula

Captain Jimmy Spock, "the Spocula," and I take the active runway at
JFK, 31 left. We are bound for TLV, Tel Aviv, an eleven and a half hour
flight, and the plane is maxxed-out, taking off at maximum gross takeoff
weight, 820,000 pounds. It's already late, about two in the morning in
New York, and the weather is shitty. A nasty rain is falling, and there is
a low, skuddy ceiling of clouds. The RVR (Runway Visual Range) is
greater than 600 / 600 / 600, so we are legal to go. We file Philadelphia
as our takeoff alternate.

After numerous delays already this evening, we're finally taxiing out to
the active runway. Cleared for take-off, Spock brings the power up,
and we start rolling down the runway. At rotation speed, about 185
miles per hour, Jimmy lifts the nose-wheel, off the ground. Just then his
entire instrument panel, hinged along it's bottom border, swings down
against his control column. With his right hand he calmly pushes the
panel forward, away from his yoke, while continuing to fly the departure
with his left hand. I am stunned, unable to help him at this most critical
time of flight, unless he tells me to take control of the aircraft. Not
wanting to distract him, I remain silent, bringing up the gear on schedule.

Jimmy's doing a great job perfectly flying the Canarsie departure out of
Kennedy airport. After we climb out to reach 5000 feet, he gives me
control of the plane.

"Fuckin' maintenance guys, they forgot to put the fuckin' screws back
into the entire top of my friggin' panel!"

"Fuckin' Billy Abel, that coke-snorting son-of-a-bitch," this from Jerry
Lovell, our Professional Flight Engineer. Rumor has it that our V.P. of
Maintenance, Billy Abel, is a coke-head, and has been taking short-cuts
with maintenance items, any thing to keep the planes flying, that's why
Morris has hired him back.

"Yeah, one of our maintenance guys tells me," Lovell confides, "that the 'F.F.' (Tower Air's two letter prefix in the computers) stands for 'fuck it, fly it.'"

"Great."

Abel was originally fired a few years back, after one of our South American freighters got an engine fire indication. When the crew blew the fire bottles and the fire warning lights and bells didn't stop, they diverted and landed in Manaus.

There had been no fire, but an inspection revealed that none of the bottled fire extinguishers on any of the engines (two per engine, and one in the tail for the APU) were filled with any Halon at all, they were empty. During every walk around, our flight engineers are trained to look for a green disk on each engine nacelle, indicating that the fire bottles are full, that they've not been discharged. Somehow these bottles were empty, even after having been inspected by Maintenance.

Billy Abel, head of Maintenance, surrounds himself with his own boys, his *goombas*, guys who value their jobs and money over morality and ethics. He was recently hired back by Morris Nachtomi for reasons unknown.

"We don't have the big picture," Spock assures me.

Jim Spock pushes the panel back into place, as Lovell works over his shoulder, tightening down the screws with a Phillips head screwdriver. I am flying out now, being radar vectored from present position direct to Bancs, a navigational fix in Canada, enroute to the North Atlantic tracks.

We have just almost died. Had Jimmy Spock not caught the heavy panel in time, it would have wedged behind his yoke. Neither of us could have controlled the plane. At more than 800,000 pounds, the aircraft would have pitched up radically, stalled, crashed and burned, no doubt about it. We are carrying almost 500 men, women and children, and 325,000 pounds of Jet-A fuel. I grow very cold inside.

With the situation stable now, Jimmy asks me, "What's the last thing that goes through the co-pilots mind as the plane crashes?"

"What's that, Spockula?"

"The Flight Engineer!"

The mood has been lightened somewhat, and we're on our way to Israel.

These flights to Tel Aviv are the longest that we have, eleven hours eastbound, and about twelve hour westbound from TLV-JFK, pushing against the jet stream. At this time, Tower Air flys more Hasids to Israel than *El Al* does, with nine scheduled flights per week. Jimmy Spock, who is the number one pilot at Tower Air, has been flying the New York-Tel Aviv-New York run for seventeen years.

Jimmy has his own method of flying the 747, and although we are dispatched as a PRD flight (a planned re-dispatch), in seventeen years, Spockula has never yet had to land at his original, shorter dispatch point and stop for fuel. That is, he has always had the fuel necessary at the planned redispatch point to be allowed to continue on to Tel Aviv. No matter what the flight plan or the engineer's charts call for in way of power, speed or settings, Jimmy just adjusts the throttles to give us a two and a half degree pitch attitude. He claims the plane is most efficient long range that way, and he's never been wrong.

Getting proper rest is always a problem in Tel Aviv. From the time we land, till we get into our rooms, three hours are gone, and it's nine P.M. Tel Aviv time. If we went to bed right away we would sleep until early the next morning, and be unable to get back to sleep during the day in preparation for our long, *long* flight back, all through the night.

Spock has also developed his own unique system for overcoming sleep-disorders and back-of-the-clock problems. With only twenty hours in Tel Aviv, Spock has taken me under his wing, and his routine goes something like this:

Upon our arrival at *Ben Gurien* Airport, we still have to clear Customs and Immigration, find taxi-service to the Sheraton and diddle with the hotel reservation clerks, since s*crew*-scheduling forgets to make our reservations half the time.

Spockula checks into his room, showers, changes, and we hit Joey's Bar, which stays open all night. To call Joey's eclectic, would be to do it a grave injustice. It's an acid-trip of neon, wall art, and a polyglot of every ethnic and sexual type, crowded into one tight spot. Jimmy and I drink until just before dawn. By six A.M., we head back to the hotel for our breakfast.

Daylight never touches Jimmy Spock, ergo "*Spocula*." We've finished a breakfast of made to order omelets (no bacon) by eight am, and head for bed. We've now been up for thirty hours. When our heads hit the sheets at 9 am, we have no trouble sleeping straight through to our 9 P.M. wake-up call completely refreshed, ready to fly back through the night to New York City.

The Bomb

We're pushing back from the gate at Charles De Gaulle, heading for JFK.

Once back in the alley, we're clear to start engines '4-3-2-1...

"Starting four..."

We have four good starts, call for taxi clearance and are cleared to taxi to runway 27.

"*Ding Ding,*" the interphone rings, it's the purser. The flight attendant at *five-right*, in the far aft right side of the airplane, has reported what appears to be "an unknown devise" in the lav sink, as pointed out by a passenger.

I radio ground and tell them that we have to hold position for a few minutes. Captain Sheamus O'Conner sends Jerry Lovell back to take a look.

Five minutes go by very slowly. Jerry finally comes back and reports that there is a cylindrical device with what appears to be wires sticking out of one end, that is submerged in filthy water in a stopped up sink in the aft lav. " I wouldn't touch it," Jerry advises.

"Alright," Sheamus says, "we are going to taxi to a remote area, tell ground we have a possible bomb on board, get us instructions as to where they want us to go, for remote, and tell them the bomb is only a possibility, we don't want to panic our passengers unnecessarily. Once we stop," Sheamus instructs the purser, "start moving people forward, away from the tail, get them up into the aisles, I don't care if there are seats available or not."

"Should we evacuate! '*Easy Victor*'?"

"Not yet," says Sheamus adamantly, "more people get hurt during evacuations then anything else. We're not ready for that yet."

As we taxi to remote, it becomes apparent that DeGaulle ground, disregarding our instructions, has called out everybody. It seems like hundreds of fire engines, ambulances, riot-police, sirens and blue flashing lights are surrounding our airplane.

Sheamus moans "Oh shit, those fucking Frogs! We told them to be discreet!" The French, as always, do things their way, they know best, they are French after all... "We have invented Aviation, and the language of Aviation. "...*fuselage, empennage, aileron....*" All French words, they point out. The Frogs refuse to speak English to each other on the radio within the dense Paris area, creating a hazardous situation for all the English speaking others, who now have no clue where the French planes are, or what they are up to.

Three hours later, the bomb squad has safely removed the device. It was only a toilet paper cylinder, complete with a glop of remaining toilet tissue still wrapped around it. Someone from maintenance had removed the tube, rested it in the lav sink while replacing it. In their haste to get off the plane, the tube had been left behind. Then someone had used the sink, clogging it with dirty, soapy water, submerging the roll, and creating what appeared to be a threatening device.

Most of the passengers were now demanding to get off the plane. We had no choice but to taxi back to the gate. Zeezu, our French-Israeli Station Manager in Paris, well hated for his abrupt manner and demeaning treatment of pilots and crew, has cancelled the flight.

Zeezu, now feverishly dealing with hundreds of pissed-off New York/French/Jewish passengers, tells us that "we are the least of his problems." Under the circumstances, he is truly not to be envied. Hours later, having found flights or hotel rooms for our former passengers, Zeezu has deigned to get us hotel rooms back at the Sofitel, Saint Jacques. This bag-drag ends eight hours after the bomb threat, as we exhaustedly enter our new hotel rooms.

Dinner that evening became a communal affair. The entire crew of pilots and flight attendants, all nineteen of us, managed to pull a few tables together in the Mussel restaurant. All was going well, huge bowls, heaped full of garlic mussels were delivered all around, all except for Capt. Sheamus, whose placemat was left empty.

Finally, and with great fanfare, a huge covered tureen is placed before the Captain. The table grows silent as the Maitre D removes the silver cover from Sheamus' bowl. There, floating in soapy dishwater is a toilet paper roll... *"Surprise!"*...bedlam.

Nineteen shitfaced crewmembers party till dawn, celebrating the rescue effort and our new notoriety. Sheamus and I stagger back through the lobby of the Sofitel, trying to avoid the plague of Japanese tourists in Paris on holiday. We enter an elevator, along with a Japanese matron and her husband, both dressed-to-the-nines, and silent. The elevator remains paused at the lobby level, when I notice that big band music is being piped into my consciousness.

As the doors close and we begin to ascend, I take the Japanese lady's hand and I start to dance. She is so startled that she automatically follows me through my Arthur Murray routine. Her husband and Sheamus are rolling with laughter, as I time my dip and my bow perfectly to coincide with my exit from the elevator, which as chance will have it, is the first stop.

I replay, and enjoy, my own performance as I drift off to sleep in my room.

"The Rabbi"

During my first year flying the Jeddah Hajj, the Muslim Pilgrimage to Mecca and Medina, the excitement soon gave way to the boredom of routine.

Islam, I am told, is a wonderful religion. One of its tenets decrees that a Muslim must make at least one Hajj, Pilgrimage, during his lifetime, in order to get to Heaven. This requires a visit to the three holy sites. Two of these Holiest Islamic sites, all part of the ritual of the Hajj, are located in the Magic Kingdom, Saudi Arabia. King Fahd and his family are the official Custodians of these Holiest of Muslim Holies, located in the cities of Mecca and Medina.

Saudis, by virtue of arbitrary geography, (thanks to T.E. Lawrence and the Brits) play host to two million Muslims a year, all entering and leaving through the Hajj Terminal, a corner of *King Abdul Azziz Airport* in Jeddah; and all this during a three-month period each year. As the Landlords of Islam's holy sites, the Saudis look down their prodigious noses at the Foreign Muslims, who travel from all over the Muslim World to make the Pilgrimage.

The deal to enter Saudi Arabia, The Kingdom (*The Magic Kingdom* to most of us, or *The Sand-Box*), is that you must be invited, you must obtain a visa, you must be sponsored by a Saudi company… this all requires a lot of time and patience… oh, and you must not be Jewish. I am Jewish…. though most of my colleagues don't know it.

Each year, when assigned to fly the sandbox, every crewmember must fill out a million forms to have the entry visa stamp affixed to their passports. One of these forms asks for religion, and an answer is required. No answer, no entry visa!

The first year I was a Catholic, the next (off of probation) I became a Druid. This year, feeling feisty, I listed myself as a Pedophile.

A day long wait in an airport holding area in Jeddah is commonplace, while strutting Saudis with clip-boards disappear with your passport. They may only take a few hours, between meals and prayers, and return *Inshallah,* with your passport and visa.

As hard as it is to enter the Magic Kingdom, leaving is even more difficult. You must first get an exit letter from the Saudi government, before you can even attempt to leave. Think of the movie Casablanca. Ingrid Bergman, her Resistance-Hero husband, and the entire population of the city, it seems, is trying to get exit letters. The letter cannot be obtained until you can prove to the Saudi's that you owe no money to your hotel or to anyone else, that your sponsor is allowing you to leave, and that you have paid passage out, already in hand.

Effectively, we are hostages in a very hostile land. The majority of the population detests our presence. We are non-believing, infidel devils, here to do their work, yet polluting their culture. Osama Bin Laden, heir to a Saudi fortune, is bent on driving the American Satan (us) from Saudi Arabia. He, and other Muslim extremists, have the resolve to kill us, but are still working on the means (weapons of mass destruction). We have the power and the means, but not yet the will to fight their kind of fight, at least not yet. Most Americans have no idea to what extent these people hate us, and would do anything to destroy us and our way of life... but we are stuck here, for the money.

Eventually, even these exotic new destinations become mundane…..
Jeddah to Algiers and back, Jeddah to Medina and back, Jeddah to Damascus and back….. the problem was the "and back." We flew to Delhi, Bombay, Karachi, Lahore, Islamabad, Dhaka, you name it, we went there, and back!

For us flying prisoners of Jeddah, breakfast became the highlight of our days. A wall-to-wall buffet of eggs, beans, rice, fruit, cheeses, and more, was available all morning. The local daily, The Arab News, was read over coffee, each morning. This slanted rag, the Royal Family's personal Pravda, is so transparently biased, that it became our focal point of amusement, written for our personal pleasure.

One popular feature was "Ask Achmed," a religious column dealing with the nit-picky issues of Islamic fundamentalism:

Dear Achmed:
My ten-year-old son likes to draw figures in art class. I discourage him, or try to get him to separate the heads from the torsos. His art teacher says this is not necessary in an art class. Am I right in Islamic law?
Signed, Metuffash W.

Dear Mrs. Metuffah W.: You are correct. As you know, Islamic law forbids the drawing of full figures of people or animals. Therefore, try to get your son to draw geometric patterns or landscapes. If he insists on drawing figures, make sure he separates the heads from the bodies. Talk to the school administration about this art teacher, since he is leading children away from the correct Islamic path.
Sincerely, Achmed.

Tired of our Kingdom prison, we fantasize aloud the ways we intend to escape the Saudi sand-box. We have been advised by Saudia, for whom we fly the Hajj contract, that no one will be allowed to go home during the hiatus, the break between the first and second "wave" of the Hajj. We will all be stuck out her for the full ninety days... not going home, not seeing family for three months.

I've just finished reading the "Ask Achmed" column, and I say: "I know how I'll get out of here. I'm going to start an "Ask the Rabbi" column in the Arab News. Maybe I'll even put a classified ad in the Arab News, *"Rabbi available to give Bar Mitzvah lessons at the Sofitel Hotel, room 206."*

None of my companions yet know that I'm a Jew, since there are no Jewish pilots, they think it's a joke.

Mark Lippi laughs, and volunteers that he's sure I'll be out of the Kingdom real soon. "Rabbi," Mark says, "you can be the Chief Rabbi of Saudi Arabia... briefly!"

"Yeah, Rabbi, they'll ship you home head first   ...body to follow!"

The other guys all add their comments, and I am forever dubbed "The Rabbi." This nickname is particularly amusing to me, as the secret in-kingdom Jew. It's a joke on the Saudi's as well, but it's a more subtle joke on my (mostly) Jew-hating comrades.

The real joke is of course on me. Loving, and being loved by a group of guys who might hate me, if they knew my hidden label, is tough to live with. The worm always eats at my soul, when I allow the anti-Semitic venom to lap around me, without fessing up. I am, after all, selling out my mother and father, my kids and all my family for acceptance, which for all I know might be mine, regardless.

Sitting in the midst of these friends, some my undeserved enemies, my mind plays with the ancient riddle. Jew, Jewish, Semite; Sand-nigger, Mockie, Kike; God, Hatred, Love and Death. How the fuck do any people get from God and Love, to Hatred and Death?

My mind wanders further back now, back to my earliest recollections.

"Stevie, I'd like you to meet your Uncle Harry, and Uncle Benny, and this is Uncle Moishe. Your uncle Davie is still in the hospital, but you'll meet him today when we visit." I was five years old, and World War II had ended. My mother had nine brothers and sisters, and all the men had been away for the duration. I was now meeting my uncles, my new-met heroes, for the first time.

This vivid scene has stuck with me through all the years, as only certain childhood memories do. The significance of what I was witnessing didn't register 'til well into my adulthood. Only my father, with two kids, and bad vision, had remained behind. All the other uncles and uncles-in-law had been off fighting the Nazi's and the Japanese. Remarkably all eight of them had come home alive.

Moishe, a strapping, natural athlete, had been a Pacific marine, who landed on Tarawa and Iwo Jima. God knows what he saw and did, since he's a quiet man, who settled down, raised a family, started a business and never talked to any of us about the war.

Davie, the uncle who was finally released from St. Albans Naval Hospital months later, had been a radio operator on a bomber in the Pacific. He and his five crewmates lived, played and flew together. For years, they fought their missions, marauding the Japanese fleet. During the last of their missions, towards the end of the Pacific campaign, they were blown out of the sky.

My Uncle Dave's chute somehow opened, and he was machine gunned across his throat and down one leg, while dangling unconscious in the parachute harness. A navy PBY swooped in and plucked him from the ocean, flying him to an American held island base. Business at the field hospital was light that day, so the triage surgeon allowed him to be worked on. He was the only member of his crew to survive. This story comes to me from his wife, my aunt Helen, since I've never heard war stories from Davie, either.

The rest of my uncles, all Jews, of course, fought in the Italian, French and German campaigns. Except for the foreign coins they gave me (very exotic stuff for a kid at the time), I never heard a word about the war from any of them. Years later, I learned of the family members back in Germany and Poland, whose correspondence suddenly stopped, forever.

The family was very close, all living within walking distance of each other, and this large, ethnic clan would kibitz, and scrap, tease and laugh over impossibly large meals, bustled to the table by my Grandma Minnie, my mom, and aunts. I had tens of cousins close in age to play with, and the warmth and camaraderie was an encapsulating cocoon of love and support.

In the nineteen fifties, The Bronx, New York, was a peaceful blend of Jews, Irish, and Italians. My being Jewish was no big deal. Although my family, especially on my father's side, was orthodox, the fact that I was Jewish had been only that to me, just another fact. I was male, American, a kid, and I also happened to also be Jewish. I thought everybody's home had meat dishes, milk dishes (*milchiks and fleyshiks*), along with the Passover plates, pots and pans, to be used only for that occasion.

It wasn't until I was about nine-or-so, and being sent to Hebrew school, that the loathing and terror of my Jewishness took root, quickly consuming, and finally overwhelming any spirituality I might ever have developed.

The Rabbis that taught Hebrew school at Temple Beth Elohim made it very clear from the beginning. We Jews were God's chosen people. I was given no choice, I was chosen, period. That being initially (and continually) emphasized, we were taught the litany of cruel tortures and deaths that Jews over the centuries had suffered to retain their Jewish ness, this "privilege" of being God's Chosen. From the flaying alive of Rabbi Akiva, the tortures of the Spanish inquisition, to the *pograms* throughout history, all culminating with that grandest of grand finales, Hitler's Nazis, and their European executioners.

By the 1950's, when I was the student-target of this mayhem of information, all the facts were in. We were treated to detailed accounts of the atrocities committed at the various extermination camps. We were shown the pictures of the piles of gold teeth pulled from Jewish mouths, the piles of Jewish hair used to stuff mattresses, the stockpile of soaps made from Jewish bones. I was treated to all this horror, and told to be proud to be Jewish, and to resist to the death any attempt to un-Jew me. The films of the concentration camps' Jewish inmates were particularly unforgettable as a nine, ten and eleven-year-old. "Never again" was the watchword, "Not me!" became my motto.

As a result of the mind I was born with, the sensibilities of delicate youth, and these wonderful examples of the positive nature of religion, I was thoroughly traumatized. At once, I was ashamed of being Jewish (why didn't those millions of people defend themselves and their children?), terrified of being Jewish (I never, ever admit to being Jewish under ordinary circumstances), and had no use for God - mine or anyone else's.

My Mother's Affair

My mother was having an affair as far back as I can remember, and I'm sure my father never knew. It started out as a "radio affair," but at some point it went to TV. Bronx housewives were all enamored with Arthur Godfrey. Vacuuming, dusting, *Balabustering,* all to those honeyed, soft-southern tones of "The Old Redhead."

Life flowed smoothly in the fifties, as we all stayed abreast of the lives of Holli-Loki, Julius La Rosa, Arthur and his wonderful home-away-from-home, Godfrey's Kennelworth Hotel on Miami Beach.... every Jewish housewife's dream.

In 1959, at age sixteen, remarkably, and beyond belief, Mary Keshner allows me (her precious high school graduate son) to drive to Miami and back with three older friends. I've got $109, and I will stay as long as the money holds out.

The drive down was fucking torture, and we all learned to sleep upside-down, our heads down in the leg-well of Kenny Berkowitz' ancient Ford. It was hard not to notice the "Kollard" and "White" only outhouses behind the gas stations, throughout the South. The white only and colored water fountains in public areas in Florida.

But, best of all was passing the fabled Kennelworth Hotel, that Miami dream, Casa Godfrey. The large, billboard sign facing A1A read, "No dogs, Niggers or Jews allowed." The unreality of it all short-circuited my brain's emotional synapses.

All I could think about was how they came up with that particular order?

dogs
niggers
Jews

Were dogs their first hate? Were Jews a bigot's afterthought? I couldn't stop wondering about the order of hatred on the sign.

131

I never told my Mom, or any of her friends in our tenement building. The Florrie Chuzmirs; the Minna Taylors; the Betty Adlers; the Anne Brills; Mrs. Kolk; Lilly Friede… I could not bring myself to break their spell.

Was I afraid nobody would believe me? The love of that Old Redhead, Arthur Godfrey continued through the years, with many Jewish women's prayers chanted over the Friday night *Shabbas* candles for his full recovery from cancer, of that I'm sure.

Even as a kid, I had no problem with a world without God. My little genius mind was unable to discern why so many people were so quick to decide that they had deciphered all the mysteries of life, assigning same to a God. Though I was able to see that people afraid of the "nothingness" of death needed to create some meaning for themselves, to lessen their fears, I could never accept that any God assigned the 'all good and all powerful' role, would be sadistic enough to fuck with His little creations, for His own self-amusement.

In other words, at my young age, I was, and knew myself to be fucked. I didn't fit. I had massive fights with my parents over my reluctance to join the ranks, and was therefore taught to feel guilty for not believing in something that everyone was expected to believe in. I went through the rote expectations of being *Bah Mitzvah'd* as an automaton, having no control over the rules governing me, waiting only for that day when I would be old enough to not have to mouth words, and pretend feelings, put there by others.

By my seventeenth year, my independence of spirit could no longer be suppressed. My father and I were having another of the many arguments we seemed to always have, regarding the "Nature of Man" (read in, versus the nature of me). It boiled over in the kitchen of our apartment, when my father, red-faced with exasperation screamed at me that "the difference between man and animal is religion." Composing myself, I said, "You've known me all my life…have you ever known me to purposely do wrong, to purposely hurt anybody? Am I an animal? Because I don't believe what you believe, am I an animal?"

My father started crying. I believe I saw in his face, finally, the tyranny he realized that I had been subjected to. I believe he broke through, and heard the words, and the meaning of what I had said. I left the room, the apartment, and his life, for years to come.

Not caring what became of me, wanting only to break free from the weight of the generational layers of expectations I felt suffocated by, I had myself thrown out of college, and I joined the Marine Corps.

I was a strong kid, who had worked hard, summer jobs as a bell hop. We carried massive quantities of suitcases in and out of mountain cabin resorts, over miles of trails. The Waldemere Hotel, on Shandalee Lake checked out 1200 guests every Saturday, and received 1200 new arrivals every Sunday.

There were no carts, there were no elevators. We four bellhops lugged and carted tons of luggage, from sun-up to sun-down every weekend. We could not eat those days, because we would puke it up from exhaustion. We discovered that we could hold down grapefruit juice, so we lived on a few sips of juice those two days a week. On the city streets, we played tackle football with no equipment. When we got hurt, we kept playing 'for the love of the game.' For the year and a half of college I had, before being thrown out at age seventeen, I was on the Hunter College wrestling team. Though only 5'7" tall, and 140 pounds, I had the indestructibility of youth.

But Parris Island, South Carolina, in the sixties was not Kansas, Toto. Upon our arrival to boot camp, we were terrified into immediate, silent obedience by the Drill Instructors. We did not talk, we did not sit, we did not 'eye-fuck' the area. We were assured that the D.I.'s did not care if we lived or died. We knew that sometimes recruits did die. Standing at attention for hours at a time, we were told that we would leave Parris Island as "Marines," or we would leave dead. We believed it.

On one of the first few days as a recruit, we were all standing at attention in front of our racks, studying our General Orders. A voice boomed, "Who doesn't believe in God?" Again, louder... "Who doesn't believe in God?"

"The Marine Corps believes in God! Your ass belongs to the Marine Corps, but your soul belongs to Jesus. Any maggot who doesn't believe in God will stay behind with us, by the time you shitbirds get back, he will believe in God!"

"Give me my Protestant Pussies!" some guys fall out.

"Give me my Baptist Bastards!" more guys fall out.

"Give me my Catholic Cock-suckers!" I am now the only one left standing at attention in front of my rack.

"You, what the fuck are you?"

"Sir, Private Keshner is a Jew, Sir!"

"A what?"

"Sir, Private Keshner is a Jew, Sir!"

"There are no fucking Jews in the Marine Corps, you go with the Catholic Cocksuckers!"

I fall out with the Catholic Cocksuckers, and attend Catholic services for the next thirteen weeks.

I can honestly say that the Marine Corps discriminated against no one. Only the sick, lame and lazy caught it in the shorts, and only competence impressed the Corps.

As small as I was, I excelled at hand-to-hand combat, academics, and most important for the Marines, I fired highest in the company on the rifle range, scoring 232 out of a possible 250 points. I left Parris Island with a stripe, one of only four promotions given to our out-posting company.

I was now officially a Marine, a Jar-head, a Leatherneck, just like all those heroes I grew up on, from my uncles, to all those wonderful leading-men in the propaganda movies made during World War II.

Getting off the Greyhound at Port Authority Bus Terminal, west of Times Square, I remember thinking, no, actually believing, that I could step off the curb, hit a bus with the side of my hand, and stop it dead in it's tracks. The mind of the young is fertile ground for battle fodder.

Although the Marine Corps was a vehicle towards legal independence, it didn't mature me emotionally, cure my spiritual void or make me any wiser (I am, however, the only Marine I know without a single tattoo). The downside of pushing away from my parent's advise was that I pushed away from all advise, theirs or others, good or bad.

The folly of living exclusively within your own head is that you meet only one person there (if you're lucky). I greeted my father's caution against marrying too young, and the benefits of a good education, with the same enthusiasm as I had his earlier, religious counseling.

The next ten years were taken up with a youthful, ill-fated marriage, the birthing of two kids, and the pursuit of endless pussy. My biological maturity coincided perfectly with the advent of the pill, the free-love generation, drug-chic, and a world without permanently damaging sexual diseases.

Although I finally got serious about college, finishing a degree in accounting at Fordham University at night, I blew off parenting my two, beautiful children, for the pursuit of personal happiness.

Caryn and David had made the unfortunate mistake of timing their arrival twenty years too early. These poor kids suffered my desertion of them because I was too stupid and immature to maintain my proper role as their father. I found countless 'good' reasons to justify my absence and neglect. In the end, my disappearance from their lives wreaked the havoc on their hearts, minds and souls you would expect. They were left to roam in the rubble of their psyches, obliterated by a missing father, trying to find some peace and meaning for themselves. Over the past fifteen years, I have tried to reenter their lives, with only moderate success. The damage is done, and the road back to trust and relationship is hard, if not impossible.

Careening through my twenties and thirties, I tried different careers, jumping from accounting to importing, to money laundering, "muling" millions of other peoples dollars and diamonds all over the Orient. Back in the States, I sold used cars by day, taught at Jones Business College at night, and took a stab at producing a Hemingway play on Broadway... I should have taken a stab at the three Hemingway sons, and their lawyers, instead.

The idea of flying an airplane, actually piloting a plane, had never occurred to me.

Sheamus Businesses

"Hey Rabbi, I'm selling some of the original party napkins from Jesus' Bar Mitzvah."

"Oh God" I think, "this is going to be an interesting month." I haven't flown with Captain Sheamus O'Conner for a couple of months.

"Hey, Sheamus, I wonder what became of the Rabbi who performed the circumcision on the little baby Jesus... that child-god must have been pissed."

Sheamus is a twisted, big-hearted schemer, and a great pilot.

We have completed our pre-flight duties on the 747, loaded the INS's, and have time to catch each other up a bit. Our plane is still about forty minutes from pushback at the Tower Air gate at JFK, still being loaded with "Chassid" bound for Tel Aviv.

Sheamus is busting to fill me in on some of his latest businesses. "I've developed a line of designer condoms. We've got paisley, plaids and stripes. I'm calling the company *Sergio Preventos*.

"Sounds great, Sheamus, sounds like a wiener."

Now at altitude, already "coasted out" over Gander, our next radio call isn't due until 50 west. We have our VHF radios set to monitor "guard" on 121.5, "air-to-air" on 131.8, and the HF's are tuned to receive any "selcalls." All of this means that we are now established on tonight's "Natrack" over the North Atlantic, and have forty minutes free to chat, as our eyes automatically monitor the nav and engine instruments.

Wayne Denze, our PFE (professional flight engineer) is still busy with his engine readings, fuel calculations, and paper work.

"Rabbi, you must know why the Israeli's don't have a space program? I've figured it out... No Kosher food in space. So, I'm working on 'the

Kosher Kosmos,' I figure it's a great niche market. I can cater Kosher food into space, sell it to the Jews, maybe get some start-up capital out of Morris Nachtomi."

"Can't miss, Sheamus, ...'*O'Conner's Kosher Kosmos*... has a certain Semitic ring to it."

Sheamus is a large man, always on yo-yo diets, now he's bigger than ever. "Brucie," suffering from extreme cock-in-mouth disease, is working the upper deck tonight, and he's just entered the cockpit with our coffee.

"Brucie, did I tell you I'm working on a new weight-reduction business?"

"No shit, Sheamus, what ever happened to your *Scratch and Sniff* diet business?"

"Shit, I had to fire my de-frocked perfume chemist! No, no, this one's much better. I've got a door-to-door lipo-suction truck. I haven't come up with a name yet, but we're thinkin' *We Suck, Inc.* "

Bruce has already finished his first service in the back, he's got some time and some advise.. "You know, you've got to be thin to make it in the gay world, so between that name, *which I love*, and the thin-is-in gay community, you should start your immediate sucking in San Francisco, really."

"Hell no" offers Sheamus, "We're gonna build up a quick customer base following the Dominos Pizza delivery trucks all over New York City."

Wayne, who has finished his fuel calculations, has tuned in to this conversation. "Hey, Sheamus, I got an idea that'll definitely improve your profits."

"What's that, Wayne?"

Wayne, forever the bigot, "why don't you back-haul the truckloads of sucked-out fat, sell the lipids to the World Health Organization in

Geneva, and they can use your famous O'Connor Lipo-Pump" to squirt a dose of fat into all those skinny niggers, you know, the real skinny ones on them food lines over in Africa... give 'em a coat of fat for the winter."

"You can call the sales end of the bid'ness *'Sharing The Fat of The Land'*," I add.

Brucie has had enough, and quickly turns on his heels and flees the fight deck as Wayne continues, "yeah, you can make money on both the sucking and the pumping... probably get a Nobel Peace Prize out of it, too." Sheamus turns towards his fight bag and makes some quick notes.

Wayne says "we all know why dogs lick their balls, right? Because they can.... but do you know why lions lick their assholes?"

"No, why?"

"To get the taste of the niggers out of their mouths!"

"Holy shit, Wayne," I say, "give it up... you don't say shit like that in front of 'N1' and 'N2,' do you?"

"Sure I do... they know they're niggers!"

On our aircraft, N1 and N2 are gauges for engine rotation speeds. At our Company, Tower Air, with only two black pilots, these are our *"nig-names"* for our two gents of color. Most pilot's don't really give two shits about race, religion, or such. Pilot's are loved, or truly hated, based only on competency. "Shit-hot" guys are loved... "weak-dick" pilots are detested.

"Wayne" I ask, "why don't you start calling them Canadians, like everyone else does?"

Sheamus asks me "What's with this *Canadian* shit that everyone is spouting?"

"Sheamus," I say, "the L.A.P.D. uses *Canadians* on their radio calls now, to avoid being accused of racism. Everybody loved it, that's all we call them now."

The INS alert light comes on, we're approaching 50 west, and we all go back to work.

"Gander, Tower Air three-one, position on 8736."

"Go ahead with your position report, Tower Air three-one."

"Tower Air three-one checks 48 north by 50 west, at time 0431, flight level 350, mach decimal 84. Estimating 50 north, 40 west, 0512, next 50 north, 30 west. Fuel remaining, 110.4, go ahead."

Gander reads back our position report, it's correctly repeated, and we are free again for another forty minutes.

"Sheamus, what happened to that Guam business of yours, *Nippers with Flippers*, did you sell it?"

"Yeah, I had to when we stopped going to Guam a lot, and I was doing great with it, I sold it to that Air Mike guy, you know."

"The Continental Air Mike guy with the Beef Jerky Business?"

"Yeah, that's the guy, the 'Redwing' shoe distributor for Guam and Saipan."

When Sheamus and I worked for Continental Air-Mike, before Tower Air, we would check into the Hilton on Tumon Bay for a week. Then fly day or night turns, between Guam-Saipan and Narita or Nagoya.

Guam and Saipan are only three hours from Japan, tropical Marianna islands. A flood of Japanese escape their bitter winters, vacationing on Guam's Tumon Bay, now more built up with hotels than Waikiki. Tumon Bay, a once beautiful crescent of beach, with great snorkeling reefs and beautiful fish, is now polluted by the effluents of the Hilton and the Pacific Star hotels. Most of the signs and billboards are written exclusively in Japanese.

While the rest of us would lounge at the Tree Bar pool, drinking beer and trying to get lucky with some young, giggling Japanese secretary on vacation, Sheamus came up with "Nippers with Flippers."

Sheamus brought in hundreds of pairs of flippers, and snorkel masks from Hawaii. He worked out some rental arrangement with the pool-boys at some of the larger hotels, naming his business "Nippers with Flippers."

The Japanese loved it, not seeming to mind the racial reference. Happily, Sheamus would stroll the beach each week, collecting his rent. Over the years, this was the only business idea I've ever seen Sheamus act on.

Bruce is back... "Your crew meal choices tonight are a pasta something, a rice-vegetable something, and the mystery meat."

I'm on the radio with Gander, reporting 40 west. They tell me to contact "Shanwick" at 30 west. Sheamus and Wayne are groaning at the choices.

"Aren't there any first class meals left over?" Asks Sheamus. We all know that the fifteen flight attendants have already scoffed-up any leftover first-class food. Bruce, innocently says that there was no extra first-class food.

"I'll have a large pepperoni pizza, and a fine Merlot wine," I order.

Bruce, having heard this from me a hundred times over the years... "Funny, which meals do you want, it's busy back there. Those fucking New York Jews are just driving me crazy."

Sheamus opts for the pasta, Wayne settles for the rice and veggies, and I get stuck with the mystery meat.

Wayne asks, "Do you remember the cartoon show years ago, 'The Jetsons'?"

"Yeah."

"They just developed a new show, same concept with an all black cast, know what it's called?"

I bite: "No, what?"

"Niggers!"

"Holy mother of God," Sheamus shouts, "I wonder what became of the tip?"

"What tip?"

"The tip of the circumcised baby Jesus' little Jewish dick! Don't you realize there's an un-risen portion of the body of Christ sitting somewhere in the dirt of Bethlehem? This is worth a fortune..." Sheamus starts pulling out charts, "...Fuck the Holy Grail, man, I'm going after that little piece of the Son of God!"

"Hey, Rabbi, you going on the Hajj this year?"

Wayne's question takes me by surprise.

"Oh, man, Wayne, the Hajj is only two months away, and it's snuck up on me again, shit! Ninety days away from home, but that's where the money is. I guess I'll have to go."

Wanda Decker, "The Pussy of Thunder herself," who is working business class tonight, and is tonight's lead Flight Attendant, has sent up a new girl to the cockpit. The new meat has been told to introduce herself to us (and to be set up for her initiation rites, though she doesn't yet know that).
"Welcome, welcome".... All that shit, then we lay it on her..... " Hey, kid, we need for you to take these white garbage bags and tie-ties and

collect ozone samples for the Feds at different flight levels…. Did Wanda tell you how to….?" "No, oh, that's o.k. it's easy, here's what you do… each time we change flight levels we'll have you take a sample bag-full of air, for the Feds, for the Ozone test. Here's a magic marker…. Just walk through the cabin and get a great glob of air in a bag, tie it off, write the flight level on it, and by the end of the flight you should have five, maybe six sample bags. … some Fed will meet you at the jetway in the terminal… just hand it to him, and get a receipt. Give the receipt to the head of your In-flight department. Easy, no sweat…… thanks."

Watching any Newbie Flight Attendant walk off an airplane holding four or five worthless bags of air, waiting around for some non-existent Fed has always been a hoot… the shit crews do for laughs.

Ahmed Slitherian

I love to be home. It's so rare that I get to enjoy the house, my wife, and kid. My time home is precious to me, so I sure as shit ain't going to spend it with any assholes.

Ahmed Slitherian, one of Iranian P.F.E.'s is the complete asshole. Obnoxious and backstabbing when sober, he becomes even more arrogant, and abusive, whenever he drinks. Ahmed is unliked by everyone, including the "Iranian Mafia," our contingent of Persian pilots and Professional Flight Engineers, all terrific guys.

During a Miami turn, Ahmed informs me that "We are neighbors, now." He has moved his family to Daytona Beach, not far from my home, since his son is attending Sandler College in St. Augustine. Thrusting his phone number at me, he insists that we have to get together. "Shit," I think, and throw his number away as soon as I can discretely do so.

Every few months, on the phone with Geri, she tells me that "some guy called, with some funny sounding name, and he's left his phone number." "Throw it away," I tell her, with no explanation.

Months pass before I bump into Ahmed again, this time in JFK Flight Ops.

"Hi, Ahmed," I say.

"Oh, you don't like me!" he booms.

"Don't like you?" all innocence, "Why wouldn't I like you, Ahmed?"

"You never return my calls," he says, invading my space. Ahmed is one of those people born with no sense of personal space. A close-talker.

"You called me, Ahmed? I never got any messages," I lie. "I get home so infrequently that I just have enough time to pay my bills, do my laundry and re-introduce myself to my family." This is no lie.

Years pass with no further attempts at home contact. When I do fly with Ahmed, every few months, we are always politely proper with each other, but I know that he knows, that I don't like him, and that I don't care that he knows.

Ramadan-Pederast

"Allah ooAckbar," the call to prayer, blares me awake. It's 5 A.M. and the loud speakers all over Jeddah are calling the faithful to morning prayer, the first of five daily prayers.

God, I'm tired. The music, fire alarms and kids running through the halls pounding on doors, have kept me up most of the night. It's Ramadan, a forty-day holiday in Islam, where it's decreed that nothing may be done during the day. No eating, no work, no sex. I don't know if the original rule was forty-days of total abstinence and fasting. If so, the Saudi's have perverted the intent, by simply reversing their life cycle. The wealthier Arabs make a holiday of it, filling up our luxury hotel, different rooms for different wives, kids, *Filippina aupairs*, the works.

Daytime's not a problem. We're out flying the scheduled Saudia trips during the day. But our evening sleep, the rest we need to be fresh for these daytime flights, has been a disaster. The kids run wild at night, riding their bikes, pulling the fire alarm handles and pounding doors. The adults at poolside pay no attention. Arab "music" blasts from giant speakers, the men pull smoke through their hubbly-bubblys (hookahs), while their women wade in the pool, holding the hems of their black *abayas* modestly up, enough to keep them dry. It is pitch black outside and I can't fall asleep.

We are in Jeddah on a nine-month "wet lease" contract. All but one of our five planes have been painted to perfectly match the Saudia fleet, except for the American "N" registration numbers, they are indistinguishable. All except for the "yellow banana," one of our planes cheaply painted by Morris Nachtomi in Mexico, using the wrong shade of yellow.

We've had a few weeks of this Ramadan under our belts and we are all frazzled from lack of decent sleep. Complaints and calls to hotel management have gone unheeded, "What can we do? It's a holiday." The poor Egyptian hotel staff, in Saudi Arabia on five-year contracts, are right. It is a holiday, and our protests be damned, the Saudi's will celebrate as they see fit.

This is my fourth month in Jeddah, getting home to Florida for a few days every other month. The strain of maintaining a relationship as husband and father is worsening. The senior guys avoid the Magic Kingdom like the plague, and as a junior puke, I've already been to Arabia on three annual 90-day Hadj's. Now this, Ramadan.

We were flying a regular Saudia flight to Islamabad. Out of Jeddah, south briefly, then east along the length of Arabia, over the Emirates, still east along southern Pakistan, hanging a left over Karachi, north past Lahore, following the fence and the no-mans land stretching north-south, defining the border between warring Pakistan and India. We land in daylight at Islamabad, the most Orthodox of the Islamic cities of this very Muslim country.

The plane is parked in the "Boonies," way out on the ramp. I've got two hours to kill during fueling. The 747 burns 25,000 pounds of jet-A fuel an hour, we need 150,000 pounds of fuel, including reserves for the return. The "Packies" have to run our fuel to us in 5000 gallon trucks. It's going to take a hours.

I drift toward the grass perimeter, lighting a cigarette as I meander. Captain "Bubba" is kicked back in first class, catching 'zzzzz's.' Wayne Cunningham, our Flight Engineer is busy with paperwork, fueling, weight and balance and such, while I'm relaxing on the ground with my smoke.

Two booted, cammo-clad soldiers approach me, machine pistols slung over their shoulders. Their faces are serious, definitely unfriendly.

"What is your religion?" one asks harshly. Shit, it's Ramadan, and I'm smoking during the day.

"I'm a Pedophile, I respond, feeling the need to remain consistent with my Saudi Visa, which is stamped in Aramaic in my passport, and I have no clue whether it lists my religion, or not.

"What?"

"I'm a Pedophile."

"What is a Pedophile?" they both demand.

"It's the same as a Muslim, but we do not practice Ramadan." I respond. They accept my explanation and walk away, leaving me to my smoke.

Captain Bubba has long, greasy hair, usually unacceptable in the industry, and a smirky, cynical demeanor. He is a PHD in music, who back up-home in Tennessee, plays the violin with the Nashville Philharmonic.

On our way back to Jeddah, Bubba asks: "Hey Rabbi, what's the definition of a New York minute?"

"The amount of time it takes between the traffic light turning green, and the first car honking?"

"O.K., O.K., What's the longest, most painful 'pilot-minute'?"

"I give up, go ahead."

"It's from the time you blow your wad, till you get the bitch out of your room!"

"Unfortunately, Bubba, I'm old enough to know what you mean!"

Wayne has been whittling away, perfecting his "hooey-hooey" sticks.

"Sa'alem Alechem, Saudia control, Saudia 41, fight level 390."

"*Sa'alem Alechem*" Saudia 41, squawk 3432 and give estimate for Medina."

"Saudia control, Saudia 4-1, 3432 coming down estimating Medina 1315Z, *insh'allah.*"

"Roger Saudia 4-1, maintain FL 390, *Shukran, Ma'as Salam*"

"Hey Rabbi," Bubba asks, you sure give good A-Rab, you sure you're not a Sand-Nigger?"

"No way, Bubba, my momma is pure Eye-talian and Daddy's a German" I lie. I can be taken for Italian, Greek or Spanish. Olive complected, salt and pepper black hair...more salt than there used to be.

I start daydreaming about Geri and Kiley. Geri and I've been married 13 years now, and it's been mostly good. Only being away from home so much has done damage to our friendship and love. Kiley is our eleven-year-old daughter, a smart, good natured girl, who adores and misses me. During these multi-week or multi-month trips, I fantasize about how it's going to be when I get home.

The reality brutalizes the fantasy. They've got lives they're living, and trying to re-mesh the gears of our family is hard work. Nobody drops everything when Daddy comes home.

"Hey guys," I'm back from my reverie. You know what the worst part of this job is?"

"No, what?"

"Every few weeks they tear you away from your loved ones and send you back to your wife and kids!"

"You got that right, Rabbi."

149

I'm trying to think of how to pay the bills and make enough money to stay home, permanently. Can't come close to the money we need with any kind of work in St. Augustine. In the past few months I mentally count up the guys I've bumped into who've gone through divorces. Mikey Marks, Jaime Pinto, Dennis Reedy, Mike Lauro, and now our latest addition, Charlie PreMantis.

"Did you hear what happened to Charlie PreMantis?"

"The divorce, you mean?"

"No," Bubba grins, "The way it happened. Charlie comes back from three-month in the sand. He drives home to Connecticut, and his keys won't open the door."

"What did the bitch do, change the locks on him?" asks Wayne.
"No, better. He's knocking on the door and some stranger opens the door and asks, 'Can she help him?'"

Charlie's wife of 28 years had sold the house (for $60,000 less than market value), and moved out, lock stock and barrel. Address unknown, except for her attorney's name and number.

"Shit," I say, Charlie's a pain in the ass 'Felix Unger' type, but a 28 year marriage, to end that way..."

"How'd the bitch sell the house without his signature?"

"She used his 'Power of Attorney.' Pilots like us, 'freight dogs' who are away from home a lot, usually give our wives or parents power of attorney forms, in the event of the unexpected.

"Can't trust those bitches no how." declares Wayne, now asking me to test out his "new, improved hooey-hooey."

I take the two sticks in hand. One of the hooeys, a piece of rough wood about the size of a drum stick, has a propeller fixed to the end of it. The other hooey is the same shape and texture.

Holding the hooey stick with the attached propeller horizontally, I rub the other hooey across it's brother, back and forth, near my hand. We're all staring at the propeller. Nothing happens. Nothing ever happens when I try to operate Wayne's hooey-hooeys.

"Here, Stevie, let me show you how," Wayne says taking the device from my hands. He starts to run the 'hooeys' together and the prop starts to spin, faster and faster. "Now watch, I'll make it reverse direction." Sure as shit, the propeller slows, stops and starts spinning the other way. I'm carefully watching everything Wayne is doing. He's not blowing on the prop, he's not moving the steady hand, nor twisting it. I've been trying to work at the trick of the hooey-hooeys for four years, and still can't figure how he does it.

"Magic!" Wayne grins, more gum than tooth. He's never told anybody how it's done, but has whittled and given away a dozen sets in the time I've known him.

"Hey Rabbi," What do you call a recently divorced Jewish woman?" Bubba asks.

"What?"

"A born-again cocksucker!"

Wayne says, "This boy and his dad are in the drugstore and the dad is teaching the kid the 'facts of life' about the condoms there…"

"Here we go," I interrupt. We're all smiling.

"So, Wayne continues, "the boy asks his Dad what's the different packs for, ya know? How come a two pack, a three pack and a twelve pack? The Dad says '…son, the two pack, that's for high school kids, you know, getting' it on Friday and Saturday nights. The three pack, now that's for college kids…they got the weekends and such … now the twelve pack, that's for married men…you know, son, one for January, one for February, one for March…"

"Man…..do married people get laid every month?"

Islamic Justice

Jerry Lovell, Herr-Lippi and I are shopping at the _zook_ (say sook), the gold market in downtown Jeddah. Jerry's been coming to the same jeweler for twenty years down here, both he and Mark have flown for different Sheiks in past lives.

The minarets start to wail their call for noon prayer, and the shopkeepers, hundreds of them, chase their customers out and close-up shop. They lock their doors and pull across their metal security gates.

Khaki clad, heavily bearded _Matawah_, religious police, pass quickly through the streets, ensuring compliance with their orthodoxy.

Yesterday, one of our male flight attendants was busted, and shipped out of the Kingdom. He had made the mistake of sitting on a public bench adjacent to a female who wasn't his wife or blood relative. He wasn't talking to her, just sitting, resting. Sometimes the _Matawah_ sweep through American or Brit compounds looking for booze or drugs. Often, they set-up roadblocks checking the work-documents of all the Packies, Egyptians, Bangladeshies, or whoever else is in the city, making sure their work visas haven't expired.

Suddenly, we are surrounded by _Matawah_. We are force marched without explanation towards the central square, across the street, near the mosque.

"Oh shit." says Jerry. "What day is it?"

"Friday."

"Fuck," Lippi says, "it's chop-chop time."

The crowd gathers, and the _Matawah_ make sure that all us western infidels are pushed up front, the better to watch Islamic justice. The prisoners are marched out. This is going to be my first viewing of a public execution. We all know that, except for during Ramadan, all

Islamic justice is meted out every Friday, immediately following noon prayer.

The kneeling man's eyes are fixed, as are ours, on the executioner standing before him. He is holding a long, scimitar-style sword. In the blink of an eye, the man's head is in the basket. No one ever noticed the second executioner step up from behind and swing his sword.

Today we're in for a treat. A Muslim husband has accused one of his wives of infidelity. Worse yet, as Jerry works out from the crowd, she's been caught being unfaithful with a non-Muslim. She will be stoned to death. Lucky for her, however, Jeddah, unlike most other Muslim cities, has gone 'high tech.' We watch as she is lowered into a prepared pit, about 10' x 5' x 8' deep. The throaty rumble of the tractor is enough to clear a path for it through the side of the crowd. We watch a front loader full of huge chunks of rock and concrete pieces lifted high above the pit. At a nod from the Imam, the tractor operator releases his load. The woman is no longer visible, buried beneath tons of rubble and dust.

"Man, it was much worse in the old days," says Mark. "They used to have the husband and his male family members and buddies just throw rocks at the bitch until she died. Took forever."

We manage to sidle out of the crowd, and escape back into the maze of the *zook,* before the next beheading or hand chopping. "I'll be more careful to make sure what day of the week it is before I zook-it again," I tell the other guys.

"Hell," says Jerry. "Sure keeps the crime rate low." He's right, but Islamic justice can be a little too arbitrary, from where I stand, as a non-Muslim (and secret Jew).

Herr Lippi asks, "know what they cater their beheadings with?"

"No, Mark, what?"

"DeCap-achino!....get it? Get it?"

Dead Hadji's I have Known (The Wrist Watch)

"Is the gear down and locked?" screams Captain Troy Cupps, finally losing patience with our stand-in Flight Engineer, Bruce Quinn.

"1000 feet above field elevation." I call out.

"Bruce, is the fuckin' gear down?"

No response from Bruce, a total asshole of a guy, who takes pleasure torturing new hires during ground school and sim sessions, but has frozen-up in the real deal.

"300 feet above minimums." I announce.

"We're going around," announces Troy, "Flaps 20, set go around thrust," and he blasts us up and away from our landing at Islamabad.

The _Packies_ are screaming in the back of the plane. Apparently some of the bodies have started rolling down the aisles, as we pitch-up to our 15° go-around deck angle.

We started the 'second wave of the Hadj' returning the Hajjis from Arabia to wherever they've come from, all over the Muslim world. A Muslim (to get into heaven), must do one Hajj in their lifetime. Since most are pitifully poor, villages all over Pakistan, India and Bangladesh take up collections to send their old, sick and dying for their one pilgrimage. The rules are that if a Muslim dies during the Hajj, he automatically ascends to Heaven.

We invariably have four or five die (out of 500 Hajji's on the 747) on the way in, during the "first wave." However, when the millions of old, sick Hajji's from all these countries are concentrated in the packed tent cities erected for the Hajj, then go through the rigors of the journey, many more die during the actual pilgrimage, or on the "second wave" heading home. The corpses of the already dead are taken into the plane, for the return trip home. These bodies, shrouded, are laid out in the aisles, and are prayed over by fellow passengers, who stand in the aisles, chanting.

Today, fifteen dead Pakistani's, and 480 live ones, are returning to Islamabad, and our violent go-around has corpses rolling down the aisles, creating Islamic havoc.

Leveling off at 1500' AGL, Troy asks me to take control. It was his leg to Islamabad, but responding that "I have control," I am now flying the airplane.

Troy, calm now, turns to work the landing gear problem out with Bruce, while I notify Islamabad Tower Control of our "missed approach." They vector me around in a pattern to avoid terrain and buy us time to resolve our situation.

Troy satisfies himself that all eighteen wheels are all "down and locked." All is safe, the crisis is just an indication problem, and the inability of an inept Flight Engineer to correctly determine what he was looking at.

Troy resumes control of the airplane, we land smoothly, uneventfully and taxi up to the terminal.

We pilots in the cockpit, Bruce escaping Troy's wrath by going down onto the ramp to do his walk around - the inspection of the exterior of the craft.

Neither Troy, nor I have said a word about the incident, each mellowing out in our own thoughts. The aircraft is now empty of all passengers, both living and dead.

One of our flight attendants enters the cockpit, a young lady so swathed in her *Abaya*, that I don't recognize her. She is holding up a man's gold watch.

"Do either of you know anything about watches?" she asks.

Abruptly pulled back from our thoughts, neither Troy Cupps nor I answer fast enough.

"Do you think this a good watch, do you think my boyfriend would like it?"

Troy and I disbelievingly catch each other's eye, then turn back to look at this girl. In our hearts, we know that she has robbed one of the corpses. She leaves the cockpit, thoughtfully, softly closing the door.

Jeddah

Easter was approaching, and so was *Father* Larry Jacks.

"Uh oh," says Wally Hudson, *Al-Wahlid*, as he pushes back his chair, the breakfast table clears in a hurry. Soon it's only me and Father Larry, a devout Christian horse-rancher from Montana. He was wearing his only outfit. Every day, the same washed-out, yellow knit shirt. That same pair of khaki shorts, with his bony, pale legs ending in black socks and brown leather sandals.

Everybody avoided *Father* Larry, like a Biblical plague. He was a nice enough, decent man, but the faith was his only topic. Early on I had answered "yes," when Larry asked if I was saved? Big mistake. Father Larry has me down as a brother now, and I don't have the heart to hurt his feelings now.

"Stephen ," this is in a stage whisper. We're all alone in this immense hotel dining room, and Father Larry is whispering to me..."we've formed a group to conduct a secret Easter service, I knew you'd be interest."

The Saudi's do not permit the possession of holy books of any faith other than Islam, no Bibles, no crosses, no nothing. You would be unable to buy a cross, or to wear one in Saudi Arabia. Very tolerant people, the Saudi's.

Apparently, Larry is a member of a Christian cabal, which meets secretly in different hotels, or homes, every Sunday. They intend to celebrate an Easter service, which is punishable by *Allah* knows what, if the *Matawah* get wind of it. My memories go back to a gentleman on his knees, facing his executioner. Saudi prisons are not fun, either. It could be weeks or months before anybody actually finds out that you are in a Saudi Jail. Prisoners cannot bathe, and are not fed. If nobody you know brings you food to the prison, you do not eat.

I try to express these concerns to *Father* Larry, but he's not listening to me... he hears a higher voice. His demeanor reminds me of an old time

Victor Mature movie I once saw. As the Christians were being fed to the lions, one devout Christian drops to his knees, a beatific calm reflected in his face. He is going to meet Jesus, dying gladly for his faith. This is the radiance glowing now in *Father* Larry.

"Come meet and pray with us, Steve… it's Easter and the Lord has risen."

"No thanks, Larry," I say as I push away from the table. "But do say a prayer for me." I leave the room.

Take Me Home, Country Road

Kiley's alone this time. What is she doing driving the car? Just outside her car window is the black box, that menacing master of modernity. Any human contact is well hidden behind the looming smirk of this machine.

The hum and buzz of technology manifests itself in the sudden explosion of human voice into the open car window: _"FRIES WITH THAT?"_

Garbled, but somehow decipherable through the webs and crackles of wires and static... _"FRIES WITH THAT?"_...and Kiley's answer, somehow now very important: words spoken and recorded on the other unseen end by the push of a button, these same words recorded again only morphing now into the fries themselves: calories; lard; complex carbohydrates; mono-unsaturated linseed oil; pooling and sinking into the dimpled yellow sad limp fry, recorded not on paper but on flesh. No longer a fry, but clumps of cellulite, folds of fat and dimpled wobbly flab... born from the grease that feeds our drive-thru generation.

Floating, I watch as in it's digested form it clings to thighs and bellies and arms, desperate and maniacal, a Marine to clinging to his fallen flag. This _Fat_. Worthless, inanimate and pointless, not just an additive or an ingredient, but **_it_**... of and from and by.... polyhydrogenation!

And finally this: this box, screaming and roiling, shaking and over and over the voice: _"FRIES WITH THAT?" "FRIES WITH THAT?"_ And Kiley too, shaking and cowering, all at once hating the lumps of polyunsaturates that feed her and ruin her, forcing her generation to try to squeeze into their acid-washed jeans and cheap polyester tube tops, stretching over rolls of stomach.

Kiley answers, softly at first, but then louder, finally drowning out the relentless blare of the microphone: "I DON'T! I DON'T! I DON'T WANT THE FRIES! I DON'T WANT THE FRIES!"

"KILEY, HEY!" I cry out, waking with a jump.

Oh man, I've got to get home… I've got to get home, my mind keeps repeating over the splash of pee I'm donating free of charge to my Saudi toilet. I lean against the bathroom wall, watching the stream in the mirror.

I've got to get home I announce to the aging, sagging face looking sadly back at me.

Asleep again, now I'm on a checkout line at Winn Dixie.. I know I'm asleep, I know I'm watching myself advances on the line. Then I see *The National Enquirer* and I know my time is near. The *Enquirer* is just like death… you try not to think about it, but it's always there waiting for you right above the *Tic-Tacs* and there's not a thing you can do about it!

When my turn came, I was all alone on a grassy knoll at the front of the store, facing the cold hard stare of the checkout girl, the girl with Kiley's face.

I placed the milk of the lower fat persuasion, all two and one-half pounds of swordfish, and the stuffed dog on the fast moving blackness of the conveyor belt.

"Is that all?" she asks in a manner some checkout girls with the rank of Assistant Manager use. It was a kind of dialect, but I understood it well enough.

"Isn't it pretty to think so my little rabbit?" Now I was pleased not to have left the stuffed dog unbought on the shelf.

"Paper or plastic?"

This was the question I hated. I never knew how you were supposed to answer. My wife Geri always knew, but her cell phone would be turned off. For a moment I felt the responsibility of the whole environment on my shoulders and this was maybe the toughest thing I'd ever have to do.

"Shit, nothing, nothing" I screamed, exiting quickly through the automatic sliding doors into the warm suburban air.

There is never any end to suburbia. "Maybe suburbia is what we have instead of God?" I would ask Geri, she would know…maybe I could page her.

The Hajj Breakfast Club

Pilots love to bitch, and breakfast at the Sofitel in Jeddah during the Hajj, is always a bitching session. Fed up with Saudi Arabia, Arabs, and the Saudis in particular, Islam is usually the butt of our jokes.

Mark Lippi, "Herr-Lippi" poses this question to us..."what do you call an Arab with a slab of pork on his head?... 'Ham-head,' and what do you call an Arab with two slabs of pork on his head? ... 'Mo-Ham-head'.... and what do you call that same fuckin' Arab with two slabs of pork on his head, squattin' on his vibrator?... 'Sheik Mo-Ham-Head,' get it?"

"This is my 37th day without a beer," moans Wally Hudson, "fuckin' sandbox!"

"Herr-Lippi" asks: "What were Mohammed's final words to the Arabs, before he ascended to heaven?"....silence, Mark's on a roll....."Act stupid until I return!"

Not to be outdone, Bubba adds: "Hey Mark, Mohammed returned... He told them 'I didn't mean that stupid!'"

"Fuckin' beans and rice again," Wally complains.

Mark...... " Moses and Jesus and Buddha are meeting for coffee and donuts.... They're discussing their comparative religions.... One of them looks up, looks around, and asks 'where's Mohammed?'..... 'Oh yeah, says Moses, ... Hey Mohammed, more coffee!'"

Jimmy Lynch, with his mouth full of rice, "The fuckin' Saudi's and their fuckin' squattin' attitude. They invented nothing, developed nothing. The Brits and Americans found the oil, and did it all for them. Look at them, strutting like Allah's fuckin' chosen people."

Herr-Lippi leans forward and pulls his glasses loosely down to the tip of his nose. "Hey, Bubba, what did Moses say to God, when God offered that the Jews become the chosen people?"

"What?"

Mark feigns studying the contract presented by God for Moses'
signature. Mark peers left over his shoulder (looking at the Arabs).
Then looks down closely at the "contract." Looking over his right
shoulder, at God, Mark says: "Moses says to God" (this in a pretty good
broken Jewish/Yiddish accent): 'Now let me get this straight...THEY
(the Arabs over his left shoulder) get all the oil...and WE get to cut the
heads of our WHAT off?"

Al-Waleed, turning serious now, "Al Brandon is great for the pilots, but
fuckin' Lithgow is a snake, a fuckin' opportunist, he'd sell anybody out
for money!"

"Yeah," I volunteer, "for a quarter of a million a year he's gonna get
someone killed. Lithgow's gonna' force someone into a dangerous
situation and it'll bite him in the ass someday….. look at Jesus, He was
an opportunist, and look what it got him!"

"Rabbi, you got too much Jew showin'" says Sheamus O'Connor, as he
relieves me of the podium.

"Jesus was no opportunist," Sheamus continues, "He was a young
schmuck, duped by his own parents. Jesus was an unwitting patsy."

"Oh shit,"…*Father* Larry's had enough. Gruffly bidding the room
goodnight, he storms from this sacrilege towards his room.

Sheamus continues his argument, "Jesus' parents were con-artists, con-
men…"

"No, they were *con-menschen*," (I can't let the opportunity pass).

Unfazed, Sheamus continues, … "Do you think that because this all
happened 2000 years ago, there were no con-artists? Human Nature's
never changed, for a full 3600 years before there ever was a Jesus, Jews

were crawling out of tents every couple hundred years or so, claiming to be the Jewish Messiah."

We were all beaming now, not knowing exactly where Sheamus is heading, but sure it'll be a bruising, brilliant and fun ride.

"Mary and Joseph were a couple of Jewish kids who got pregnant on a road trip, so to speak. The carpentry business was slow at the time, so they came up with the virgin birth routine. All that attention, man it was great in the beginning, meeting Kings and wise men. Free meals, housing, and the limelight, man, the limelight… fame is a powerful drug… they rode that scam for all it was worth."

Sheamus pauses to sip from his Swann's fake beer. A pink mole of a tongue burrows out of his lips to tidy up his mustache, then retreats.

"Their only problem was that Jesus bought into the story, hook, line and Torah!" He smirks, leaning forward, knowingly, "One night in bed, Mary whispers in Joseph's ear that she's troubled, she's worried about Jesus …. 'He's starting to believe that he really is the Messiah, and Joe, our baby's going to get into trouble.' Joseph tells her not to worry, 'when the kid's a little older, when they think he can handle it, they'll tell him the truth.'"

"They just waited too long," Sheamus explains, "Yeah, poor, dumb kid, he got hoist on their wooden petard, permanently!"

"You are saying that our Lord Jesus Christ was not the son of God? Is that what you're saying?" Father Larry demands, having returned (smelling sweetly of *Sediki)* to bravely defend the faith.

Al-Waleed answers for Sheamus, "Jesus was a pain-in-the-ass Jew Rabbi. He had this holier than thou attitude!"

"Look Larry," Sheamus says, trying to calm him, "Don't get into a snit. If Jesus was the son of God, He was into getting himself crucified. If he wasn't, he's just some delusional kid that came along, like they did every couple a hundred years or so for those first 3700 years, His crucifixion just cleaned up the gene pool a bit. The poor dumb kid was on a trip started by his parents, and their scam overtook them. After all, it was only the most gullible Jews who took up the "Christianity thing," strengthening the pure Jew-gene pool, by removing a considerable contingent of fools."

Father Larry groans, gut-shot, stalking once again towards his room.

"Hey Sheamus," I ask, "is this the philosophy that led to your t-shirt and bumper sticker business... *Body piercing – Jesus loved it!* ....And by the way, how're sales?"

"Rabbi, you're gonna' roast in hell" Sheamus winks.

As I head for my room later that day, Father Larry intercepts me in the deserted hallway.

"Steve, Steve, com'ere."

"What's up, Larry?"

"Really, I know you were kidding earlier, right? You really believe in Jesus."

"Larry, I think I'm actually an atheist. I don't actually believe in a God."

"Not even in a Jewish God?"

"No Larry, not Jesus, not Jehovah, not Buddha, not no one. I'm okay with it."

Larry gets feisty now, his face reddening. "You are a character, and... and you have NO character," he spits at me.

"Look Larry," trying to calm him some, "character and integrity, that's really about what you do when nobody's looking."

"I agree, that's good. I agree."

166

"Okay, Larry, so now we agree on something. But, I contend that the only true person of character and integrity is the atheist."

"What…. where you comin' up with that shit from?"

"Simple. If one of your *believers* does the right thing when nobody is looking, it could be because you think that God is always watching, keeping a secret tally of your sins. See, you always feel you're being watched. Your doing the right thing, but you feel you're under God's constant scrutiny, like you can't cheat.

"When an atheist like me does the right thing when no one's watching, and there is no God watching, then that atheist is a true person of integrity and character."

Father Larry seems stunned. "Devil's spawn," he declares, marching away from me, up the hall.

The Zam-Zam Scam

I'm on lobby duty with P-Brain and Herr-Lippi in attendance. It's early evening and our guys in Jeddah take over the couches in the lobby of the hotel, to schmooze and gripe for hours.

Lynn Barkley and Jerry Lovell come down the stairs, excitedly carrying their empty _zam-zam_ jugs. These are five-gallon plastic containers, labeled as _zam zam_ and a bunch of Arabic script. Jerry broke the code on getting laid in Malaysia and Indonesia. _Zam-zam_ water is the holy water of Islam, coming from the official well that Mohammed drank from before ascending to Heaven. Unavailable to most Muslims, _zam-zam_ is worth more than the blood of Christ, it's "worth it's weight in come," as Jerry would say...adding "life is good!"

Lynn and Jerry have snagged a trip to K.L. tomorrow, Kuala Lumpur, where the beer is flowing, and the women fuck your brains out for a five-gallon jug of _zam zam_ water. Jerry, Lynn and the rest of the guys put the empty containers in their flight bags.

After checking into their rooms in K.L., they will fill the jugs up with ordinary tap water from their bathrooms and head out on their eternal quest for LBFM's, Little, brown fucking machines. The _zam-zam_ scam is alive and well in Malaysia.

"Lucky bastards," Mark says. "I haven't gotten a layover in K.L. yet!"

"Still playing with yourself, Rabbi?" asks Lenny Craig.

"No, Lenny" I say, "I'm non-hormonal... I was startin' to worry about why I'm not jerking off as much as I used to, but I discovered the reason. When I lay down now (pointing at my huge gut), I don't see my pecker anymore...out of sight, out of mind...it's over the horizon," I conclude.

Lenny advises, "Rabbi, my philosophy is very simple. If I wake up and I see a fist in my bed, I fuck it!

"Mark: "I have to pour beer on my hand to get my date drunk."

Schwarmer-time in Jeddah is the social event of the evening, and timing is critical.

The group would meet in the lobby of the Sofitel at 6:30pm, allowing for the fifteen minute walk to *Jaw's café*, gave us forty minutes to eat between evening prayers.

"Great White" is the patriarch of the Turkish family that works the *Schwarmer* stand. He would greet us on the sidewalk with a big smile, his gleaming teeth and juicy gums extended impossibly forward somehow, giving the place it's name.

Every evening, as we marched in and took our positions, Charlie Pickles' nasal twang would sing-song out, "Two chicken *Schwarmers*, extra pickles....Pepsi."

By the second month of the Hajj, all the Turkish brothers, Stinky, Reeky, Jaws and *Achmed* were singing along with Charlie (and the rest of us):

"Two chicken *Schwarmers*, extra pickles....Pepsi."

Charlie Pickles, of course, became Charlie "extra pickles", or just plain "extra pickles."

The Mountain Comes to Mohammed

The Spocula, Jimmy Lynch and I are tired as shit. We've just completed another bag-drag, delivering hundreds of thousands of pounds of leftover luggage to Islamabad. After eight hours of flying, and three hours on the ground waiting for the _Packies_ to unload the crap, we've just landed in Jeddah.

The Saudi's, always the perfect hosts, want the Hajji's leftover luggage out of Jeddah. "Just take it anywhere" the Saudia Ops man orders, "Take it to Islamabad!" O.K.

This leftover luggage is actually mostly personal effects, bundled up into prayer rugs or cheap straw bags, and tied up with twine. When the Hajji's are herded through the Hajj terminal and onto airplanes for their return to Allah-Knows-Where, their luggage either makes it onto the plane, or doesn't, _inshallah_!

A mountain of these leftovers has been growing out on the tarmac, adjacent to the Hajj terminal, as the waves of faithful finish their pilgrimage, and return home.

The only cargo we now have on board is Royal Dalton China, ordered by one of the Saudi Royals, some Saudi Prince.

Now, taxiing to the gate area, it becomes apparent that we have some kind of "Royal Priority." Someone must have tipped off the tower and ground controllers as to our cargo and its destination. Suddenly all traffic at _Abdul Azziz_ airport is stopping, giving way to us.

We are instructed by ground to proceed to Hajj Terminal, Gate A-1. Approaching the ramp area we are overwhelmed by the looming Everest of bags, rugs and suitcases. Rising from the ground, up higher than the roof of the terminal building, a vast pyramid of personal flotsam now occupies an area the size of a soccer field, on the concrete apron.

Another 747 had just pushed back from the gate we were to occupy. It was just starting to move forward to taxi towards the active runway, as we entered the ramp and turned towards our now vacant gate.

The Saudi ground controller orders the other aircraft to give way to us, that we have priority, because of one fucking box of dishes, for one fucking Saudi Prince, who eats with his fucking fingers. We all realize that there is not enough room for us to taxi past the other aircraft. Spocula says "Tell that ground guy to allow the other plane out, that we'll wait for him. We can't fit through that space."

"Jeddah ground," I say, "Saudia 806 requests you allow for Saudia 800 to continue its taxi-out first, so that we may, *Inshallah*, have room to enter gate A-1, *shuckran.*"

Bubba's voice, obviously the captain on Saudia 800, says, "Thanks Keshy."

The ground control, insisting that we "have royal priority," orders Bubba's plane to make a right 360 degree turn to get out of our way, and come up behind us.

A loaded B-747 can weigh up to 830,000 pounds. The amount of power needed to get it rolling straight ahead is pretty impressive. The power needed to 'unstick' the same airplane, allowing it to make a tight 360 degree turn, is much greater. Not wanting to damage any ground equipment or vehicles, Bubba tries again:

"Saudia Ground Control, Saudia 800 request taxi straight ahead to runway 36L. We will be out of the way of Saudia 806 in a minute."

"NO! Saudia 800, immediately make a right 360 degree turn. Allow Saudia 806 to enter gate!" The manager of the ground control staff is now screaming on the radio. He will show us infidels who is in charge of this airport…indeed in charge of this Kingdom!

"Rabbi, do you know how much thrust these Pratt JT9D's deliver?" Spock asks me.

Of course Spocula knows that we all know the answer to that one, he's just starting the verbal drum-roll for what we all know is about to happen.

Playing along, I respond, "Well, Captain, I believe each of these four engines is capable of delivering about 45,000 pounds of thrust, about 90,000 horsepower, …a grand total of 180,000 pounds of thrust, or 360,000 horsepower."

"That's correct!" agrees Jimmy Lynch, now pushing his face between ours against the windscreen, preparing to see the show.

We all watch as Bubba sets his parking brake on Aircraft 800. We listen as he powers up to near take-off thrust. Our plane is shaking and throbbing in syncopation with the now deafening blast. We all smile, as Bubba releases his brakes. Saudia 800 makes a tight, sweeping, right 360'. As it does, 180,000 pounds of thrust blast into the Himalayan pile of luggage on the ramp. We blink, the mountain of luggage is gone and the apron is spotless.

"Now you see it, now you don't," drawls Bubba over ground frequency.

For miles around, hanging from buildings, airplanes, roofs and trucks, bits and pieces of laundry, straw and rugs litter the landscape.

Not one word is heard on the radio from Jeddah ground or Tower control as we taxi into our gate.

"The Mountain has come to Mohammed" announces Spock, as we climb out of the cockpit.

More Ahmed Shithedian

We've been months trapped in Jeddah on contract. I'm sitting in the dining room with Herr-Lippi and a flight attendant, and in walks Ahmed, in uniform. We all know that he's connived a few days home (sucking up to the schedulers everyday), and that he is waiting for the hotel bus to take him to the airport.

Unable to resist rubbing my nose in it, he plunks down at our table, and says, "Steve, I will be home for a few days. Can I do anything for you, should I call on your wife, and tell her 'hello' for you?"

"No Ahmed, thanks, that won't be necessary."

"Oh," louder now, "so you don't want me in your home when you're not there."

Leaning close, I hold his forearm now, look him in the eye, and say, "No, Ahmed, I don't want you in my home even when I am there!"

I see the steam exploding from Ahmed's ears as he jumps up from the table. Watching Ahmed storm from the room, Herr-Lippi shits himself. I grin. The flight attendant seated at our table, not attuned to cockpit politics, is non-plussed.

The tale of this confrontation spreads through our pilot pool with the speed of an Ebola virus in an Zaire infirmary. The story becomes a classic, and I am an instant hero. I've made a dangerous enemy, however, and I'm going to have to watch my back carefully, for some time.

Life in Jeddah…The Grand Illusion

My father's big hand lets me go and I run towards the tank full of boats. Dad has taken my sister Helene and I to a carnival that popped open, mushroom like, in the Bronx.

I climb into a boat, hoping I will be alone at the wheel and in the boat. Before the ride starts, I notice that each boat seems attached to a spoke of metal emanating from a central hub in the vast tub.

The ride starts, gasps of surprised glee from all lucky children in command of our own vessels. I turn the wheel, and the boat doesn't respond, only going around in circles strapped to the arm of steel. I spin the wheel, madly now, in the opposite direction. No change in course.

The other children in their boats are smiling, happy, playing with their steering wheels, not seeming to mind that the boat goes where it wants to go, without help from you.

I am upset that I have no control. At the age of five or six, I am already wondering if life isn't like the boat?

"Hey Rabbi, wake up, it's *Schwarmer*-time!" Where am I….oh, fell asleep at the pool… Oh God (whose, which one?), I'm still in Saudi Arabia.

The Sandbox is Forever

As weeks drone by, the Saudia flying dwindles to zero. Other companies with Saudia contracts, have reached the correct corrupt official, and have been awarded our trips. But we are still there, prisoners of Jeddah.

The snorkeling along the Red Sea reef, the endless games of "spades" while enjoying our _Cohibas_ and _Partagas_, have given way, finally, to dull, bitching sessions. We're not flying, we're going crazy, what the fuck are we still doing stuck out here in the sandbox, away from home? Night after night, the same old routine: the walk for _Schwarmers_, then having eaten, back on lobby duty, twenty pilots, unable to leave the Kingdom.... ("flying can start back up at any time," says _screw-scheduling_).

We are tired of each other, and of any further conversation. We all just sit around with the thousand-yard-stare, beginning to hate each other.

Jaime Pinto, in full "commercial travel" attire, comes flying down the hall, his wheelies and his flight bag clipping behind him. Heading for the check out desk, he yells, "We all have twenty minutes to check out and to make the airport bus. We're going home!"

Startled, staring at each other, we all jump up. Jaime stops, turns to face us, and starts to laugh. It's a practical joke. Unbelievably, Jaime has gotten us all, the mood is broken, and our hearts and spirits are back.

Our crew members are not alone at the _Durrah Al Aroos_ Resort Hotel. Saudi guests fill a majority of the rooms, and much of the lobby is taken up with Arabs, enjoying their tea and breakfast.

The morning after Jaime's joke, Captain Charlie extra-pickles takes center stage.

Post-breakfast lobby duty is in full swing, when a loud, nasal singing fills the echo-chambered hotel, moving along the balcony, overlooking the entire lobby.

"Another openin', another show..." doing his best Ethel Merman routine, dressed in shower cap, bathrobe and flip-flops, Charlie finally appears at the top of the carpeted, marble staircase.

Everything stops. No one moves, Muslim nor infidel make a sound. Without pause, Charlie dances a few steps down, and one or two up, down, then up the staircase...he is Shirley Temple and Bo-Jangles, now singing, *"There's no business like show business."*

Extra Pickles times it perfectly, he arrives at the bottom of the stairs at exactly the same time as his closing notes, *"... let's get on with the show!."* He ends with a flourish, arms extended.

Pandemonium....the room erupts with applause. All the Saudi's, and all the foreign Americans devils have jumped to their feet, and are wildly applauding Charlie extra-pickles performance. He's beaming, he's a hit!

Charlie, Lovell and Barclay head for Kuala Lumpur, leaving Mark and me stuck in Jeddah, the "Land of No". We decide to meet up in my room in half an hour, and head for dinner somewhere.

"...Hilary Clinton? Who the fuck believes anything she claims to stand for? Make believe, lying, obvious bitch... with her desiccated, pinko-hippy agenda!"

"That's it, Rabbi," Herr-Lippi says, "Don't hold back. Tell me what you really feel about the Clinton-cunt, as in *C.U.N.T.,* cant understand normal thinking!"

Lippi laughs, he's hangin' in my room, waiting for me to finish washing out my underwear in the bathroom sink. I squeeze the last of the water out of my three pairs of skivvies, and hang them to dry on a towel.

"Why don't you use the same inside-outside-backside-frontside routine Al Waleed uses? You'll get four uses out of each pair."

"Right, Mark, and I'll smell like camel-shit, just like Wally Al Waleed does."

"You've noticed."

"Hey, I actually got a bunch of those paper panties they sell in Jakarta, seven to a box, check 'em out. 5,000 *Rupes* a box, that's about forty cents a box, about five cents a pair, think you can afford 'em? I even gave them the Rabbi's' liquid and fart' test, in the Hilton pool, fuckin' amazing, they held together."

"Paper panties, you sweet little-girl Rabbi you. Still playing 'you bet your shorts' when you think you've got to fart? Fuckin' Indonesian food, I never know if I'm gonna' fart, shit, or let a liquid-bubble go in my drawers."

"Herr-Lippi, you're a class act……"

"Thanks, Rabbi, speakin' of paper panties…. know what Grandma pussy tastes like?"

"Okay, I'll bite."

"Depends!"

"Depends!, I got it…Depends!… thanks Mark, I'll be sure to tell that one to Geri's mom, Beverly, she'll love it."

"Mark, when I turned fifty my dad told me, "….son, there's three things you want to pay attention to now….. never turn down a chance to use a bathroom, never trust a fart, and never waste an erection"

"Sounds like good advice… who've you been flying with lately?"

"Mark, I can't remember who I was with, but I can tell you that I was in Room 1018 in Luxemburg, triple-4 in Dubai, and now I'm in 1212 in Jeddah."

"Anything interesting going on out in those garden spots?" Mark wants to know.

"Well, I watched the Millenial-2000 Airshow in Dubai, from the roof-garden of my hotel. Spectacular. The commentator was talking in Arabic and French."

"I watched the Scotts beat England in soccer, narrated in German, in Luxembourg, and I saw the Holyfield fight in Paris on TV, blow-by-blow in French. That's good, 'blow-by-blow in French,' get it, get it? Come to think of it, I must have laid over in Paris at some point last week."

"Lipster, those fuckin' bathtowels in Paris? They always smell like cod-liver oil to me, you ever notice that…. not that nice, fishy-pussy smell, but the ugly, mediciny smell? "

"No, Rabbi, I've never noticed," Mark smirks, "But you've got that magnificent, sensitive Jew-nose." Mark is one of the few guys I've told the truth to about my Semitic heritage. He's cool, making racial and ethnic slurs about everybody, harboring no real hatred towards anyone.

"Hey, I finally ate the *Pizza Pescatore* you always mange in that place next to the Sofitel. It was great. Man, they heap on the scallops, shrimp and mussels. I hit it with the hot-pepper-oil shit, *mierde, fabuloso.*"

"That's *fabeyeux in* Paris, Rabbi."

"*Right, d'accord*, fabeyeux, vraiment! Let me practice my limited French, Herr-Lippis of Marcos."

"Well, get that fat Jew ass of yours in gear, before the rag-heads close down the *schwarmer* for evening prayers, I'm getting hungry."

"What's going on with you and your old lady….. seeing your kids at all?"

178

"The bitch is hanging on, waiting for my settlement to come through. I see the kids once in a while. The little one is building a computer and teaching me about the web."

"Jesus, those kids 're great." I say. "Kiley's very special, and we miss each other a lot. Man, I've got to get away from this shit, and get home, do something that'll keep me home."

Lippi agrees, he's got two young kids, and we're averaging only eight days home a month.

Home

"I'm the only broke Jew I know." My hands grabbing more dirty dishes from the dining room table.

Geri adds, "Yeah, I married a Jew, and got the only one without any money."

Our gang of friends seated around the dining room table laugh at the joke. The parties are usually at our house, a three story glass and deck beach house, whose space, and personality makes it the perfect host. It's the house and my profession as a pilot, that have our buddies believing that we have money.

As I scrub the dishes and plates, a pile of dirties still waiting their turn next to me at the sink, I think about "the joke." Only Geri and I know the truth, the joke's on us. We don't have a dime set aside, we live paycheck to paycheck, and forced retirement is less than three years away.

I am juggling while walking a tightrope, Philippe Petit without a net, high over the financial chasms of ruin. To keep our personal and family life whole, I need to stay home as much as possible. Earning only minimum guarantee. We can't pay our bills on minimum guarantee, so I have to sacrifice our home life to fly extra trips to make the bill payments.

Always juggling bills that need paying, versus time home as husband and father, I place one foot carefully in front of the other on the unstable wire.

But even our tightrope ends in less than three years. Washing and stacking more dishes and glasses, watching the pile of dirties grow next to my right elbow, I hear the party, the music and laughter, raging around me.

What the fuck am I going to do three years from now? My first and second mortgages combined are $2000 a month. It costs us $4000 total a month to live.

All my flying buddies are now turning forty. Entering their peak earning period, they have twenty career years left to accumulate wealth, to build up retirement accounts. I'm fifty-eight (and ½) years old, only one and ½ years left, until the age sixty mandatory retirement rule kicks my butt.

I'm chained to the oars now, having volunteered to row on the slave ship too late in life.

"Stevie, this is a great party, again!" Stella chimes, leaving more dirty glasses and dishes on the counter.

"It never ends," I think. "Anybody need another Marguerita?" I ask, rejoining the group of smokers and tokers on the deck.

Watching Clint, his brother Mike, and Sheila sharing a joint, I bitch, "I can't believe I had to give up drugs for my lousy profession, ain't fuckin' worth it!"

Sheila laughs, coughing and choking on the smoke she's trying to hold in. Clint throws out the proverbial pothead adage, "You don't cough, you don't get off."

Next day, I'm prioritizing bills to pay now. Piles of stuff, junk, intermingled with what might be important, litter my desk, waiting to be deciphered. I've been home for a week, and I'm moody now, melting down. I'm getting ready to leave for the Hajj. I'll be gone for the better part of three months. Geri and I are arguing over petty shit. My lousy disposition leaks out, causing me to bark at both Geri and Kiley. I bark, I apologize, I bark, I apologize. Poor Geri's trying not to react to my mood, we both know the symptoms and the cause.

"Kiley, I'm sorry honey, I didn't mean to snap at you like that. I was wrong." This in the spare room, Kiley watching a Lucy rerun on Nick at Nite.

Kiley hugs me, holding me close she says, "That's all right Dad, I love you."

"I love you too, Sweety, I'm sorry."

Leaving home is becoming harder and harder for me to do. Being home, an actual member of the family, feels so comfortable, so good, that the pain of impending separation is searing my soul.

"I hate this shit!" I tell Kaput, the black kitten napping on an office chair next to me. Kaput has no advice for me.

Alan Quine and Christmas in Paris

Alan Quine, Newt "Neutron" Silva and I are getting fucked up every day for Christmas week in Paris. The Sofitel St. Jaques crew room is the scene of this marathon crime.

By 2:00pm we show up, each of us with a couple of bottles of excellent twelve-fifteen franc merlots and cabernets, *mutard*, fresh *baguettes* and *fromages* are pulled from plastic shopping bags.

Flight attendants and pursers come and go, drinking and schmoozing with us, as we sit drinking from our $2 bottles of fine French wine, smoking Cuban cigars, and *kibitzzing* through the night, every night, until the restaurant opens for *petite dejeuner* at seven am.

Changing venues, we gorge on Nova Salmon, omelets to order, *café au lait*, we are wrapped in the aromas of *Chocolat chaud* and fresh linen. Then its off to bed. At 2:00 P.M. we start the cycle all over again.

This decadent Parisian orgy lasts through Christmas and New Years, broken only by one flight to *Al's Garage (Al Kharj)* and back to Paris. Eugene, one of our more popular Pursers, a gay gentleman, has brought his professional dancer live-in of thirteen years, along with him on this trip. They are celebrating not only the Holidays, but the Purser's 40th birthday.

Miguel, the boyfriend, is a fiery, no-holds-barred Broadway dancer, who we all immediately take to. Miguel arranged for forty bottles of wine and champagne for the birthday party. We pot luck the rest, and by midnight a home-made carburetor of ganja is being passed around a crowded, well lubricated room filled with flight attendants and two crews of pilots.

Alan and I are talking about Vietnam. In the Marine Corps, my job was carrying a double-E-8 radio with a whip antennae sticking up, announcing to all the world that if you shoot in the direction of this antenna, there's sure to be a lieutenant or captain nearby. The job is usually given to the loudest wise-guy in the rifle platoon.

Al Quine had the same job for the army, with their equivalent radio, the Prick-8.

"Prick-8's" for two loud-mouthed, wise guy pricks," we agree. Miguel, working the room, but overhearing this discussion, is suddenly transfixed. "What was it like, what was combat like?" he must know, he must!

Alan leans back, a cigar in one hand gently held, one white eye-brow cocked, says. "…we were flown for hours (it seemed), and the choppers dropped us in tall grass. Then we listened to sounds of the helicopters getting further and further away."

He makes sounds of receding blades, finally disappearing… "whump, whump, whump, whump, whump…."

"Now we're out there all alone, in the middle of this stinkin' jungle. Then a guy says 'I've got to shit!' Then the next guy says he's got to shit, and the next…" Looking at me but mesmerized by memory, he smiles, "Is that how you remember it?"

I can only nod. Alan takes a puff of cigar.

We look at Miguel, he is very still, transfixed…he has never been this close.

What's to say? Underwhelmed, Miguel moves on.

The Purser's 40th birthday was a major success. Fifty people have crowded into the crew lounge, and the wine and champagne have been flowing liberally. An improvised carburetor, fashioned from an empty cigar tube, is being passed around among the flight attendants, in a moderately discreet fashion. Captain George Bolus, now no longer drunk and wanting to kill Neutron Silva, is peacefully sleeping on a folding chair though the din.

Asshole-in-chief, Captain Bob Foreskeen has been pinching nipples at random, mine included. Warning him to cut it out, warning him again (what's that all about?), finally I have to deck him, to the approval of all. Perhaps in cowardly retribution, he orders three hundred dollars of cheese platters up to the party, and when it arrives, he signs the name and room number of some girl flight attendant.

We all find out about this a few days later when the girl is in tears. The hotel management is calling all our rooms to try to find out who actually did it, and Foreskeen is trying to get Al Quine and I to believe that the culprit was Newt Silva.

Thankfully, Miguel, our gay purser's *Caballero*, identifies Foreskeen as the culprit; Miguel actually saw that asshole sign the check when the cheese arrived. Almost fucking us out of a very good deal with the Sofitel (the use of a crewroom, free coffee, fridge, free movies,a and so on) Foreskeen winds up paying the entire tab with a credit card… hopefully it was one of his own.

The young lady flight attendant, the original butt of the *fromage* fraud, brought a gentlemen friend along with her for that week in Paris. Apparently, she was no longer enamored by his company, since in honor of her liberation from her credit problems, she removed all her garments in the crew lounge (so long as we all did the same), and she allowed Quine, Newtron and I to study a very interesting mole on her ass. Merry Christmas!

Engine Failure

Next day I'm paired up with the mean-prick of a Captain, Psycho-Saroyin again. He is aptly named for his Jekyll-Hyde tendencies. We will be doing a "turn" to Mombai (Bombay), a long day, about five hours in each direction, and believe me I'm not looking forward to it.

Saroyin hates everybody and everything. As we meet up in the lobby this morning, there's no greeting And unlike the rest of us who try to be friendly with the cabin crew, Psycho just walks right through them. No "hello's," no eye-contact. I usually hang back and apologize to the cabin crew on his behalf, after he disappears up the air stairs.

Herr-Lippi sees me out to the hotel bus, and as I'm about to board with Saroyin. "Hey Steve , know what Psycho told me his Golden Rule of life is?"

"Gee, Mark, what's that?" I'm not very happy.

"Psycho's Rule Numero Uno states that _If Psycho sees a blind man on the street he kicks him, because why should he be kinder than God?_"

"Thanks, Mark, makes sense." Mark laughs and waves goodbye to me as I board the bus.

The day is shorter than I think it will be. Taking off out of Jeddah, the # four engine blows, engine parts explode through the compressor and turbine, spraying the runway and the dessert with fragments. It's my flight leg, I'm flying, unconsciously my left foot has put in enough rudder to adjust for adverse yaw, and we're on a correct runway heading, level, but barely climbing out, with a temperature inversion taking it's toll on our available power.

The cockpit is silent. "Positive rate, gear up," I say. Saroyin brings up the gear, announcing into the radio "Jeddah Tower, Saudia four-five… we've lost an engine! Request straight ahead and level off at 800' AGL."

186

"Anything you want, Saudia four-five, you own the airspace." Thank God it's a Brit Controller on the radio.

At eight hundred feet AGL, I call "altitude hold." I level off, allow the speed to build up, and request the flaps be brought up on schedule. Now the airplane is "clean," gear and flaps up and I start a gentle climb, calling "3000' alt sel, max continuous thrust…In-flight engine failure checklist." Everything is going textbook, the hours of sim-emergency drill has kicked in automatically. The Captain and Flight Engineer turn off the fuel to the engine and complete the checklist. I fly the plane and handle the radio.

Mikey Palamino, Jr., "Baby Mike," our engineer, has already calculated that our dump time is twelve minutes. That is, since our take-off weight far exceeds the structural limits of our max gross landing weight (on this flight), we must dump fuel in order to quickly as possible get us down to a structurally safe landing weight. Dumping fuel at a rate of about 5000 pounds /minute, "Baby Mike" tells us we need twelve minutes dump time. I level off at 3000' and call for the 'after take-off' checklist. "Psycho and Mikie finish the "after take-off check", and Saroyin gets back on the radio.

"Jeddah Tower, Saudia four-five needs vectors to a dumping area."

We complete the dump, which actually, at the speed we're going, vaporizes the kerosene into the air. We complete the 'descent checklist,' the 'landing check-list' and we come back in for a 'normal' landing at *King Abdul Aziz Airport*, that is, Jeddah.

The 747 flies great with one of its four engines gone, depending on its weight of course. Losing an engine, maxxed out during take off (just past V1) is the tricky part. Once the plane is 'clean,' and if it's light enough, I've flown 747's with two engines gone on the same wing.

Truly, "Psycho" Saroyin and "Baby" Palamino have performed perfectly. We all acted in concert, knowing what to do, and what to expect from each other. Our flight to Mumbai was cancelled, and we hit the bus back to the hotel.

Of course, everybody already knew about our "air return." Guys swapping horror stories of their own experiences.

"Cheated death again," announces Saroyin.

"The beer's on me all night," calls out Herr-Lippi, bringing the crowd to a howl, since there is no legal alcohol in the sandbox, "The land of no!"

The Jakarta Hajj-The Land of Yes

The senior guys bid the Jakarta Hajj. Whereas Jeddah is called "the land of no" (no beer, no pussy), Jakarta is called "the land of yes." Guys wait nine months to get back to Jakarta, where the alcohol flows, and the pussy is plentiful. The cherry on top, is how cheap it all is.

During stable times, Suharto kept control by subsidizing rice, gasoline and public transportation, "the *Rupe*" (the Indonesian *Rupiah*) was always about 2000 Rupes to the dollar. A great meal, at a fancy restaurant, would run about $10 US Dollars. The "*Kupu-Kupu-Malaam*" (literally "Night Butterflies") cost nothing (usually), just a night in a five-star hotel bed, breakfast, and cab-fare home.

This year, Indonesia was in turmoil. A few months before our arrival, Suharto had played the highest stakes, single-hand of poker in history with the World Bank, and had won (temporarily). He was able to blackmail 35 billion dollars (about the amount that he, his family, and cronies had stolen) from the International Monetary Fund, but the *Rupe* still plunged, now trading, at the time of our arrival from 8-15,000 Rupes to the dollar. That meant that instead of being millionaires by Indonesian standards, we Americans were now billionaires.

A meal for two of lobster, French wine, Cuban cigars and Irish coffee, at Jakarta's best restaurant, still cost about 100,000 *Rupes*. Last year that would have been about $50. Now, it was less than $10. A massage and a blow-job, quickly ordered to your room with a simple phone call, cost three or four dollars.

The "Breakfast Club" was in full session. "Bubba and the Ball Walkers" were teasing Lynn Barclay's Bottom Feeders" about who wound up with the ugliest whom last night. It was our day off, but Johnny Rivers kept checking his watch. I was a late arrival at the table. "Johnny," I ask, "why do you keep looking at your watch? Are you flying today?"

Everybody laughs.

"No," Johnny says, "I got 'the weed-wacker' coming up at ten." Weidja (the 'weed-wacker') was a massage-blow-job girl, whose reputation for inducing "the scrotal scream" was legend.

"Why so early?" I asked, knowing that as a member of "Bubba's Ball Walkers," Johnny was recovering from a late night of drinking and sex at the "Tavern" or the "Tannemore."

"Because I have a second broad coming up at 1 PM, and a third one at 4. Then, we're hitting the Tavern about 8 PM."

"Holy shit, how do you do it?"

Flight Engineer Jerry Lovell explains: "Hey man, the "Pfizer Risers." Jerry has turned the guys onto this drug he gets from some Indonesian doctor. Horse pills, that induce large, blue-steel erections within twenty minutes of consumption. Jerry's cornered the market on "Pfizer Risers," and has been dealing them out to about twenty of our pilots and engineers.

"How did you get into that business without Sheamus getting there first," I ask?

"Sheamus is in love." Jerry says, while the group collectively smirks.

I haven't seen Sheamus in months, so they set out to fill me in on 'the latest.' Joe Berry, a sweetheart of a man, who looks for all the world like a parakeet in need of a shave, explains that Sheamus has met a Kupu-Kupu, fallen madly in lust with her, and has taken to the mattresses. All business ventures have been put aside.

"Holy Shit," I say, "Sheamus, no business?"

Johnny says he'll explain to me one day the 'power of positive pussy.' For now, he tells me: "One pussy hair is stronger than a locomotive."

Johnny, a big, garrulous man whose mustache makes him look like a walrus, says to the table of ten guys, "Did I tell you I celebrated my 25th wedding anniversary?" His soft, Carolina accented voice carries across the table. "Yeah, I take the wife to a fancy Eye-talian restaurant. Red check table cloth, linen napkins, china, the works. The band's at our table playing the anniversary waltz, and Francis puts her hand over mine." Johnny shovels some more steaming *nassi goring* into his walrus-mouth.

"People at other tables are paying attention to our going's on. Francis looks soulfully at me through the candlelight and says 'Johnny, I just want you to know I've been just as faithful to you over these 25 years as you have!'"

Johnny says, "I talk to the guy at the next table who's overheard her and say, 'How'd you like to be married to a slut like that?'"

"Johnny, you didn't," asks Wayne Cunningham, the 70 year-old-flight engineer, master of the hooey-hooey sticks.

Johnny just grins.

Most of these guys (including me) are married, and I get my daily dose of sex at the breakfast club table, listening to all the details of the previous nights' action. How much of my fidelity is due to my love for my wife (considerable), my aging, non-hormonality, or my fear of all the life threatening diseases out there, I'm not sure. Only Herr-Lippi and I are the two "virgin holdouts" of the group, subject to a lot of good natured teasing by the rest. I don't know how these fellas take the risks they do, morality aside. They never use rubbers, so they claim.

"The Tannemore" is a three-ring, Indonesian circus. The entire basement level of a high rise hotel, it consists of a central bar, which branches off to three larger, lounge areas. One of these rooms is for "straights", the other two are exclusive to homosexuals who gather in one, while transvestites frequent the other. Mingling, floating between the three rooms is common, with only good-will prevailing. As vast as the Tannemore is, the establishment is always comfortably full, with a great live band providing dance music, heard throughout.

This bar, and The Tavern, are the two main hangouts for all our cockpit crews. The company is jovial, the language is English, and the conversation is not exclusive to sex, but is worldly and wide-ranging. I've been to the Tannemore and the Tavern a number of times, enjoying the comradery of our group, and Indonesia's great local liquor, *Arak* I was having a "*Arak* Attack," when I noticed our Brit First Officer, Peter Vallie, walk into the place. This was his first Jakarta Hajj, and it was apparent the way Peter was taking in the scene from the entrance way, that this was his first visit to the Tannemore.

Our group sat at the side of the "straight room," and Peter didn't notice us. He started heading in the direction of "Transvestite Kingdom." Pointing him out to Bubba, who was sitting next to me, I started to rise to intercept Peter. Bubba held my arm down, stopping me from getting up... grinning, he gave me a wink. Then he passed the word to the other ten or so of our guys, that Pete was heading for the wrong room. They all stayed low.

The "women" in the transvestite bar are more beautiful than the real thing. Most Indonesians are thin, small-boned, attractive people. The transvestite's are gorgeous. If you're not expecting it, you'd never know that you're flirting with a biological male. An apple-cheeked, single Brit, Peter is a bit dry, does not actively socialize with the guys, and must have come alone, by cab. We forget about Peter, distracted by the progress of the evening.

The next morning, Peter became an accepted member of 'The Breakfast Club.' Shyly, he approached the table, joined the group, and told of his "interesting evening."

"I successfully interested a beautiful young lady in accompanying me back to my hotel room," he begins. "We kiss in the elevator as we ascend." Peter, blushing during the telling, explains that he found out "rather late in the game," the true gender of his partner. Ever the gentleman, rather than tossing the T.V. off his Hilton balcony, Peter accompanied the "young lady" back to the Tannemore, by taxi, picked up an "actual" woman, and consummated his quest. Peter's candor, gentility, and self-effacement actually wins over this rough group, and he was instantly adopted as a charter member. Lynn says "we've got to start him off slow, this is the Majors, and he's still a scrub rookie." All agree.

Bubba is passing around Polaroids of "Poppa Don" and Larry Kent, jabbing huge dildos into the receiving ends of two Indonesian girls. The girls are side-by-side, doggie-style on a bed in one of their hotel rooms. Flight Engineer George Loman has another stack of Polaroids working their way around the table from the other direction.

"Why, this looks like 'the weed-wacker'," moans Johnny Satin, feigning indignation. "I thought she was faithful only to me!" Poppa Don loses his coffee through his nose.

"*Salamat Paghee, abaka bah?*" I ask the Hilton desk clerks. Good morning, how are you?

"*Baiek, Baiek!*" they invariably answer, they are well.

My limited Bahasa allows me to go a little further with them. Since I am a short, quite overweight pilot, whose uniform buttons always threaten to explode, I know that they think I am *kandut*, grotesquely huge, as opposed to *gamuck*, which is simply heavy. Out of kindness, they hide their mirth at the ridiculous figure I cut. Indonesians are a wonderfully warm, polite people, easy to befriend, genuinely nice.

Used to dealing with Europeans, or Americans of a more serious nature, these desk clerks are not used to any self-deprecating humor. Straight faced, I inform them that "I am not *gamuck* and I am not *kandut*. I am a member of the American *Nassi-goring* Championship Eating Team." *Nassi-goring* is their national breakfast staple, eggs over fried rice. They finally cannot contain themselves, they are in love with me, a fat man, with a heart large enough to make fun of himself, all in good humor.

I am waiting in the Hilton lobby for Charlie extra-pickles and Flight Engineer Jerry Lovell. We've flown these past three weeks of March, together, making many trips from Jakarta to Jeddah, and back. Today's flight is the end of the first wave of the Hajj. Meeting up, we're all in good spirits, knowing that we will be heading home as part of this pairing. Today's flight will be ten+ hours to Jeddah, carrying the last group of Indonesian Hajjis into Saudi Arabia, to start their pilgrimage to Mecca and Medina. Upon our arrival, we will be on the ground at the Hajj Terminal for an hour or two, fueling and doing paperwork, then 'tail-end ferry' the empty airplane to Singapore (another nine hours flying).

Under other circumstances, the F.A.R.'s would not allow pilots to fly this many hours in a twenty-four hour period. "Tail-end ferry" however, means that as a 'non-revenue flight,' (no passengers, no freight and in this case, no flight attendants), the leg from Jeddah to Singapore falls into the F.A.R. Part 91 category, and does not affect 'duty time' rules as apply to F.A.R. 121 carriers. Legally, the flight leg does not exist. In real terms, however, we know that it will be an exhausting day. We're up about it, however, since we know that we will spell each other in a series of sleep breaks, across the entire empty rows of seats in the empty 747.

Also, we know we will be 'chi-chinging,' that is making extended duty pay at the rate of $60/hour for every hour of duty over 14 total duty hours. Today we will earn an extra $700 over and above our flight pay. This extra is our 'chi-ching' (the sound of a cash register opening). Finally, upon our comatose arrival in Singapore, we will be checked into a five-star hotel, rest for a day and a half, and fly as business class passengers on Singapore Airlines, heading east towards home. I'm for my scheduled vacation, April 1 - 15.

"April fool," says Charlie at poolside. I've just got a FAX from the company. They've cancelled our tickets home, they're desperate for pilots in Jeddah, and we're it!" It seems we've just been shanghaied back to Saudi Arabia to fly the Jeddah Hajj until we've "timed out," 120 flight hours, max, in one month. Then we can go home. This is no joke.

We still get our days rest in Singapore, making the best of things at Raffles bar, and at poolside.

The next evening we're first class passengers on "Saudia," heading to Jeddah. Charlie and Jerry and I discuss the progress of the "Lust affair" that Sheamus O'Connor has himself involved in. It is not the first time a pilot has gone off the pecker induced deep-end.

A standing joke in the industry (I've been married three times myself), that you are not ready for "Captain upgrade," if you don't have at least three marriages.

One week later, still in the sandbox, in walk the 'Siamese Twins,' Joe Rudder and Bob Hollis. Both former Eastern pilots, they flew for Air Siam after the strike, and seem always in each others company.

Joe: "Hey Steve , we were just best man and maid of honor at P-Brains wedding."

Bob: "And we have the pictures to prove it."

I am blown away...we all are.

Captain Phil Brain Phil ('P-Brain' to one and all), a bitterly divorced, confirmed misogynist, and I had dead-headed to Jakarta together four weeks earlier. Realizing the bargains now available in Indonesia due to the devalued rupe, we decided to go into business together. Both of us live in Florida, so we decided to collectively buy Indonesian wooden sculptures and container same to Miami. We would then split the cost of the container, the cost of the extremely cheap inventory, divide up the artwork and peddle the stuff independently.

P-Brain was to price out freight-forwarders and container costs. My job was to locate and select the wooden carvings.   I had done my job, but had not seen P-Brain in four weeks. I was expecting to consummate our business deal upon my return to Jakarta in May.

"Holy shit, what happened to my partner," I ask?

The Siamese twins explain that in a three week period, P-Brain met a *Kupu-Kupu Malam*, bedded her, dated her, fell in love with her, married her, and was now in the process of adopting his new wife's six-year-old daughter.

195

"Good grief!" Charlie exclaims.

"Life is good," says Jerry Lovell.

I shake my head in disbelief, I am struck mute. The Jakarta Hajj has struck again!

Charlie Pickles invents Live-Heading

Coming Awake, the darkened interior of the empty 747 was cavernous, echoing shadows, not sound. We three cockpit crew, along with the fifteen Indonesian flight attendants, are deadheading back to Jakarta from Jeddah, on this otherwise empty airplane. We had spread ourselves throughout the beast, and I staked out about ten rows of nine seats wide as my territory. I stretched out across an entire empty row of seats and fell fast asleep.

Now awake, thanks to my fifty-year-old bladder, I crept silently forward, looking for an empty lav. I was already abeam Charlie's Cheshire smile before I noticed the girl's head moving purposefully in his lap. Capt. Charlie, wearing his bright red Jodhpurs, was getting a chi-ching blow job, God bless him!

A few days later, Charlie confides that this is the first time in his twenty-five years of flying (after all the stories he's heard of others' experiences) that he's gotten sex on an airplane. "She was great," he exclaims in his distinctive, nasal style. "I didn't do anything...she asked if she could lay down next to me and use my lap as a pillow, the next thing I know she's got my pecker in her mouth...it was terrible!" he grins.

"Yeah," I say, "I saw part of your act...you looked like the _Mona Lisa_ with attitude."

"Did you really?" all happy now that he's got a witness to part of his good fortune. Charlie blurts out that she finished him off, had a handkerchief ready to delicately pat him dry and put him away. "But she didn't need it," he smirks, "she was so neat and thorough. Keshy, the best part was that she asked me for my room number in the Hilton, so she could come by the next day to do it again." He answers my unasked question by saying, "Yeah, she shows up in a Mercedes, her husband must have a business, does me twice more, without wanting any return favors, and about 3P.M. she says 'I have to leave, I have to be home to fix dinner for my husband'...then she shows herself out of my room."

"Perfect," I say.

"Perfect," Charlie agrees, "those perfect little Indonesian girls. They have such a wonderful and different view of sex."

"Yeah, a different view…hey, Charlie, do you know the difference between a gynecologist and a proctologist?….point of view."

Charlie grins in agreement. Thinking aloud, he does the sums, "…you know with the extended duty we got for that trip, I got to sleep-for-dollars, a blow job, and $800 extra dollars for that leg."

"Charlie, you just invented a new 'chi-ching,' 'Live-head' pay, instead of 'dead-head' pay."

"Life is good," Charlie agrees, using Jerry Lovell's punchline.

The Intellectual

I'm one of the few pilots considered an intellectual, since I'm forever reading. Let me amend that, I'm now reading Forster's *A Passage to India*, while Yul Laviv, our only Israeli flight engineer is studying *Penthouse Forum*.

"Hey Chubby," Charlie Pickles turns towards me in his Captain's chair, "You know about Salmon Rushdie, don't you?"

"Charlie," I declare puffing up slightly, "I'm the only person I know that actually read *Satanic Verses,* cover to cover."

"No shit?"

"No shit, and it was brilliant, but a bitch to get through, all those references alluding to London and to Islam that I had to look up."

"Well then, Rabbi, you probably know that those *Imams* lifted the death sentence on old Salmon."

"Yeah, Charlie," now smugly, "I've seen Rushdie interviewed a few times on those PBS interview shows."

"Then you must have heard he's just written another book?"

"No, No, I didn't hear that."

"Yeah," Charlie informs me, "It's called *Buddha is a Fat Fuck*!" Yul howls, I redden as I laugh, my ego sucked me into that one, and Pickles was masterful, as ever.

Yul and I were turned around upon our arrival in Paris, told by the Station Manager that we had to commercial to Athens. We had time to change into our commercial attire, sports jacket, tie, and slacks, and head for the first-class lounge. All our overseas repositioning of crew, "commercialing" is business class or better, when available.

Yul Leviv and I check into the lounge, now comfortably ensconced in plush couches, drinks in hand. "*Ve haff tree oors 'till dee Olympic flight to Ahhthens,*" Yul literally sprays this advise at me, taking another strong pull on his *Absolut.* "What?" I ask Yul repeats it, and this time I get it., we have three hours to kill. I'm half deaf, but Yul born in Europe and raised in Israel has an accent which defies anybody's first hearing. The more you ask Yul to "say again," the more excited he gets, and the worse it comes out. He spits his 'plosives, to boot!

Yul's an older man, with white, close-cropped hair and the lips of 'froggy the gremlin.' This will be the first time I've ever spent any private time with him. He quickly knocks back three more of the free double vodkas before we go to the gate. On the plane, Yul leans towards me to advise me, in confidence, "*Portnoy iz a hamosexl*!"

"What?"

"*Portnoy,*" he spits, "*is a hammosex'l,*" more spray, "*Ee lives wid a mann, he haz breazts.*"

"Oh," I say.

Yul leans back in his seat, satisfied now that he has alerted me to this crisis, and is at once asleep.

In Athens now, the young Greekin and reekin' cab driver, excited to be driving two such distinguished Americans to their hotel, animatedly engages us in conversation. I'm conversing, Yul is snoring.

"How long will you be in Athens," he asks?

"About 16 hours."

Not sure that he has used his English correctly, he repeats the questions, "No, no... How many days is your holiday in Athens, in Greece?"

Tired myself now, "Less than 16 hours." I'm on autopilot now, trying to disregard the heavy Athens traffic, the hotel check-in process yet to come, the whole bag-drag we're still faced with.

"What, you come to *Athenie* for, for less than one day? Why you do?"

"To eat at Chicken George's," I respond. Yul smiles at this, his eyes still closed, he is awake.

I have been truthful, though enigmatic with the taxi driver. After a shower and a nap, we will eat at Vasili's place, known to the airlines as *Chicken George's*. Whenever we layover in Athens, *Chicken George's* is a must. Now I'm glad Yul is with me, since I've gotten lost trying to find the restaurant, on foot, the last few times I've been out here. It has no street address, and nobody knows the real name of the place, only that Vasili and his family run it, and that the food is terrific.

Sitting at *Chicken George's* later that evening, we are stuffed. We've consumed barnyards of roast chicken, huge Greek salads, gallons of unsweetened ice tea. Rubbing my big belly, I confide, "I fly for food." Yul agrees that he thinks that I do. Leaning forward, Yul says, *"Have I told you that Portnoy is a hammosexl?"*

We throw the chicken bones and leftovers to the stray dogs that lurk about the place, tired of shooing them and the aggressive hornets away from our food and sodas, we stumble tiredly back to our hotel.

Jeddah Contract

I've been keeping in touch with Geri primarily by FAX, with the occasional $100 phone call.

Our pilot pool is made up of former Continental, Pan Am, Eastern and Braniff guys, as well as old 'freight dogs' who never managed or cared to get on with a major carrier. Not one "scab" among us, we're proud to say, enabling us our valued "jump-seat" privileges with other union airlines.

Since we are all "born-again virgins," having had to start with Tower Air late in our careers, our pay is low. I'm making $65/hour in my fourth year with the company. This may seem like a lot of money to some, but Federal Aviation Regs. mandate "flying no more than 1000 hours a year". That means that I can't make more than $65,000/year under ordinary circumstances. Thankfully, our contract provides for "dead-head" pay and extended duty pay (blood-money), which add a bit more to my salary. However, after taxes, hotel rooms in New York (our base), and meals/expenses on the road, our net income is still low. It hardly compensates us for being away from home an average of 20+ days a month, flying the world's largest jet airplane on international routes. Not at all the outside world's perception of the rich airline pilot.

Geri has been desperately trying to reach me. Communications between "The World" and "The Kingdom" are difficult, at best. I get a message from the front desk that a FAX awaits me at scheduling. A phone call to scheduling, across the compound, alerts me that, "your wife wants you to call home, it's an emergency." The original FAX from Geri is days old! My heart in my mouth, not knowing who's dead or dying, I try to call home. No answer at my home, none at my folks, nor at hers. I am in a panic, trying to remember my sisters' phone numbers in Boston, and Neenah, Wisconsin.

After hours of trying, I reach my wife. Thank God nobody's dead, it's not that kind of an emergency. I normally pay the bills each month, but since I haven't been home in months, Geri's taken over that duty. During our last conversation, ten days earlier, she asked me "how much can I send out?" The fifteenth of the month was approaching. Knowing I had a terrific month, and should be receiving nearly $6000- this 15th, I instructed her to send out $3000- worth of checks, clearing our financial decks.

She tearfully explains that "all our checks have been bouncing," she has no cash for food, and the bank has been hitting us with $26 NSF charges for each bounced check, hundreds of dollars of extra charges, on top of the havoc to our credit with mortgage banks, credit card companies and the rest.

Seems that the new CEO at Tower Air, Terry Holcomb, has instructed payroll to withhold most of the money owed to the pilots and flight attendants, and only $1500 of what was due me was direct-deposited for me, against the $6000+ I was owed.

Mutiny. Twenty guys all with shortages between $4000 to $10,000, are in my same financial boat. Phone calls are made to the V.P. Ops and the Chief Pilot's office. A petition is drafted and signed by all, implying that not a throttle will be moved until we are paid, and we are coming home now!

To be fair to Tower Air, I have to say that this was the first time the Company has ever been late with, or withheld pay. It's still not a good sign however, and I get home in time to have to deal with all this shit.

The Company cuts me a "personal loan" check for $3000 to tide me over "until we get this payroll mess straightened out..." (nobody yet admitting any intent), with a promise to reimburse us all for any NSF bank charges we've experienced. Joe Berry, on the flight home, says, "Tower Air isn't a company, it's an 'Outfit'...and the 'Outfit' I'm gonna retire from, hasn't even started yet!"

He is referring to all the "scumbag outfits" we've all collectively worked for in the past. We're all holding our breath, not wanting to start over again, on the bottom of another 'Outfits' seniority list. Unlike other professionals with years of solid experience to sell elsewhere (

pharmacists, lawyers, C.P.A.'s and such), out-of-work, or unhappy
pilots cannot up and leave for the same, or a better, situation. Chained to
the Seniority System, an unemployed pilot, with 10,000 hours of hands-
on experience lucky enough to be hired elsewhere, must start at the
bottom of the new company's seniority list, the lowest pay rate, in their
worst city, flying the shittiest schedule.

Bangladesh Prisoners – Hadj

We were parked in "the Tulies," and the ancient busses were pulling up near the plane. Jeddah desert temperatures were nearly 110°F, and we were instructed to fly "the prisoners" to Dacca, Bangladesh.

"Holy Smoley," high-pitched, nasal Charlie Pickles declares. "What's worse, a Saudi prison or Bangladesh?"

"What's the third choice? *'Chop-chop'*, I'd ask for *'chop-chop'* square," is my reply.

Jerry Lovell, our Flight Engineer says, "No man! Even death by *bugga-bugga* beats those alternatives!"

We pilots are pouring over our charts, neither Captain Charlie nor I have ever been to Bangladesh. Jerry is working out how much weight we can get off the ground today, it's 100 ° Fahrenheit right now, and it's still early morning. Our zero fuel weight, subtracted from the Max T.O. weight allowed from Rwy 3-6 center, will determine if we'll need to stop in Karachi, Pakistan for more fuel.

Mike, our only straight male purser, comes flying into the cockpit. Ever polite, a former Marine, Mike yells, "Sir, holy shit Captain Pickles, Sir, have you seen those prisoners?"

"No," collectively. We all look out the window. Shackled hand and foot, these concentration camp victims are struggling up the air-stairs. Unshaved, unbathed, unbarbered and unfed, this mass of emaciated unwashed are being driven from the buses by uniformed Saudi *Matawah*, beating them with riding crops.

Unthinking, I say "*Cosh* that *Schwog*."

"What?"

"Cosh that *Schwog.* That's Bronx Jew for the suggestion to beat the nigger with a truncheon. Where I come from, if you didn't want the Gentlemen of Color to know what was coming, you talked 'white.' You've heard Jews call blacks *'schwartzas?'*

"Yeah."

"Well *Schwartza* is actually shortened from *Schwartza Cholerian,* Yiddish for Cholera, the Middle Ages "Black Plague!" When the blacks became familiar with that expression, we shortened it to *shwog!* It went from the root *'schwartza'* to *'schvatza'* to *'shvoogie'* to *'shwog.'* A *cosh,* is of course a truncheon, and we knew the niggers would never know that!"

"'Keshie, where'd you grow up?" asks Lovell, bemused.

"The deep South Bronx," I explain in my finest Southern Gentleman accent.

"What was that like? Was it tough?" asks Charlie Pickles, whose youth was spent on a Virginia horse breeding ranch.

"Fort Apache? Let me put it this way," I explain, "I joined the Marine Corps and went to Paris Island, South Carolina to escape The Bronx.

"Actually, when I was a kid, The Bronx was a great place to be raised. My neighborhood was a mixed bag of Jews, Italian, and Irish. Nice people. Then along came "Hizzona," Mayor John Vashel Lindsey, elected from some silk-stocking district in Manhattan. He had that bullshit political charm of our past President Billy, and the dashing, high-cheek-boned good looks of a young Robert Redford...he was beautiful. He won the election, then he really fucked up New York City.

"Lindsey was a Liberal tinkerer, one of the first 'social engineers,' you know the type. He immediately doubled welfare payments, and eliminated any residency requirement to collect benefits. Can you guess what happened? Yeah, you're right! All the Southern Blacks and a trillion Puerto Ricans flooded into the city. Those people were like animals, no normal, conventional, middle-class values. Suddenly, our apartment houses stunk…. urine soaked hallways and garbage everywhere.

"The City built these brand new Projects, high-rises, to accommodate the flood of new poor. They had the copper wiring stripped out of them within weeks, to sell for drug money. Garbage was thrown out of windows, or dumped in halls. And the Gangs! I was a teenager, with two younger sisters, and there were the "Egyptian Crowns," "The Medallion Crowns," the "Fordham Baldies" I used to have to fight to *not* join a gang!

"The whole white, middle-class world I knew fled for Clearview or Whitestone, or some other suburbs, we got stuck there, no money to move. The '*Shwogs*' filled the vacuum, and the rest is history. Look at all these fuckin' inner cities. Black, and 'people of color' on the inside, white, suburban bedroom communities around the outer perimeter. That's the fuckin' liberal, fuckin' democratic, mother-fuckin' Social Tinkerers for you!"

I'm hot. Nobody has ever seen me ever like this before.

"Hey, don't hold back, Rabbi, tell us what you really think."…this from Lovell.

Charlie is just staring at me in hypnotic, wide-eyed amazement. He's never experienced **his** mother being punched in the face through a subway-car window, by some black man, on her subway ride home. He hasn't experienced the thrill of his aging Grandmothers' apartments being ransacked, and one of them being beaten during the occurrence, for the fun of it, by our beloved people of African-American descent.

I calm down, and explain some of all this to him… "Hey, Charlie, when my folks, and most of the Italians, Irish and Jews came here from Europe, it was the turn of the century, about 1910…. They had never seen a black person before, no less brought slaves into an already free society…. what the hell did they have to do with the plight of the blacks already in America? They paid their taxes, supported welfare, walked picket lines to end discrimination, then they got shit on by the same colored bastards they'd been trying to help. Ask Farrakhan how many Americans were in the U.S.A. at the time of slavery? Better yet, ask him which Black Chiefs sold their own people into slavery in the first place? What the hell do we have to do with slavery, for Christ's sake, other than having to feed the *black pigeons* now, now that they've developed that lovely "gimme more, gimme more, I'm a victim attitude?"

"I can't believe it man," says Charlie.

"Believe it!"

The trip to Bangladesh is uneventful. These prisoners are the unlucky bastards who overstayed their work permit expiration dates, trying to send a little more money home to their families, and were nabbed by the religious police, the *Matawah.* In jail for months, they stink and are infected with lice and fleas. "This cockpit door is remaining shut, period," we notify Mike. "Maybe we'll leave for a piss break, but that's it, and don't let them use our upper-deck lav!" Charlie commands.

Mike, the Purser, keeps the entire upper-deck clear of our human cargo.

No matter, Jerry Lovell, Charlie Pickles and I still wind up flea bit around our ankles. We've hardly left the cockpit. Some of our cabin staff came down with some weird-shit type of T.B., and other exotic ailments. I don't know how the flight attendants put up with what they're forced to deal with.

"Hey Rabbi, you know it's not politically correct to use the term "lesbian" anymore?"

I've been discussing my opinions regarding Janet Reno and Hillary Clinton.

"So, what's the P.C. expression now?"

"Vagitarians!"

"Damn carpet-munchers, they get more pussy than I do." This from Captain Charlie extra pickles.

I bitch about not getting laid much. Geri and I are friends, and are more like brother and sister, than husband and wife. Whenever one of us asks the other if our lack of quantity sex seems abnormal, we placate each other with "our relationship was never based on sex, to begin with." We started out as friends. But when we do occasionally get around to it, it's always great...we always wind up asking, "Man, why don't we do this more often?" But today I'm feeling sorry for myself, sharing my gripe with D.B. and Jerry.

"Hey, 'Chubster,'" Jerry asks, "You know what rodeo sex is?"

"No, what?"

"When you slide up behind your wife, slip it in nice 'n gentle, grab her around by the tits, and whisper in her ear that she's not as tight as her sister...then you got to try to hold on for 10 seconds!"

"Hey, Jer, once a year if I wake up and Geri's already up I pretend I'm still sleeping, stay real still. Then I slowly 'come awake,' look over at her like I'm still groggy, and ask. 'What base did you say you were from?'" Geri always falls for that one, gets her real pissed-off, and I always get a punch in the arm, or something!"

"Chubby Stevie," this from Jerry, "you're getting to be as big as Sheamus O'Connor!"

"No wonder you don't get laid a lot, Rabbi!"

I pose, a la a body builder, "No way, Jose, I'm on Adkins now! Stevie SchwartzenKeshner."

Charlie asks us, "Know what pilots use most for birth control?"

"What?"

"Their personalities!"

"No dick, shit Tracey!" Jerry Lovell is about sixty, but a well-earned reputation, well earned, as a smooth talking, ladies man. He's been divorced for years, is the single parent to a little girl he adores, back in Texas, and between his *Zam-Zam* scam and his personality, he gets laid alot.

We're heading out on a military charter to Guam and we will have 36 hours on the ground before continuing to Kadena and Yakota in Japan and Okinawa. I know Jerry's got some female phone #'s in Agana, and he's already set himself up with a 'cheap date."

"Yeah boys," he rubs it in, "I'll take her to Shirleys for fried rice and coffee. She loves Shirley's fried rice."

So do I, but jealously, I keep it to myself.

"...then we'll head back to her place" smirks Lovell, ... "life is good!"

Zeppah Zaydeh-Revelation

Not even the loudspeakers' overlap wailing, jarring their echoing prayers, nor the smell of cheap paint and the over-chlorinated pool can upset my tranquility this day.

My head is reeling with new emotions. I have finally flown with Zeppah Zeydah, the quiet Captain with the riveting, intelligent eyes. Zeppah has a gentle, loving spirit, is a multi-faceted, thinking, caring man. The hours I've just spent with him flew by with our animated discussions about Persian history, the revolutionary overthrow of the Shah of Iran, Rehza Pahlevi, and its effects on Zadeh, and his family. We talked of our children, his Bahai Faith, our mutual love of Italian opera, classical music, impressionist painters, and of racism.

I unpeeled my defensive layers for Zaydeh, and he awakened in me not a hope for some kind of a faith, but for some kind of dignity! You see, unlike me, Zeppah has been able to create a Disease-Free zone around himself, within which he will not permit racist thoughts or remarks to be made. Neither will he suffer sexist feelings, nor foolish, sloppy thinking.

Yet, Zeppah is admired by everyone, pandering to no one, and does not sell out bits of his soul for acceptance, as I do. Believing that part of our different approaches to acceptance might have to do with his Faith, I have asked him to provide me with literature about Bahai, which he has graciously done…. but have not yet had the courage to broach what I perceive to be the major difference in our souls….. I'm not yet ready for him to discard me for my weaknesses.

Why do I allow myself to be corrupted for acceptance, while he is strong enough not to bend to the need to fit, to bond with the bullshit secret-handshakes of Racism, and of Us-ism against Them-ism? As I get to know Zeppah better, I will plumb him for his methods, the secret of his Self. Meanwhile, I will observe from a distance, trying to learn, and revel in what I see now as possible.

I am glad that Zeppah, my Jonathan Livingston Seagull, has come to show me what is possible, and more importantly, what is not necessary.

Sheamus - World Cup

We're on our way to Paris, Sheamus's Mexican Company has booked the charter, Mexico City - JFK - CDG, and return. Two planes, 1000 people, total.

This year, France is hosting the world-cup soccer matches, and Paris is packed.

"Seriously, Sheamus, how'd you pull it off?"

"Easy, Rabbi," he explains. Two planes, round trip, a total of about 50 hours of power. I figure Moe's costs are about seven grand an hour, so I offer him ten grand an hour, a total for both flights, round off to about $500,000 for the charter. I use my Mexican company's name."

"What's that?"

"*Manana Air.* Any way it was easy. My partner Paco did the negotiating, so that Nachtomi won't connect it to me. Paco and I put up $25,000 each, 'chump change.' We drafted a contract calling for a 10% deposit, ($50 grand), <u>refundable,</u> if we cancel out more than ten days prior."

Sheamus and his buddy had sold lottery tix in Mexico for $40 U.S. apiece out of the major supermarkets in Mexico City. They promised twenty million Mexicans a chance to fly to Paris to see their beloved Mexican soccer team play in the World Cup matches. These people have never been out of Mexico City before, no less flown to Paris to see the World Cup playoffs. There will be 1000 lucky winners.

"We had rules," Counting on his fingers, "Rule #1 - no suitcases, no baggage, no hotel room."

"What? How's that possible, Sheamus?"

"Easy. The deal is that the lucky 1000 wet-backs would fly to JFK – refuel / recrew, fly to Paris, get on buses and be taken directly to the soccer arena. After the game, it's back on the buses, back to the plane and the flight home, period!"

"How much did the soccer tickets in Paris cost?"

"We picked up 1000 cheap seats for $20,000 total. Nobody wanted to see Mexico play!"

"Yeah, except your Mexicans!"

"Got that right, Rabbi! We started selling those tickets six months ago. Sold more than 50,000 of those babies, raised $2,000,000 in no time. We gave the supermarkets $2 a ticket for selling them. $500 grand for the planes, 20 grand for the busses. So, we netted 1 million four.

I've got about $700,000 U.S. dollars waiting for me in Mexico City.

"Jesus, Sheamus!"

"Rabbi, the best part was that our original risk, our actual exposure, was only the $50K for the planes, and the $20K for the tickets and buses. The rest came out of receipts, even the $50K would have been refundable if the tickets didn't sell well in Mexico City."

"So you and your partner had an actual exposure of what, only $12,000 each?"

"Got that right, Rabbi.... Stevie, do you know the difference between a speculator and an investor?"

"No Sheamus, but you'll tell me."

"I'm an Investor.... all the other guys are Speculators!"

Serious now, I ask, "So what're you gonna do with your $700,000, retire?"

"Well, there is a slight hang up, so I'm not sure yet about timing my retirement."

"What's the slight hang-up, Sheamus?"

"I can't seem to get in touch with my partner, Paco."

"What's Paco's last name?"

"Rodriquez something, or Gonzales something..."

"Oh."

When we arrive, Paris is ecstatic. The timing of our 48 hour layover includes France winning the World Cup, and the Bastille Day celebration in one shot. France explodes in double celebration, and we join the jubilant crowds on the *Champs Elysee*, cheering the bus carrying their hero soccer team. An outpouring of millions of people, greater than the liberation of Paris during World War II. Sheamus is "up," having fully recovered from his riches to rags descent. We have great big bowls of garlic mussels at a favorite restaurant, *fabeyeux!*

Next week, back in New York, Sheamus is trying to get me to invest in a new venture…"It's seed money, baby, just chump change."

"How much are you talking about, Sheamus?"

This during a five minute break from Recurrent Ground School training, two boring days of torture, conducted by Engineer-cum-asshole Bruce Quinn, everybody's "hero." Word about Bruce's inability to tell whether the gear was down and locked going into Islamabad, had traveled quickly. This class he was just slightly less of an asshole, apparently embarrassed that everybody knew about his "incident."

It seems that Sheamus is in lust again, another Indonesian *Kupu-kupu* he met on the last Hajj. He's keeping her in a Hotel in Kuala Lumpur, and has lost a ton of flesh, he's down to dating weight. He pulls me close, we're now alone in the hallway, whispering, "I'm thinking of bringing her into the country, down to Miami, and into my home. Tell my wife that she's the new maid, just got her from some Indonesian Au Pair service. Rabbi, I talk to her every day on the phone....I'm teaching her three new words a day.... today's words were 'dog,' 'cat,' and 'blowjob'."

"You're not a real pilot, Sheamus."

"What?" Sheamus taken aback.

"That's right. A real pilot would bring the girl into his home and tell the wife that now she (the wife) is the cleaning lady." I turn back to the classroom as I watch Sheamus' mouth drop open.

Home

Home, at last, this is going to be a good one, a long one, the flying has slowed some. I've resolved to be more gentle, less controlling, in my relationship with Geri and Kiley.

We're a one-car family, and we like it that way. Geri has picked me up at the Jax airport, and the ride home has been light, pleasant banter. No bullshit yet about money problems, or the honey do's that need to get done around the house. Geri drops me at home, and returns to work.

Showering, scrubbing off the dust of a few continents, I change into shorts and a t-shirt. I get the washer started, and Emma, our male cat, is suddenly underfoot, rubbing, walking between my legs. Following his castration a few years back, Emma has become heavy and lazy, sleeping on his back in the sun after meals. I'll never forget coming home and Kiley, all of about four-years-old then, rushing out to confide to me... "Daddy, daddy, Emmie had his balls cut off today!"

"You're a chow-hound, Emma," I accuse. If you overeat, Mommy's gonna be all over me...but you're wounded...and I know how to take care of veterans," as I fork more tuna into Emma's dish.

I find that I'm talking to the cat more often, enjoying the conversation, but wondering if there's something wrong with me. I dismiss it, I'm content at being home.

"There was this Princess, who was a prisoner of a wicked Sultan..." Kiley's rapt, I've got her attention. "...to save her life this princess, Sheherezad, comes up with a plan. She starts telling these very interesting stories, one each night, to her evil captor. All morning long this Sultan keeps thinking of last night's story, and by afternoon, he can't wait for tonight's new tale. So Sheherezad comes up with 1,001 tales." I'm driving Kiley to school, a morning ritual which we both love. "If you want, I'll get the book out of the library, and we'll read it together at night." Another of our rituals.... I usually fall asleep faster than she does, but not before she elbows me awake a few times..."Dad!...DAAAAAD!"

Kiley says that "yes," she'd like to read those stories with me.

"On one condition," I put to her, "that you let me play one of my 'uckie' CD's for you afterwards, called "Sheherezad," by Rimsky-Korsakov." Kiley laughs, knowing that she's being taken. "After we read some of those stories, I want you to close your eyes while you listen to some of the music."

"It's a deal," she says, high-fiving me as she gets out of the car.

"Parent pick-up," I call after her. She smiles, and waves, she knows it's parent pick-up when I'm home.

Kiley loves 'Bare-Naked Ladies' and 'Mambo #5,' and tolerates my Italian opera as I make pancakes and bacon for her and her sleep-over buddies on the weekends.

"I need to hear Italian opera when I cook," I explain. "I can't cook without Italian Opera."

Kiley comes up to me, looks me in the eyes lovingly, and says, "Dad, I'll never understand you." Then she wraps her arms around me, hugs me and kisses my shoulder.

"I love my wife!"
…Pilot humor…

Temptation

"Geri is a wonderful, beautiful person. We're very lucky, because we were loving friends for a few years first, having been partners with other people in a group for about five couples. We all partied with each other all the time. Then we discovered that we loved each other."

I was the only passenger in first class, and the flight attendant on this short flight to Atlanta seems genuinely interested. She had initially commented on my wedding ring, telling me how beautiful the three colors of gold looked. Then she got me talking about my wife.

"After a few years, my marriage to Ilsa had broken down" I continue. "Geri's relationship with Larry ended, and we realized that we were in love with each other. It sounds messy, but it wasn't," I explain, "There was never any hanky-panky beforehand."

The flight attendant, an attractive thirty-something with real class, seems mesmerized, fascinated to meet a pilot who loves his wife and is actually monogamous.

As we begin our descent into Atlanta the lady straps herself in, asking if I'd like to join her for a drink at her hotel this evening. Not at all suspicious of her motives, I explain that I start reserve at midnight, and have to get back to my crashpad, but thanks.

"There's a phone in my room," she chides. The elevator in my brain finally reaches the top floor…her remark means (a) I'm invited to her room, not just the hotel cocktail lounge, and (b) the offer of the phone suggests I'm invited to spend the night.

I am flustered, I just spent forty-minutes enjoying the telling of my personal love story to this woman. A tale of fate, good fortune and

219

faithfulness, and I am now being asked to spend the night cheating on my wife.

"Thanks anyway, some other time," I say, graciously allowing that she just wanted to continue the conversation.

"Okay, well nice meeting you," she concludes.

A few weeks later, I'm in San Francisco, returning from dinner to my room. In the corridor, a girl is carrying an ice bucket.

"I know you," she smiles, "the pilot who's faithful to his wife."

"Right," I respond, trying to remember her name.

"Joan," she says sticking out her hand and rescuing me, "and you're Steve."

"That's right," shaking hands now, "You have a good memory. You look so different out of uniform."

"Well, now you have no excuse. I was just going to fix myself a drink, and you have to join me, I want to hear the rest of your story."

There's no harm in it, so I tell her I'll be by in a few minutes, I need to go to my room first. Joan tells me her room number, and I agree to be over in five.

Letting myself into my room, I pee, wash my hands and face, and dampen my hair with the excess water still on my hands. I regard myself in the mirror, as I run a comb through my hair.

This is all very innocent, I think to my reflected face in the mirror. She just wants to chat, I just want to kill some time, and besides, I instruct myself, I can always just leave if it becomes something else. My reflection agrees with me, as I turn to leave the room.

"This is very nice," I say, admiring the two club chairs facing each other in the corner of her room. A bottle of Absolute, two ice filled glasses, and an ice bucket wait for us on the little table in between.

She fixes two drinks, as I plunk myself down in the comfortable club chair, my back to the corner.

"Cheers" she says, lifting a glass. "Salud," I respond.

Joan starts telling me about herself. She has had a failed marriage early on, "No kids, thank God," she adds. She's dating a cop in New York, a police detective.

Great, I think, this is going to be fine. We spend about an hour swapping personal stories, some airline jokes, and start a second drink.

Joan grows quiet, as we lapse into a comfortable silence.

She leans slightly forward as she says, "Why don't you just get into that bed and let me fuck your brains out all night?"

"You don't understand, I've done all that shit. The coke, the 'Plato's Retreat,' the threesomes and moresomes."

"So have I," she challenges. "Last week, on a flight from Denver to Honolulu, we passed right over my ex-husbands house, it was my fucking house, that creep was banging my girlfriends in my bed. Well, fuck him! I took my panties off, pulled out the flight engineer's dick, had the Captain and co-pilot take turns fucking my cunt and ass, while I sucked off the engineer. Right over the top of my old man's house, felt great getting even with him, that bastard."

"Shit Joan, I was a prick, just like your ex-husband. I used to fuck women in my ex-wife's bed...crazy shit. One woman, Teri Herrin, we finish and I'm driving her home. She says her gold wristwatch is missing. We drive all the way back to my place. I leave her in the car, and run back upstairs into my bedroom. I had remade the bed before we left, everything nice and neat. We had this white goatskin shag carpet in

221

the bedroom. I'm down on my hands and knees, my fingers going through this rug, all the way around the bed. No watch. Not in the bathroom, not on any dressers or tables, no watch. I try under the bed, and all the way around on the carpet again, no watch.

I don't know what made me do it, but I lift up my wife's pillow, and there it is. Dead center under that pillow, perfectly positioned to be found.

I hand Teri back her watch, tell her where I found it, and ask her what the deal is? She says that she wants me, she wanted Ilsa to find the watch, Jesus Christ!" I take a drink.

Joan giggles now, she liked that story, as I continue:

"I'm different now, older, done that shit, and I love Geri. She took a real chance marrying me, knowing what a slut I had always been. But when I fell in love with her, I never wanted anyone else again. I feel guilty just thinking of the shit I've done, before we were married. I don't even think about sex or anything with any other woman. I'm just glad I don't have to hide anything, lie or cover up anything, I couldn't handle that kind of crap anymore. Thank God, I got all that out of my system before marrying Geri. Our relationship's never been about sex, anyway, more like we're brother and sister."

"So, what are you saying, that you guys don't sleep with each other, don't have sex with each other?" She's becoming more genuinely interested now.

"No, we still fool around occasionally, not too often, that's true, but whenever we do, it's great…we always say 'why don't we do this more often?'"

She's up pouring us another drink now, getting another pack of cigarettes from a carton in her suitcase. "Pardon me for a minute," she says, heading for the bathroom.

I start to think back on Geri and me and sex..... times we shared my mattress in Stigo's apartment... he would come in and catch us all the time, always laughing and pretending to be covering up his eyes, looking through his open fingers, the way kids do... "excuse me people," he would announce, going slowly by, getting a good, honest look. We would laugh along with him, not caring, it was only Stigo, and we were in love.

One morning, after Stigo pulled that routine of his and headed for the shower, Geri and I quickly decided to get even with him. "Let's see if he can handle it." We both got completely naked, snuck into the bathroom, pulled back the shower curtains and casually stepped inside with Stigo. "You don't mind, do you" we asked, both of us starting to lather up. That fuckin' Norwegian freaked, I'll never forget the look on his face, and how he blushed... I laugh to myself, thinking how we blew him away...

Then, that one time in Honolulu, it was Geri's birthday... I told her to get into her tuxedo, I got into mine, and I surprised her with the Limo for the evening. Up at the top of Tantalus, standing through the open sunroof, watching the sunset, we started fucking around. I was eating her out while she stood there, the Limo heading for the nightclub now. For the thirty-minute ride back to downtown Honolulu, I'm pounding into her from behind, both of us trying to see if the driver can tell what we're up to, through the partition's smoked glass, neither of us really giving a shit if he could.... man, we were hot and that Limo reeked of sex, I tipped him bigtime as we got out, barely back into our clothes.....

Joan's frowning now, as she lights another cigarette, easing into the seat across from me again. "You're going to sit there and tell me that you don't find other women sexually desirable? A woman like me, for instance...I'm opening my legs a little, like this, and you don't feel anything?"

"No, I honestly don't."

"What about now," she gathers her skirt up around her waist, knees wide open, bringing her legs over the arms of her chair. "What do you feel

223

now… you're watching me. You're watching me slide my fingers into my pussy. It's pretty, isn't it? I shave just the lips," holding them open with the fingers of one hand now. "I sometimes sit on the floor in front of the mirrored closet doors in these hotels, watching myself slide these fingers in and out of my pussy…don't you like to watch?"

I am watching, unable to look away… "You are beautiful, you are sexy, and it is fascinating to watch you play with yourself like that, but I'm not going to get involved."

"You're not going to get involved? You are involved! What's sex? Do you think it's only sex if these were your hands? Your tongue?" She brings the slick moisture down to her rectum now, arching her hips up for easier access.

God, I am mesmerized, watching her wet finger travel between her pink, splayed pussy, and her asshole. She's teasing her own ass now, slowly sliding a fingertip in, twisting it. Removing her hands, she does this little trick with her asshole, puckering and unpuckering it. I watch as a film of her moisture stretches across the open rim, and I think she's about to create a bubble, it looks so like the rainbow pattern on a kid's bubble pipe, just before the pursed lips blow…

"No," I finally answer through my dry throat. "It's not sex for me… I could be looking at a penthouse magazine, or even playing with myself reading the Penthouse letters and looking at the pictures, and that wouldn't be cheating on my wife. I would just be getting myself off, relieving the tension, but I wouldn't call it sex."

"So, I'm just a living fantasy for you, a three-dimensional centerfold, that's all… right?"

"Well, yeah, that's right."

"What about my smells then, Steve ? Can you smell the musk of me?" Her hands are back now, churning her flow into cream. "Come on, I can see you're affected, don't you know how all this tastes, smelling my pussy, and my naughty, forbidden asshole?"

She laughs before I can respond, "It wouldn't really be sex if you took your dick out and played with it, while you're watching me, would it? After all, I'm just a magazine fantasy, right?"

I don't say a word, reaching for one of her cigarettes, attempting to hide my nervousness. As I light up, I haven't smoked at this point for years, Joan continues:

"I'm going to suck your balls. I'm going to slide my tongue in and out of your ass. I want you to spank me raw… to pinch my nipples hard… harder, as you butt-fuck me…I want you to pull it out, and finish in my mouth."

"…I love my wife," is the best I can do under the circumstances. I push my chair back against the wall, struggling to get up.

"You're lying to yourself" she chides.

"I've lied to everyone else all my life," I say, "why shouldn't I lie to myself?" As I approach her bed, my body is shaking, sodden with sweat. I don't bother to pull the covers off, I don't remember hitting the mattress, only the slow motion falling, falling…

I jump awake, my erection is a painful reminder of the vivid dream.

"Jesus," I say to my bathroom reflection. I'm so hard, it hurts to push my cock down and coax it to pee. "Man, what was that all about," thinking aloud again, doing more of that nowadays, in empty hotel rooms. Splashing cold water on my face, a mixture of guilt, pride and loneliness affect me, and I start to cry, alone in my room.

Home Again

"Folding wash is all the therapy I need," I realize, angry at the lateness of the revelation. Geri is the only one really trying, and I'm marking time, getting by, quits.

Except for Elton John singing about (or to) _Daniel_ in the background, I'm alone in the house. I stopped folding the wash, thinking that "the seeds of our own destruction, or the seeds of our own salvation are always within us."

Geri and I had worked out at the gym together, yet apart, not in itself significant. Dropping her off at her therapist, Dr. Levine's office, came the question I'd been anticipating for a long while…."will you take therapy together, if I ask Levine?" "No, I don't believe in that shit," I blurt out. "Well, if it means saving our marriage or something, of course I'll come talk to him with you," I say now as I see Geri's face clouding up.

"Been there, done that," I think, pulling away. All I could really think, escaping the situation, was that people say things to each other in the presence of a therapist that might not be conducive to keeping a relationship going. " I don't feel like having sex; maybe I don't feel like having sex with you; maybe we don't like each other so much anymore."

I know there is no fucking way I'm going to let this relationship reach separation or divorce, but it has more to do with Kiley, than what my relationship with Geri has become. All these thoughts blow through my consciousness, register, resonate and are instantly suppressed back into the soup of my unwanted feelings. These thoughts are there and gone before I reach the first traffic light.

I breathe a sigh of relief just to be away, on my own in the car, (the Captain, in control?).

Now, after one more fight in the car (from the Doctor to Geri's job), after making fun of the simplistic drivel Geri's picked up from Levine (have

226

more sex, put more fun in your life as a substitute for overeating, drinking), I've got her in tears, with my "No shit, but what about 'you don't feel like having sex,' or 'you don't feel like having sex with someone you don't particularly care for as a person?'" Just my sarcastic tone, even before my unfortunate logic, deflates Geri before my eyes. Shit, she's crying and unhappy again.

"Look, we've got to try to communicate. We've got to spend more time with each other, not just sit in front of the TV every night," Geri manages, drying out her nose, wiping her tears.

"First we have to come to like each other again as people and then as friends again," I volunteer. "That requires thinking the best, not the worst, of the other person's motivations. I've always thought only the best about your motivations, but when there's a need to make assumptions, you only think the worst of me," I point out accusingly.

"We have to work on it," we both agree, as she gets out of the car to go to work.

Jesus. Driving home, it's all washing through my mind, unbidden. I am happier away from her, and from Kiley, for that matter... what's the deal?

Home now, folding the wash, revelation hits. I feel personally, solely responsible to pay the bills, to make it all work somehow. I'm facing a shortening deadline of pilot earnings sneaking quickly up on me, driving me crazy. I cannot relax, I cannot enjoy my wife and daughter, since they are a living reminder of my problem, the mirror always reflecting my nightmare back at me... I run from that mirror.

Finally it all comes clear. Geri is the only one who has been trying to improve this impossible situation. I've been trying to "save my family," the big picture, but I'm destroying it in the process. I've allowed my encapsulated thoughts and feelings to isolate me from Geri. I've worsened the situation by not trying to improve it, avoiding, just trying to let it all go by... Rodney King's wimpy "can't we all just get along."

Holy shit, I've really fucked up. Why should I pass the days trying to skip by, waiting to be called out to fly, passively hoping that my marriage and my family holds together? Why not actively participate in improvement? Am I uncaring? No. Lazy? Yes. "An object at rest tends to want to remain at rest."

"I hope it's not too late" I think, wishing Geri were here so that I could immediately share these thought with her.

Back On The Job

Charlie Extra-Pickles is driving me nuts, trying to load the waypoints into the I.N.S.'s.

"Jesus, Charlie, you're trying to help me, but you fuck up my flow. Now I don't know what I'm supposed to be doing…"

I sense Jerry Lovell starting to smile behind me, as I hear all the familiar clicking and buzzing of his engineer panel pre-flight check.

"Jerry, how many Captains you know fuck with the I.N.S.'s?"

"'Extra-Pickles' is the only one I know, wants to be one of the boys." Jerry adds to the shit we're heaping on Charlie Pickles.

We're all grinning, this is a great crew; professional, but laid back, looking forward to each other's company, as we anticipate our layover in Athens.

"Keshy," (fake indignation now in Charlie's high-pitched nasal voice), "…I'm not trying to help you, I'm trying to remember how to use these things."

"Right, Charlie. Charlie, the registered pharmacist in three states, the military instructor pilot in 130's, you're trying to remember how to load the I.N.S.'s….give me a break."

With the preflight done, the fuel on board and confirmed by Jerry's computations and the gauges, we get the checklist out of the way and brief the Canarsie departure.

"Holy shit, no interruptions." Charlie beams. It's true, normally some galley slave, ramp guy or gate agent comes barging in during our challenge and responses, spewing bullshit, and we usually have to start all over again.

The amber cargo door lights tell us we still have time to kill.

"How're Geri, and my baby Kiley?"

"Holy shit, Charlie, you won't believe this shit….your baby."

I tell the guys about a party we had over the weekend, a houseful of our friends getting loose, with kids all over the place. Kiley is eleven, with budding young breasts, which she shyly hides behind towels, closed doors and bras.

Stuart and the other boys of the group are skim-boarders and surfer types, who love hanging at our house, so close to the ocean. The word "dude," resurrected by the wannabe teens, is being used a lot, as "segue" and "closure" are by the wannabe Cronkites on TV.

While we adults are downstairs relaxed, buzzed and catching up after a two week rain-caused hiatus, Geri goes to see what the kids are up to. Geri's back, beet red, holding back the laughter.

"I went into the bedroom, and they're O.K., just playing a word game, but this cross we brought back from Jerusalem is on the floor, broken."

So Geri asks, pointing at the crucifix, "What happened?" and Kiley says, "The Dude fell off." The sand-stone Jesus is missing….Geri asks, stunned, "So…where's the Dude?" We're all rolling…." The Dude fell off!….the **Dude**!" Geri concludes, saying "One of the kids accidentally stepped on Jesus, and he crumbled… so, I think they all stepped on Jesus, after he was already broken, to see if the house would fall down."

Stoned and well overweight Yoko Pacetti, swollen ankles propped up on a hassock blurts, "Jesus was born in a pile of shit in a barn, I don't think he'd mind being part of your carpet."

"Charlie, I can't believe it, I know that I'm emotionally bankrupt, but your 'Baby Kiley' is only eleven, and she's saying shit like "the *Dude* fell off!"

Charlie and Jerry lose it.

Zoann, our purser, has been listening to this sordid story the whole time. "I'm going to church Sunday. Anybody want me to say a prayer for them?"

"I didn't know you were religious, Zoann?" pipes Charlie, high-pitched, quizzical.

"I'm not. My mother wants me to go to church to meet men. I tell her, 'Oh mom, so now Jesus is my personal pimp?' "

That's it, this is going to be a great trip.

"Tango Oscar Whiskey 800, clear to taxi Quebec, hold short of November, runway 3-1 left in use."

"Roger, ground, Tango Oscar Whiskey 800, entering Quebec at Quebec Golf, clear Quebec hold short November."

"Disregard, Tango Oscar Whiskey 800, transition to Bravo at November. Clear foxtrot, cross 4 left, clear to taxi to 3-1 left."

We smile at the royal treatment. "Roger, Kennedy Ground, 800 clear Quebec; transition to Bravo at November, Foxtrot, cross 4 left and taxi to 3-1 left.

"Roger 800, change now to Tower frequency 119.1."

"119.1 Tower, Rog, 800."

"JFK Tower, 800 checking in, approaching 3-1 left...we'll be ready at the end."

"Roger, Tango Oscar Whiskey 800, position and hold 3-1 left."

"Position and hold 3-1 left," I respond. Charlie's heard. He nods his acknowledgement to me.

"Taxi checks complete!" declares Jerry, "and I've sat them down," moving his chair to face forward and up to the pedestal between Charlie and me.

"Before take off check," declares Charlie as we taxi into position and hold. He throws on the lights as I turn on the radar, T-cas and transponder.

"Tango Oscar Whiskey 800, clear for take-off runway 3-1 left Canarsie climb departure."

"Rog JFK tower, 800 clear to take-off 3-1 left, Canarsie climb, we're on the roll." I declare, as Charlie stands the thrust levers straight up.

"Engines stable," calls Jerry.

Charlie pushes the thrust levers all the way to the target EPR, declaring "set take-off thrust."

Jerry tweaks the throttles to even the power at take-off EPR.

"Eighty knots," I call.

"Check," Charlie.

"V-1….Rotate…" my calls.

Charlie rotates to a deck angle of 13 degrees. The nose comes off the ground at 148 knots, as the main trucks, almost two-hundred feet behind us, don't become airborne until another 1500 feet of runway disappear behind us.

"Positive rate," my call out, as the Vertical Speed Indicator climbs to the positive side.

"Gear up," says Charlie. Charlie's flying, I'm on the radio as I reach over and bring the gear handle up.

At 400 feet, we turn left towards the Canarsie VOR as tower announces, "800, contact departure now on 135.9."

"Rog, departure, good evening 800."

"Good evening departure, Tango Oscar Whiskey 800, checking, direct Canarsie VOR, climbing to 5000 feet."

We clean the flaps up on schedule, as our airspeed increases.

"Radar contact, 800, good evening, turn left now to heading 060, continue climb to twelve thousand feet, contact NY center on 123.5."

"Roger, departure, 800 continue climb to twelve thousand feet, turning left to 060, NY center on 123.5."

"Twelve thousand" I repeat to Charlie, my fingers flying to the altitude knob, twirling in 12,000 feet. Charlie acknowledges the 12,000 feet as I bug his heading to 060 and watch him turn."

"New York center, good evening, Tango Oscar Whiskey 800 checking in, now heading 060, climbing to twelve thousand feet."

"You're in luck tonight, 800, now present position direct Banc's, climb to and maintain flight level 3-3-0. Boston center on 132.5."

"Chicken George's, here we come," I declare to the guys. "Roger Center, thanks, 800 now present position direct Banks, climb to 330, Boston center on 132.5....good night."

"Boston Center, good evening, Tango Oscar Whiskey 800 is with you climbing now through 14,000 feet for flight level 330, direct Banks."

"Roger, 800, good evening, climb now to flight level 310."

"Hey Charlie, check out the fireworks!"

"800, Boston Center, do you read?"

"New York center, Boston center, do you see or read Tango Oscar Whiskey 800?"

"Negative Boston, he's off my scope."

"New York, Boston, he's disappeared off my scope also...they're gone, call somebody!"

"New York Center, this is USAir flight 217... there's a fireball in the sky abeam us....."

FLIGHT 800

RECONSTRUCTION

Figure 1 – The following are unauthorized, never before seen photos of the reconstruction of TWA Flight 800, whose parts were recovered from the Atlantic Ocean, and assembled at the Calverton, New York Hangar by the Feds.

Figure 2 – The right side of the final NTSB reconstruction of TWA flight 800

Figure 3 - TWA-800 reconstruction at the Calverton, NY Hangar – right side. Notice the fuselage "scorching" over the right wing root, the only external area to show the effects of any burning.

Figure 4 – Taken in the Calverton, New York hangar, a photo (secretly taken) of the final reconstruction of TWA-800, as seen from the left side.

Figure 5 - TWA-800 – a view into the center fuel tank from the left side. Notice the "unexploded" forward interior wall panels of the center fuel tank, the claimed epicenter of the explosion. The Feds claim that sparking by the scavenge pump inside the center fuel tank was the source of the caused explosion. no Boeing 747 pilot I've ever talked to, nor any B747 maintenance man I know, believes that.

Figure 6 – The same view of the center fuel tank, this on a "sister" 747, one owned by Tower Air (while still solvent), and often flown by me. This shows what a normal center fuel tank looks like (as a comparison), showing the scavenge pump and wall panels in normal condition.

Figure 7 - The TWA-800 reconstructed center fuel tank, showing the missing wall panel where the scavenge pump normally resides. Notice no sign of "explosion" damage to adjacent wall panels.

Figure 8 - A close up of Figure 7. Notice the wall panels intact to the right and left of where the scavenge pump would sit, and that the missing panel has been "surgically" removed. No seeming sign of explosive damage there.

Figure 9 – Left hand wing root – TWA 800 reconstruction.

Figure 10 – The recovered TWA-800 cockpit – Inside this B747 cockpit is where I normally sit..... weird feelings generated.... I've got 6000 hours living in this cockpit alone, with three different companies over a fourteen-year span.

How I got the Story and the Pix

On the evening of July 16th, 1996 TWA Flight 800 was most likely shot down with a U.S. missile made available to terrorists because of a policy/non-policy set by President Clinton and his Administration. The official version, that the center fuel tank exploded, causing the tragedy is, in a word, bullshit.

During this past year I was made aware of a gigantic hoax, and a cover-up by the United States Government, concerning the destruction of TWA Flight 800, July 16, 1996, with the loss of 230 innocent lives.

Fifteen years of research have gone into my book, "_Cockpit, Confessions of an Airline Pilot,_" a collection of the lives and times I've experienced in aviation. During these years I've been flying 747's ("the big jets") all over the world... Pakistan, India, Bangladesh, Syria, Turkey, Afghanistan, Croatia, Algeria, Saudi Arabia, Malaysia, Singapore, Indonesia, most of Africa, the Orient and South America. My passports look like a kaleidoscope of colorful visa and stamps of different shapes and sizes. During those years I have been asked to bring in a "load" from Kabul, Afghanistan (I didn't), to report on the "doings" of Suharto, his puppet, Habibe, the blind cleric Abdurahman Wahid, and the most recent President, Megawati Sukarno-Putri. (I haven't).

I've followed with painful amusement the "Presidential Christmas Amnesties" granted by Philippine President Joseph Estrada to the cannibal murderer of a Catholic priest (he and his pals ate the priest's brain). It's okay though, not to worry... the pardoned cannibal told the press that, "...although he was considering opening a restaurant in downtown Manila, he was now a vegetarian."

This past year, from the end of January through the end of April, I flew the "Malaysian Hajj," bringing Malaysian Muslims from Penang, Kuching, Borneo, Kota Kinabalu and Kuala Lumpur's Sultan Abdul Aziz Shah- Subang to Saudi Arabia for the annual Pilgrimage, the Hajj. In February of 2000, in Kuala Lumpur, Malaysia , I was called in my room in the Hilton Hotel to come down to the lobby to meet a man who introduced himself to me as, let's call him "Jim Simmons."

Jim, was a forty-ish, rangy fellow, tight-end material. He produced Federal ID for a government agency regulating communications, and had airport security clearances for the Kuala Lumpur secure ramp area, Subang, Malaysia. Ostensibly, he works in an area of sophisticated electronics.

He tells me that we have to go out to my airplane, that he needs to install some "high tech" equipment at the behest of my Company, Tower Air, and that he must demonstrate how it all works. Off we go. Ninety minutes later, now in the cockpit of our empty 747, it is apparent that the high-frequency radios and ACARs that have been installed are not sophisticated, nor do they require any real instruction.

I'm kinda perturbed, having made this unnecessary trip to the airport, but uncharacteristically, I'm keeping my pissyness to myself. Jim separates myself and him from the other pilots and support staff, arranging for the two of us to be alone in the cab heading back to my hotel. During the ride back, Jim starts telling me a story:

He was in Istanbul, working on the radios of the State Airplane of the President of Kazakhstan, a breakaway Muslim thorn in Russia's side. Noticing a wiring problem with the First Officer's radio altimeter that he felt could lead to serious problems in flight, he warned the pilots and maintenance people, but was ignored. They wanted to get home. Hours later, asleep in his hotel room, he gets a phone call direct from the President of Kazakhstan's staff….. "Big problems…we need you here, now…almost a fire on board on the flight home, you were right." A knock on his door, and tickets, $6,000 dollars in U.S cash, and a letter of authorization (personally signed by the President of Kazakhstan) arrive while he's still taking this phone call. Dress immediately, a car's waiting to take you to the airport.

Neither his company, nor his family are now aware of his movements, such was the haste of this unexpected side trip. He'll call everybody upon his arrival, fuck it, the money's right. The Turkish Air flight must transit *Sheremetyevo* Airport, Moscow, (bear with me reader, it gets better and better).

As Jim checks in at the Kazakhstan Air counter in the Moscow transit area, he is instantly surrounded by several "hard" suits who flash Russian I.D, separate Jim from his hand luggage, cash, the transit letter signed by the Kazakhstan President, and his American passport. They then lead him to a stark room off the main corridor.

He is made to strip completely, and with his arms fully extended, he is chained to pipes along the wall. The slack in the chains just allow him to sit naked, fully exposed on an ancient wooden bench, against the wall.

He is left there, naked, chained, for hours as men and women come and go through the room, paying him as much mind as a potted plant (his words).

Finally, a man in a suit, someone who seems to have some authority, begins questioning him. "Where are you from? What is the purpose of your trip to Kazakhstan? How did you get this letter from the President of Kazakhstan? This six thousand dollars cash? Where is the disc?

Jim would answer every question with only one request of his own. "I want to call the American Embassy!"

"Why?"

"I'm an American Citizen being held against my will."

"How do I know you're an American Citizen?"

"You took my American passport, you have it."

"What American passport!"

Fear finally took real hold of Jim. He got the message. His hosts were playing hardball. They were denying his existence, and although they didn't know this, Jim knew that not one soul, not his Company, not his

247

family knew where he was or where he was going, such was his rush in leaving Istanbul.

Jim started to cooperate fully, answering every question as thoroughly as he could. He could not answer any question regarding a mysterious "disc."

Six hours later, his clothes, passport, letter and cash are brought into the room. He had not been allowed water, he was not allowed bathroom privileges.

Unchained, and now redressed, he is given back his passport, letter and cash. He is then handcuffed, shackled, and chained hand and foot to a waist-chain, frog marched through the airport terminal, down the stairs, and out onto the tarmac.

There, waiting for him God knows how long, sits a Turkish Airliner, bound for Athens. Air-stairs have been brought up against the side of the fuselage. Two men, one on each arm, helped him hobble up the stairs and enter the plane full of passengers.

A business class seat had been kept ready for him. Under the gaze of all aboard, Jim, chains clanking, was placed in that seat. The main interrogator was suddenly in front of him. He fastened Jim's seat belt. Only then did he remove the handcuffs, shackles and chains.

Without another word, his captors left the plane, the door was shut, and they were airborne for Athens within fifteen minutes.

All eyes remained on Jim for the duration of the flight. Who is this guy? What had he done?

I've been listening to this story for twenty minutes, barely breathing. What has this to do with me? Before I can ask any questions, as the cab stops at a red light miles from my Hilton K.L. destination, Jim says, "I hear you collect airline stories...I don't think you'll ever get anybody to top this one." Then he steps out and walks away. The cab immediately bolts through the light, drives up to my Hilton, and stops. "What do I owe you?" "It's taken care of ," says the driver, in perfect English, as he speeds away, and down the ramp. What the fuck was that all about?

Weeks later, as we arrive in *Penang*, a remote Malaysian Island, "Jim" is seen on that airport's ramp. On our arrival at the Shangri-La Hotel, we hear that he has gained unauthorized access to our now empty 747, removed some equipment under the noses of the maintenance and security staff, and has disappeared.

Under the wonderful, lobby-long hanging dragon lantern, an Oriental gentleman approaches, hands me a thick, folded envelope, saying, "…this is from Jim," and disappears into the crowded street.

In my room, the open envelope tossed aside, I examine what appears to be a photo of the fully reconstructed remains of TWA 800. I also examine a photo of an unexploded center fuel tank, repositioned in the planes fuselage.

If what I am seeing in my room in *Penang* is genuine, the Government reports that an explosion of the center fuel tank of TWA-800 took it down is bullshit. The Zapruder films, showing JFK's head apparently being struck from the front right, proved that the Warren Commission report was a cover-up, but I've got nothing but unsubstantiated, undocumented copies, which could themselves be a cruel hoax. Not a word to anybody, I bury the photos in my map case, inside my *Jepps* charts, safely unfindable.

Back in Jeddah, late in April, I got sick enough with the "*Hajji hack*" to take myself off the flight rotation, which would have put me in *Kota Kinabalu*, an island dive resort on Borneo. It was from that hotel, on that island, that week that the kidnapping of all the western guests by the "Abu Sayeff" guerillas took place in April, 2000.

My paranoia tells whispers it was no coincidence that I could have been taken as one of those hostages. This is a radical arm of militant Muslims, not the freedom fighters of Mindanao, which has sought independence from the Philippines for years for it's Muslim population.

Back in Saudi Arabia, my Employer, Tower Air, (a Chapter XI bankrupt company as of 29 February, 2000), owes hundreds of thousands of dollars in hotel bills, fuel, and landing fees. Now I am a hostage, but in Jeddah, Saudi Arabia. The Saudis don't fool around about money. They've got my passport, they've got me. I'm a prisoner of the Sofitel, confined to Jeddah, and the American Embassy is in Riyadh, hundreds of air miles away.

During the week of April 21 – 28th I'm piling up more debt, calling home, asking my wife and my brother-in-law (he's in Washington D.C. with political connections), to get the State Department and the press involved in my release. The U.S. Consulate in Jeddah is fucking worthless, guarded on both sides of the street, believe it or not, by fucking Saudis in pick-up trucks, with mounted machine guns, I can't even approach the inner wall to ask the U.S. Marines for asylum. Someone must have paid the ransom, because I am finally allowed out of the Kingdom on April 28th, having spent the last thirty hours in the Hajj Terminal, waiting, waiting.

Now that I'm back home, I'm advised that I'm out of a job.... Tower Air is Kaput.

Two months later, as a new hire with Polar Air Cargo, whose base is JFK, but Corporate HQ and basic indoctrination is in Long Beach, California, I'm working out at the L.A. Fitness Center every day, trying to get back into some kind of shape.

A gentleman has been riding the hotel van to the health club with me daily, working out at the same time as me, both at the L.A. Fitness Center, and in the hotel's limited aerobics room, strikes up a conversation.

We talk about mundane matters for the first week or so. He's originally from NYC also. Seems that in the military in the late 60's and through the 70's he was a "Disinformation Officer" on behalf of the Pentagon.

"Oh?"

"Yes!"

"What do you do now?"

"This and that, yourself?"

I tell him I fly 747's for a living, "chained to the oars," but am writing a book, and trying to get it published, "*Cockpit,......*

"*...Confessions of an Airline Pilot?*" he finishes the title for me.

"Yes," is all I can manage, now staring at this ruddy-faced, ageless, non-descript gentleman in the sweaty t-shirt.

"We have something you may want...it's a disk...more specifically, it's the disc from a digital camera."

"Is it of pictures of the reconstructed TWA 800?"

"Yes it is, and we took them."

We meet over the next few weeks, as I am made privy to more pieces of the puzzle. These two gentlemen, who we shall refer to from now on as Mr. Deep and Mr. Throat, decided that our government had no right to decide for all of us, what we could or should be told about the TWA 800 tragedy.

Mr. Deep and Mr. Throat were the last two individuals to be officially allowed into the guarded hangar in Calverton, N.Y., before the government discarded (yes, discarded) the reconstructed 747. After years of retrieving all those bits and pieces from the bottom of the ocean, reassembling same, the U.S. Government "discarded" the reconstruction.

During their time in the hangar, while Mr. Deep distracted the Federal watchdog who allowed them access, Mr. Throat took the series of digital pictures of the fully reconstructed airplane, including the unexploded center fuel tank.

I've since spoken to both Deep and Throat, and they are willing to submit (anonymously) to a battery of polygraphers of my choice to attest to the following:

Their capacity allowed them official access to the Calverton, N.Y. secret, guarded warehouse.

They took the pictures.

They were not allowed/authorized to do so.

One of them is a qualified Captain on B747's (in addition to other official functions).

One of them is a qualified maintenance/mechanic on B747's (in addition to other official functions).

The pictures provided to me have not been tampered with, altered or duplicated in any way.

The pictures were the last taken of the actual TWA 800 reconstruction

The pictures, and what they observed, show that no explosion to the CFT brought down TWA 800.

The seats and carpeting (all placed back in their original order and positions) show no burning, singeing or explosive damage, in the area over the Center Fuel Tank.

The only singeing observed was on one exterior portion of the fuselage.

"Okay, well, what really happened," I finally get a chance to ask?

It seems that on the night of July 17th, in "hot" zone W-105 (off the coast of Long Island, New York), our Navy was testing anti-missile missiles. An American missile/or missiles with proximity switches (they explode near, but do not penetrate the target), being test fired by the U.S. Navy, accidentally killed TWA 800. Or, an American missile or missiles, obtained by and used by terrorists, brought down TWA 800.

As quickly as it happened, it was over. Flight 800 was gone, spread as a flaming swath across the ocean.

The guys say that… "All I can tell you is that by 2am on July 18th, White House staff members on conference calls, had indicated to key Federal Intelligence personnel that a friendly missile had shot down TWA 800, during a naval exercise. They had on their hands, they were told in that blamelessly antiseptic world of military corporatese, '*a situation.*'"

"But, why a cover-up? Why not tell the truth?"

I am told that now we are getting to "*Billy Clinton's Legacy in c-minor*", here's why the lie:

"Remember, you're talking July/August 1996, three months before the presidential elections. Clinton's running for a second term.

U.S. Stinger missiles that we made available to the Muslim *Mujahadin* for use against the Soviet Union in the Afghan war? It seems Clinton refused to buy them back.

Attempts to buy back 100 or more remaining missiles failed when the Clinton administration decided not to make the purchase. Some press reports claim an attempt was made to give the missiles back, an offer that was also, for some reason, refused by the Clinton administration.

It seems that when the U.S. failed to recover the remaining missiles, they were sold at international arms bazaars to the highest bidders. The buyers included surrogates for rogue states like Iran, according to "reliable military sources" and press reports.

"The United States, up until Flight 800, had never lost an airliner to a hostile missile. What the American public is not aware of – but the White House was very much aware of before July 1996, is that 26 Civilian Airliners have been shot down world-wide since the '80's, when

253

these (our unrecovered American-made) missiles became available on the open market.

The need for the Aegis class USS Normandy Anti-missile cruiser's tests that night were to defend against the use of our own missiles against us.

"Clinton and his people did not want the American voters, only four months before the elections, to know that his administration was responsible for terrorist's possession of American made missiles. That TWA 800 was brought down as a tragic by-product of Clinton non-policy at it's worst."

So, the whole cover-up was politically motivated?

"What do you think?"

"So do you expect more acts of terrorism, a *Jihad*, by fundamental Muslims, as I do?"

"What do you think?"

"What I think is that after our planes, it'll be our drinking water."

"Ever hear of Anthrax?"

"What do you think?"

This book

Mr. Clifford Cormany, an F.B.I. Polygrapher (now of Cormany Polygraph Services, Greensboro, Ga. 30642) and I spent half a day together in a hotel room at a Jacksonville, Fla., hotel, allowing Mr. Cormany to ask me any and every sort of question imaginable about my stories. This lie-detector test was independently arranged and paid for by Nash Entertainment, a Los Angeles based maker of reality television shows, which had me come out to be part of one of their programs.

This session with Mr. Cormany was the most intimate I've ever been with anyone in a hotel room without sex being involved. Cormany listened to these stories, had me write them out in front of him. Then I read the documents over with him aloud, signed each page, and swore to their total accuracy, as well as to my desire to tell him the entire truth.

Then began a four-hour process, during which he hooked me up to a Polygraph machine, a "lie detector." Testing me for honesty, he asked me his series of questions based on all that we had covered….. not once, but three separate times, stopping the process between each series, so that he might, out of my range of vision, determine if he had "valid tape." The questions for each of the three sessions were mixed up, and asked in a different order so that I could not anticipate which question would be coming next. A technique, I assume, to enhance any residual anxiety on my part, making it harder to fool the machine.

I was pronounced to have told the whole, unaltered truth.

Publisher's Note:

Steve Keshner has spent the past fifteen years flying Boeing 747 aircraft throughout the Middle and Far East. Following the demise of Tower Air, which was based out of JFK in New York City, Keshner accepted employment flying B747's Internationally for Polar Air Cargo, headquartered in Long Beach, CA.

Steve Keshner is also the author of:

The Tai Stick Sting, a farce written in 1983.

A Night at the Opera, a one act play, written in 1999.

Selections of his Haiku poems have been published in the *Honolulu Advertiser* and in the *Mainichi Daily News*, of Tokyo.

Mr. Keshner has begun work on:

FREIGHT DOGS
The Other Side of Glamour
(due out December, 2001.)

An anthology of Haiku poetry, *Cry Hawaiian Blues*, will be published by *booksonnet.com* in 2002.

Full size / full color Photos:

Full size / full color copies of the unauthorized photos of the TWA-800 reconstruction can be obtained by sending a twenty-five dollar check, along with a return address to:

Photos
P.O. Box 4522
St. Augustine, FL 32085-4522